A Crafty and Devious God

"…a great read…"

"Weirdly excellent"

"[The] writing is very natural, loose and easy, yet deep and thoughtful."

"…an engaging character study… a tale of a man who's lost, looking for his way, and a girl who knows she is destined for great things and is determined to achieve it at all costs."

"I gave it a try. And kept reading, and reading, and reading. Just very well-written, scattered throughout with concepts that made me think (which I occasionally like to do)."

After

…short stories of New Yorkers trying to make sense of their changed world in the immediate aftermath of 9/11."

"These stories are emotionally impactful but they are not grim. Each character finds some measure of hope or understanding or, at the very least, adaptation to their circumstances."

"…a masterful job of depicting the surreal dream-like state that trauma survivors inhabit…"

"Intricately woven stories of despair and ultimately hope…"

"…a tender tribute to the survivors of 9/11."

Praise for Ted Krever's books:

Mindbenders

"…a storyline that takes hold in the first few pages and doesn't let go…"
"…really fast paced…I found myself unable to put it back down."

"…dialog that left me breathless."
"…[a] global, international conspiracy of corporate and governmental politics, mind control, murder and intrigue."
"OMG!...finally crawled into bed early hours of the next day."
"This is that rare piece of fiction based on fact in such a way as to make the two seem to blur."
"Mindbenders…will make you wonder if your mind really does belong to you."

Mindbenders 2: The Fiery Sky

"…a more than worthy followup to the 1st book, fast paced, well written and exciting!"
"…takes me places that were only in my imagination - I feel like I have been to that island in the South Pacific living on the water, and I've been parched in the Aussie desert - it's all real."
"…A complete thrill ride from beginning to end…great style and substance."
"…intense, memorable scenes…"
"…seamlessly weaves multiple storylines together, delivering a powerful punch of an ending."

GREEN

"…not your typical romance…

"…a unique look into the mindset of men, rather than the typical romance, which is told from the woman's point of view."

"… a smart, witty and wise look at love later in life…"

"I found myself laughing aloud more than once, only to shortly thereafter find myself deeply touched."

"The descriptions…of Ireland are alone worth the price of the book…"

"If you like reading about horses, Ireland, friendship, love in any form…"

"Part a love story, part a political thriller, and part a satiric commentary on life and politics…"

"Green is a charming book."

Howling at Wolves

"This book, simply put…is funny!"

"Keep your tissues handy as you won't stop laughing."

"Nothing is sacred…"

"…like Garp on steroids (or maybe Viagra?)

HOWLING AT WOLVES

by
Ted Krever

Little David Publications
www.tedkrever.com

ISBN: 978-0615484747

~~~

For Joe:
I'm sure it wasn't *really* like this,
but it could have been.

~~~~

This is a work of fiction. There is no connection between this story and anything
that's ever happened to anyone, ever. No connection to any person, persons,
places, moose, institutions or countries. In real life, I never even kissed the girl.
When I use my own name, I'm just kidding you. And your lawyer. So get over it.

~~~~

One

I was doing some research and
found a review of a CSNY
concert by you. Are you the Ted
Krever that traveled on the
Michelangelo twenty-five years
ago? I seem to remember the guy
I knew was a CSNY fan. If
that's you, do you remember me—
Nora Hill?

This story has to begin with Nora and end with Nikos—Nikos
Papandreou, my teacher and second father. But I have to explain a
few things if you are truly to understand what was at stake here at
the beginning—for you to understand how much Nora's email
meant to me.

Two months ago, I finished—finished!—my first novel. My
indulgent parents sent me to Sarah Lawrence around the time Billy

Jean King polished off Bobby Riggs, because I insisted I was meant to write novels. Sarah Lawrence taught me story structure and speaking from the heart. It also taught me to regard both women and men as competition for my girlfriend's affections.

Anyway, twenty-five years after graduation, after a million wrong turns, I finally finished my third attempt at a first novel. It was a tale about meeting, twenty-five years later, the girl you were nuts about (but never had the nerve to ask out) in high school. The character was based on two women. The first was a girl in my high school class, Allison Slonim, who occupied almost as much as of my attention back then as Mrs. Emma Peel. But the main template of my tortured memory, the template created by my longing, by my awareness of what had gone missing in my life, the template I'd shaped and polished and buffed to a sheen in the fifteen years of my miserable marriage was Nora Hill.

She was an ex-hippie's dream—I was smitten within seconds of our first meeting. Blonde and blue-eyed, with a little overbite and a frighteningly cute tiny gap between the front teeth, big granny glasses and a body to die for. Sweet and smart, friendly courteous and polite in a way that comes as second nature to Canadians. Oh yes—she was Canadian. That was the rub in the end. She lived in Waterline Ontario, halfway between Montreal and Toronto. It was a long way to travel, even for her, and at that age it seemed there would always be other girls. I don't think I ever even kissed her. But I obsessed over her for two years, writing the book.

And now, in the midst of my precious rejection letters, she'd written me an email out of the blue. It was a ray of light in a sky suddenly grown full of clouds.

A month after I finished the novel, I went for my first prostate exam, a PSA. As soon as you reach forty-five, and particularly if anyone in your family has had cancer, the cash register goes off automatically every time you pass a doctor's office. They follow you down the block throwing free samples of drugs guaranteed to sooth your digestion, help your kidneys and liver and grow more hair on your head, so long as you don't mind becoming impotent as a side effect. Which I suppose would be useful if I wasn't busily pretending that I'm still twenty-five, only wiser.

I want to pretend I've never heard of liver, kidneys or spleen, prostate, follicles or anything else that might someday wear out. I want all decay to remain in the realm of someday for as long as I can maintain a willful ignorance. But now the doctor insisted I see a urologist for a digital exam and a PSA.

The urologist, Dr. Speil-something-or-other, put on a latex glove, fondled my balls, stuck his finger up my ass, then whipped off the glove and offered me the same hand to shake. "Nice to meet you," he said. The office also drew blood for my PSA. Ten days later, I was back in the office for a biopsy.

"Has it spread?" I asked immediately upon hearing that my PSA number was 'a concern.' That's what doctors call everything now—a 'concern'—as though it's Cancer, Cancer and Locusts LLC, a team of litigation attorneys in a distant state.

"Has what spread?"

"The cancer."

"Whoa—I have not diagnosed cancer," Spielvogel said. "You have a high PSA number—at the moment that's all you have. You could easily just have chronic inflammation."

"What are the health hazards of that?"

"There are none."

"I like that one. Let's go with that," I said. "Can any of these things be a result of…uh, a little too much self-love?"

He considered this a moment, though I couldn't tell if he wasn't sure about the answer or if he wasn't certain what I meant. "Not as high a number as you have," he answered finally. But I'd been divorced over two years and I hadn't been dating—I wasn't sure he really knew how much self-love I was talking about.

So a few days later, I come in for a biopsy. "It takes an hour," I was told by Speilworker. "Most people go back to work the next day." I didn't have anyone drive me—it just didn't sound necessary.

After I'd stripped down to a towel over my nether regions, I started examining the room. I did this from nerves, really. I have a lot invested in the notion that my body will work perfectly until the moment I have the final embolism and keel over in my soup at age 93. So the idea that they had to check me out—that something might actually be wrong—caused real tremors inside.

I started examining the machinery in the room, just to take my mind off my situation. The biggest gadget in the place combined a mechanical arm, a tiny camera eye attached to a metal box with a couple oscilloscopes and a little green video monitor, a second arm sprouting just below the camera eye carrying a skinny dildo with a pair of tweezers at the end and a bunch of tubing. Just the thing for removing big snakes from the electrical conduits of nuclear power plants. Robby the Snake-Removing Robot.

There were several other machines in the darker corners of the room, stuff with big widescreen viewers and the old ratchety metal knobs and florescent tubes. I wondered if they'd slipped in a consent form with the paperwork I'd signed and I was going to be the subject of a documentary on the All-Surgery Channel. Surely there was such a thing on cable now. I hadn't been able to afford cable since the divorce but considering the way things were going at that time I was sure they would by now have separate channels for ants as opposed to fleas. Or maybe the Red Ant Channel versus the Black Ant Channel.

At this point, Speilballast appeared with a blonde nurse. He began talking to me in that we're-going-to-keep-you-distracted tone of voice, as though that would fool anyone over the age of six. The nurse sat on a stool at the head of the table. He then asked me to lie down facing her and he sat down at the controls of Robby the Snake-Removing Robot!

At this point, I began replaying our earlier conversations about this procedure, trying to make sure I hadn't missed anything. They were going to use a camera to guide a probe inside me in order to take eight small samples of my prostate gland through the wall of the anus. Several days earlier, when I hadn't been lying on this cold slab looking at the big metal arm and the small metal arm both moving in the direction of my genitals, this had seemed innocuous enough. The way it now translated was: we're sticking a camera the size of an aerosol can up your ass, followed by a couple of needles the size of ocean fishing hooks (*small* ocean fishing hooks). We'll use the camera to make sure we don't miss the prostate, stick the needles through the wall of your ass and pull out little chunks of you. And we're doing all this without anesthesia.

I have a decent pain tolerance but this exceeded it pretty fast. I was grunting and groaning from the beginning. I knew I wouldn't die but I now had proof I'd never be gay.

The nurse had taken my hand and was stroking it, murmuring "Sshhh—sshhh" in what is surely taught as a comforting tone of voice in all the best medical schools. I wasn't having any. The lower arm with the needles was now cutting out pieces of me—the sound of each sample was like a giant staplegun echoing over my head.

I groaned at each movement and each small dissection. She repeated her dutiful "sshh" until I looked up and said "I tell you what—you come down here and I'll sit on the chair and tell *you* to ssshhhh. This *hurts*."

Not a word from Speilhimmler. After about seven hours on the table (I may be exaggerating slightly), I could finally feel the pressure ease and suddenly his face appeared right in front of me.

"All done," he said with an idiotic gaiety. "We'll get the results within the week—call you when we know."

The nurse stood and spoke with the vacant tone of the flight attendant showing you how to inflate the life jacket under your seat. "There's a bathroom over there. You can leave whenever you're ready—no rush." And then they were gone, leaving me alone in the dim room with Robby the Intestine-Mutilating Needle Dildo.

I continued to lie on the table for several minutes. This is not my normal response to anything. Usually I'm up and onto the next thing as soon as the last one is over, but not on this day. On this day I lay like a stump for about fifteen minutes. Everything below my neck ached but I couldn't think. It was as though they'd mistakenly anesthetized my brain instead of my body.

Having experienced their level of concern and attention at close range, this didn't seem in any way impossible, except that I knew they hadn't anesthetized *anything*. If they had, I'd at least have had another insurance disclaimer to sign saying I didn't really mind if they killed me by mistake as long as I wasn't around to notice (that's what the anesthesia disclaimer says, by the way — a lawyer friend of mine paraphrased it once for me).

Anyway, *it had taken less than an hour*, as they said. I accepted this only after checking to make sure the second hand of my watch was still turning—it was despite my disbelief. I swear it felt like seven hours. Proof positive we don't really create our own reality, though this whole experience put that concept to sleep. Anyway, *it had taken less than an hour*, as they said (circular logic is my friend). And *most people go back to work the next day*—that was the other thing they said. So after fifteen wasteful useless extra minutes on the table, I should have been able to stand up and get dressed.

I must have missed a step somewhere. I rolled over, sat up and nearly swooned onto the floor. I grabbed the edge of the table and pulled myself back into the middle of it. I lay there another fifteen minutes, sweating and sliding up the inclined back portion very slowly until I was nearly upright. Each move required time to get over the dizzy spells that followed with regularity. Go back to work the next day, my ass.

The next morning, I went to work. I felt better although I was pissing blood. They had warned me this was a normal consequence and could go on for three to six weeks. The warnings don't really prepare you for the reality. The chills that followed watching myself piss blood were enough to convince me to go to work—I didn't need to sit around all day worrying about going to the bathroom and worrying about having cancer.

I left the house early. I met my boss Kevin in the Trade Center lobby for breakfast at 7:30. He was an obese man of 35 who seemed to collect everything he'd eaten in the last 24 hours on his shirtcuffs. He had taken me on because I had learned to wrangle computers on my last job, the dotcom that went out in a blaze of lawsuits. After eggs and bacon and juice and me whining about my biopsy and him complaining about the rigors of Atkins (he had a small steak and electrolyte fluid) and the demands of his supermodel girlfriend (who apparently never left her apartment 'uptown'), I took the PATH train across to my office in Jersey City.

Kevin's company were security contractors for a brokerage house with offices on both sides of the Hudson—Kevin ran the office in Manhattan and I took care of the video in the command center across the river.

I loved the job because most of the day I just stared at a console. It was a pretty amazing thing to watch—after three weeks on the job, I still marveled at it. I had eight screens covering the partition in front of me from desk height to ceiling. They showed security camera shots in rotation from our offices all over the world. Lining the outer screens were alarms in strategic locations—some locations had so many alarms that each marker on my screen stood for ten or twenty others. I could explode each view with a couple of keystrokes to get the details.

If an alarm went off, I'd call the source and find out what was wrong. Usually, it was just a technician tripping a wire someplace. If so, I would just reset the thing and move on. If there really was a problem, I escalated to higher authority, internal or external—engineers to work the problem or the cops if we had an intruder.

The command center also held remote controls for every office in the company. I could lock and unlock doors, windows and control elevators in London, Paris, Jakarta and Tokyo as well as New York and Jersey City. I could really fuck with people's heads if I wanted to, although that privilege was usually reserved for the night shift—you don't mess with tradition. And when things were quiet—which was most of the time—I could write on my laptop. I had started another novel and it was cooking along. It was the ideal job.

It was a beautiful morning after several gloomy rainy days. I sat by the window for a while just taking in the sunlight and then returned to the console. I was writing something a bit heavier than the first book—this one was coming out a lot more personal and a bit nastier. I didn't like it but it kept coming and I don't get in the way of gifts.

I was trying to decide how to portray the last woman I'd gone out with. She had developed this very strange offshoot of namedropping—namedropping without real celebrity, or namedropping for the age of Six Degrees.

"I went with this guy—he took us to a party at Leonardo DiCaprio's brothers' house."

"I'm really friendly with David Sedaris' lover. He lives in the neighborhood—I'll show him to you sometime—he's very gossipy though."

I'm not real impressed with celebrities—I've worked with enough of them over the years—but even if I was, I wouldn't be impressed with their brothers or lovers and even less with people who took me to a party at the brothers' house—was he there? And more than that, was he interesting? Does David Sedaris' lover have a sense of humor?

What bothered me most about her was that she didn't seem to even think much about these people while she appropriated their Two and Three Degree positions for herself. I went out with her four times, unable to decide if she was actually that shallow or if she was saying all this stuff as some real hip Carroll Gardens self-parody. Then I made a few suggestions about a piece she was writing—note to self: NEVER EVER believe someone you're dating when they ask your opinion of their creative work!—and she told me she didn't really think we should see each other again. Then she suggested we sleep together before I go. Of course, being a man, I agreed.

It hit me, as I was taking my clothes off, that I'd lusted all my life after anonymous sex, in an age where it apparently was epidemic and failed at every turn to find it. And now, when I least expected it—on a date!—here it was. What could be more anonymous?

If we'd just met in a movie or a bar and gone into the bathroom to fuck without even introducing ourselves, there was always the lurking chance we'd like it—and want to do it again—and then we'd have the possibility of love and entanglements and anonymity just goes right out the window then, let me tell you. I've been married; I know this stuff.

But here we'd met for four dates. She'd told me nothing genuine about herself—too busy weaving her fourth-hand upmanship stories about gardeners to the stars and so on—and she'd never really let me get a word in edgewise. So we knew absolutely nothing about each other. And now, we'd decided resolutely never to see each other again. This was as safely anonymous as any couple could possibly be.

And the sex sucked. It was more desultory and obligatory than what I'd had after fifteen years of marriage with our son moaning in his sleep in the next room. She couldn't wait to pull me into her and I couldn't wait to get my clothes back on. I broke a sweat but I don't know how.

I'm cursed to be a romantic, I thought. In an age of irony and women who want the same thing men do, I sit on the sidelines waiting for true love, flowers and poetry. Worse yet, I have bad sex and soon, with my prostate, I may not be able to have *any*.

That was when the screen went off. A hundred alarms in three different banks. It took me a few moments, just staring at the chaos, to realize they were all just across the river. I pushed the first blinking button and waited for Kevin to pick up the phone. It was a little over an hour since we'd had breakfast—knowing him, he'd gone down to get coffee and another steak and tripped over the main cable. Or maybe he'd spilled the coffee on the console over there—that might actually account for all the alarms at once. They weren't stopping and he wasn't answering. I saw a lot of movement on the cameras now—people moving onto the staircases. My phone rang.

"Are you watching?" My friend Jim, in the Financial Center.

"Can't talk to you now. I've got all these alarms going off," I told him.

"That's what I mean," he said. The words he said didn't mean a thing, but something came through his tone of voice. There was a quaver there, a squelched note, that spoke to me. It was as though the whole world slowed down for a moment. I stood up and stepped around my wall of monitors, to where I could look out the windows across the river, at the tower burning black smoke into the clear blue sky.

You know what happened, of course. But we didn't, not yet. We figured it was an accident. A bomber flew into the Empire State Building in the late 40's in the fog, I remembered reading about it—this could have been something like that, although the day couldn't have been clearer and planes had all kinds of instruments and alarms now they didn't have then. The truth was much simpler, if you examined it, than all the things we were imagining, but somehow none of us could manage to boil down to that simplicity.

And there simply wasn't time to think anyway. I was now manning the phones, opening stairwell emergency doors and taking phone calls from employees wanting advice. I just told them to leave and call in once they were outside—we'd let them know as soon as things were straightened out. Our floors were in the thirties and forties—pretty soon, I was taking phone numbers from employees who were already outside and waiting for the all-clear. Meanwhile, I was talking to Gary at the City Emergency Preparedness Office—he was in an underground bunker and didn't have the view I did, so I was describing the things to him that were taking place right over his head.

"How far up is it?" he said. "How many floors involved?"

I was trying to count the floors but it was impossible. And just as I felt like I was getting somewhere, this other plane crossed in front of my view and obscured it.

"Gary," I said, "there's something wrong."

"Of course there's something wrong," he said. "The cops and fire department are here—they'll handle it."

"No," I said. "There's another plane." It circled around the lower skyline, low and a bit uncertain at first. As I finished speaking, I saw it heel over and pick up speed and continue banking until it went into the other tower.

This time, I heard the screams from downstairs in our office. Everyone was watching out the windows of course. They actually evacuated our building for a while—we were in the tallest building in Jersey City and they were afraid—they were afraid of everything at the moment. So we stood on the waterside and watched people jump from the towers. It was the perfect distance—close enough to see, to see in their body language when they decided to go; but far enough away that it just wasn't real.

The smoke rose black into the sky until the towers came down. We all said we missed the first one collapsing. There's no way we could really have missed it but it went so fast and the idea was so unthinkable that we all denied. By the time the second one went, nothing was unthinkable. And then the smoke ran deep red into the southern sky.

Two

October 10th—a month later—I'm sitting in the den of Nikos' house in Westchester. He is watching me flip channels on the television.

"Don't just flip—watch something," he says. "*Do* something."

"I'm not interested in anything," I say.

"Pretend," he insists. "You're barely alive as it is."

Nikos Papandreou is my mentor and second father, really. He was my writing professor and don at Sarah Lawrence and the first person that believed in me—he beat me on that score by several decades. If I would listen to anyone at this point, it's Nikos, but the hurdles seem high.

Kevin was one of the casualties when the towers went down. 3,000 stories like his out there. No reason why that we know of— he had time to evacuate. Almost the entire staff of our brokerage house made it out. No one remembers seeing him lagging behind or unconscious in a doorway somewhere. Another example of arbitrary fate, but a fateful one: he was the sole owner of our security concern. With him gone, the company went out of business overnight.

I have a little money put away—enough to keep me going for several months—but I'm out of work for the second time in a year and the economy is drying up fast. And the book—the book based on my memories of Nora Hill—keeps gathering rejection letters. They paper the wall of my home office. It doesn't even hurt much to receive them anymore—just another flap for the collection.

Meanwhile, the lab that compiled the results of my biopsy was also in the Trade Center complex. My test results are lost in the rubble. I no longer piss blood, though the memory remains fresh, but I know no more of my situation now than I did before that ordeal. I have ignored the doctor's advice to come back and repeat the experience. So I linger between sickness and health, between the living and dead.

I flip channels until I get to the news.

Al Jazeera broadcast a statement yesterday from al Qaeda spokesman Suleiman Abu-Gheith, who praised the hijackers who carried out the September 11 attacks and said there were thousands of young Muslims willing to die while carrying out more attacks on the United States.

Abou-Gheith did not explicitly say al Qaeda was responsible for the attacks, but

> investigators have said at least three hijackers
> had ties to al Qaeda, the network headed by
> suspected terrorist mastermind Osama bin
> Laden.

What kind of world is it where terrorists have a spokesman? I remember the good old days, when terrorists hijacked airplanes or murdered Israeli Olympic athletes—those guys pointed guns at anyone nearby them with a camera. Only phony terrorists like Patty Hearst played to the camera. Now they have press spokesman? Did they have craft service at the press conference? Who does the catering for Al Qaeda? Could the Jewish newsmen get kosher lunches if they reserved them ahead of time? I'm in a foul mood and nothing seems to help it.

There are funerals everyday in my neighborhood. In my unemployment, I have actually gone to a few of them, just as a citizen witness. A woman down the block that I've known by sight for three years put a sign up renting out rooms in her house—it seemed funny to me until I saw her husband's obituary in the paper.

There have been telethons to raise money, funds for the survivors. These are worthy charities. I contributed on the Internet while listening to Neil Young sing 'Imagine' on the telethon. But there are no arrangements for the witnesses, for those of us who just lost a little piece of ourselves. I put down the remote.

"What are you watching?" comes Kara's voice from the kitchen.

"It's the news," Nikos says, staring at me.

"You're supposed to be cheering him up," Kara reproaches Nikos.

"How?" he says. "I don't feel cheery either. Come on," he tells me. "Take me for a walk."

When I met Nikos in the mid Seventies, he'd already had two heart attacks. He became a long-distance runner, a vegetarian and ditched his first wife. Despite all these positive moves, he was perennially having setbacks and complications. When I moved to Colorado and California in the late 70's, I lost track. By the time I moved back in the early 90's, I was afraid to check up on him again, afraid he'd passed away.

Finally, two years ago, when I was starting the first book, I called the alumni office at Sarah Lawrence and asked for his number. The nice lady (I've since sent them money and they like me even *better* now) told me she couldn't give out his phone, but she'd pass my information on to him. I was thrilled knowing he was still alive.

I got a letter from him and wrote back instantly. Then I didn't hear a thing for four months. He'd always been a lousy correspondent, even when we were both much younger, but as weeks went by, I got nervous. I got his number from the phone book and left a message on the machine.

Two days later, I found a message on *my* machine from Kara, his pistol of a second wife. Kara is fifteen years younger than Nikos and a whirlwind. I called back and she answered.

"Hi, it's Ted Krever," I said. "Nikos was my professor at Sarah Lawrence."

"Sure," she said. "I remember you." I was surprised she remembered. I figured Kara thought of me as a friend of Nikos' pre-her, but maybe that was so long ago now it didn't matter anymore. Old wounds do wear away eventually.

A long silence followed. Finally, she said, "Yes, he's still alive."

"Okay," I exhaled.

"His students all call," she continued in her brusque fashion, which came rushing back to me, "and there's this long silence while they wait to hear the bad news. No bad news—he's still alive. He has congestive heart failure and prostate cancer. When you knew him in the '70's, he was dying. He's *still* dying. He's going to make the Guinness Book of Records as the man who took the longest to die."

I've visited Nikos and Kara every couple of weeks since. I drive up to their little house in Westchester, in a development near a golf course. He and I talk writing and we go for walks. That is, he walks—I wait for him. I could make it to the corner and back in the time it takes him to clear his front gate. The long-distance runner shuffles very slowly these days. Usually, I tolerate it because I love him and owe him. Today, his pace mirrors my mood perfectly.

"Are you going to shave sometime soon?" he asks.

"It bothers you I have a beard?"

"It bothers me that you're hiding behind a beard," he says in his gentle way. I've seen Nikos dealing with his first wife (painful), faculty politics (poisonous), his sons (guilt and resentment) and recently his conditions and doctors (frustration and fear)—I've never seen him angry. When he speaks pointedly, I have to notice.

"I'm not hiding," I say. "If I wanted to hide, I'd put on a camouflage suit and move to the North Woods somewhere. I live in New York—I walk around with a bullseye on my back like everyone else."

"That's not what I mean," he says.

"I know," I nod, trying to reassure. I've spent a lifetime trying to keep this man from worrying too much, from caring too much, afraid his wealth of feelings would overwhelm his evidently feeble body. Now it's clear that it's *my* efforts that are growing feeble. "I just don't feel anything anymore. It's not dramatic. I don't fell deadened—I don't feel like I'm *preventing* myself from feeling. I don't think I'm going to suddenly well up in tears and understand the deep hidden torment behind it all. I just look around and nothing really moves me. It's like the whole world's a disappointment. I know that's incredibly self-centered, but it's the best explanation I can make of this hollow inside. I just don't get the point of anything."

It is a sullen day. The rain doesn't fall so much as hang in the air, a futile static mist.

"At this point," Nikos says as we return to the house, having walked to the corner and back, "I live to treat my ailments. If I don't treat the cancer, it'll eat me up. But the treatments take so much time, I have no life. The radiation for the cancer saps my energy, then they remind me to exercise to combat the heart disease. I am convinced this is part of some greater plan, but so far I've missed it."

"The point is that you're still here complaining," Kara barks from the kitchen. "It's a blessing from Heaven to me personally, that you can still be here moaning and groaning about everything."

"Thank you," Nikos says and laughs. His laugh is barely audible, just a rushing of air from his lips, but his face squints into a ball and he quakes and the tears roll down his cheeks.

"Come look at this," he says to me and leads me past his office, overflowing with books and papers and pictures in frames stacked against the walls, to the back courtyard of the house.

I walk around the plaster wall onto the little tile patio overflowing with a marble table, a few chairs, empty flowerpots, tools, bags of compost, old sneakers and a rusty tuba in a corner. Nikos' little dog Orzo is barking like a three-alarm fire.

Three inches from Orzo's nose is a lizard the size of my thumb, green and orange and pink, just standing on the dead leaves and the old trowels, quivering in the face of the yapping dog. At that distance, you'd think the force of Orzo's breath would carry the lizard away, but it sticks to its place, staring back, not moving.

"This is nature," Nikos says. "It knows, somehow, that the mammalian eye tracks movement, so it stays still, waiting him out. And because it's not moving, Orzo doesn't know what to do. Given another moment, he will begin to doubt his own judgment. He'll decide it isn't really a lizard—it's a *leaf*. And then he'll just walk away and the lizard will disappear." Nikos begins to laugh, that soft laugh I remember from what seems like ancient times, laughing at this little joke, at the jokes the world slips in around the edges.

"This," he says to me confidentially, "is no New York lizard. I cannot find any reference material anywhere suggesting this is native to New York. I think one of the local kids got it as a present and lost it or threw it out the window. I have no idea how it's surviving in the cold weather, but it keeps showing up on the patio every day. I think we're domesticating it," he says and the laugh starts again.

He leads me back into the house, into the kitchen. "Okay, clear the way!" he yells towards Kara, assuming she's in the kitchen. "I'm making pizza."

But Kara's not in the kitchen. She's in the living room, reading a letter at the table. Nikos ambles by, lots of movement and energy expended for every foot of ground covered. Kara barely looks up. This is not like her. I've known them on and off for twenty-five years; nothing Nikos does escapes her attention.

"I'm making pizza," Nikos hums to himself, like it's a song from 'Our Hit Parade' that's come back to him. He is pulling every saucepan and sizeable, dangerous knife in the kitchen into a large semicircle of trouble in front of him.

"How are you?" I say to Kara, who doesn't look happy.

"My son is having problems," she says. Both of them have kids from previous marriages. Kara's lives in Florida, where the two of them should live too, except they don't have enough money left to even consider such a thing. "His company is a mess. He got a manager who didn't know what he was doing. I told him the guy was an idiot, but he didn't believe me. He believes me now," she says, holding up the letter. "I could fix this, if I was down there."

"So maybe you should go down," I say.

Her eyes flicker like I'm some naïve schoolboy. "And what do I do with *him*?" she says, gesturing toward the clanking, humming kitchen. "His radiation, thank God, is down to once a month. He doesn't have to go again for three weeks. But he's got to exercise every other day or his heart will go. After that new therapy, the doctor says he could have five more years — "

"That's five more years after telling me I had eighteen months three years ago," Nikos clucks from the kitchen. They hear everything the other says, and they talk about each other habitually as if they're not in the same room.

"But he has to do his exercise *every other day*," Kara repeats now, slowly and loudly, in the direction of the kitchen, like she's teaching English as a Second Language to a class of two. A class of two where the second student has dyslexia and ADD. "And if I'm not here, he doesn't do it. So there's no answer."

There are many types of love. There's the love of parent for child. There's the love of your lover, I suppose, of either sex. Then there's the love of parent, and in a way, Nikos made me as much as anyone.

"How long would you have to be there?" I ask.

"Ten days—two weeks, maybe," she says. "What needs to be done doesn't take long; it's just somebody has to do the dirty work, and my son—God love him, he's a good guy but he hasn't got the stomach for it."

"Go," I say. "I'll keep an eye on Nikos, make sure he does his exercise."

"How are you going to do that?" she asks. "You have an hour ride to get up here."

"I'm unemployed," I tell her. "My job hunt is going nowhere and I'm not looking that hard. All Nikos does is walk on a treadmill for twenty minutes. Either I'll stay up here or I'll take him down to Brooklyn and find a health club we can pay for by the day that he can walk in."

"Is that expensive?" she asks.

"I can get a try-out membership. There's a new one near me that keeps sending me offers. That'll give us a month of treadmills and Stairmasters."

"Keep him off the Stairmaster," she says. "He keeps wanting to try it and it'll kill him, I'm sure."

"Kara, it's New York City," I calm her. "I can walk a couple blocks with him to get lunch and back to the house and at his pace that's half an hour of walking. So he'll get his exercise."

"Go on," Nikos calls from around the corner. "I'm not such a baby as you think. Ted and I'll pick up some girls at the health club."

"Feel free," Kara replies.

"Sure—*now* she says that," Nikos says, poking his face out of the kitchen door. "The stuff they give me for the prostate cancer shrinks my penis and gives me tits. So *now* it's okay if I pick up girls."

When he slides back into the kitchen, she turns to me. "What about you?" she asks. Kara is a gutty, blunt presence. You don't cross her and you don't ask for quarter. It's what I've always liked about her. Now suddenly I discover what it's like to be the center of her withering gaze. "You don't look good. You haven't looked good in a while. You sure you can take care of him?"

If only a woman with such power was concerned for *me*. With all his problems, Nikos has made himself a good life. "I may not do much of a job taking care of myself," I tell her, "but I'd cut my arm off before messing things up for him." She lets the words register, watching my face carefully. I don't flinch.

"Did Nikos ever write you a goodbye letter?" she asks.

"Huh? No."

"Must've been just before you got back in touch with us," she says. "Four years ago, the doctors told him he had eighteen months to live. So he wrote everyone he knew letters that started 'This is the last letter I will ever write you...' blah blah blah. God almighty—I told him, 'Nikos, you could get better. At very least, you might want to write someone another letter in the next seventeen months.' But you know him. It was actually a really good thing. The next time he wanted to write someone, I made him write a retraction. I said 'You already wrote them your last letter. They love you—you probably tore their hearts out. So if you're going to write them again, you apologize for the fact that you're still alive.' And he did. It was the funniest thing you ever read—I hope he kept copies. He could make millions. But it got him his sense of humor back. It was like he had really been waiting thirty years to write that stupid 'last' letter and once he got it out of his system, he could go back to living—you understand?" She stares at me like there's some universal truth here that I should get. If there is, it's zipping right over my head.

She gets up from her chair.

"I'm going to call the airport," Kara says to Nikos, but it's a question, not a statement.

"Go," he tells her. "We'll have fun."

Three

Kara's out the door with kisses and good wishes before the pizza is done. This is no ordinary pizza, of course—it is a Nikos pizza, and therefore, comes with stories attached.

"I go to this market," Nikos says, cutting out a slab of dough. "There are three markets nearby—this is the smaller family market. The fellow that owns it bought it seven years ago. He's a very nice guy, his wife comes in and works with him a couple of days a week, you should see her, such a beautiful woman, such hips, ohh! Her name is Melinda—her family is Italian, he is Greek. His family came from Patrai in the West of Greece—a port city, taken over by the Romans in the second century BC. They had Christianity there before the Romans. Their people came here and became fisherman, worked like dogs so their kids could grow up and open restaurants. Everyone thinks the Greek restaurant is a negative stereotype—tell that to the parents. They're thrilled in their graves."

"So I went in yesterday and he says 'Nikos, I have something new—I just finished making them, it's an experiment, so you take them and tell me if they're any good. They're chicken sausages, no cholesterol, I made them myself, all the regular spices, you be the judge. Oh, and Melinda—she was there, God what tits, I'll take you over to meet her—her family is Calabrese, from Crotone on the Eastern boot of Italy. A Greek City. Pythagoras had a brotherhood there in 500 BC. I told her she's probably Greek, but she insists she's Jewish. You'd like her. They're wonderful people, they have two boys about sixteen—they're hysterical. They have tattoos and dreadlocks, both of them—one has a nose ring and is very pugnacious looking; they're both in a hip-hop band together—but around the store, it's 'yes dad' and 'okay ma' like it's 1932 and they're stuck in the family business forever. How they manage to do this in this day and age is beyond me; they're obviously wonderful parents. How he managed not to have 17 children with her around the house is beyond me too."

This is how everything goes with Nikos. There is no pizza without knowing the souls who contributed the sausage, especially if they have Greek origins or something in their histories—no matter how ancient—that filters back to Greece. And with Nikos, *everything* filters back to Greece. He made a career in a simpler age, an age when book publishing companies were owned by people who loved books, as a writer specializing in the place of

Greek-Americans, the problems of assimilation and enculturation in this turbulent, all-bets-are-off polyglot country.

"We Greeks are a people who habitually fall back on our history and rich traditions, our ancient heritage of civilization, good humor, individual dignity and democracy. In that, we are very much like the New York Yankees of the late 60's and early 70's, always reminiscing about 'Yankee tradition' and ignoring the fact that our team hasn't won a championship in years. It's not a natural transplant to take such a people and bring them to America. If America had a slogan, it would be something like 'History—so what?'" (*The Angry Son*, Simon & Shuster, 1974)

Nikos belittled the image of souvlaki stands and tuna fishermen, or worse, the anonymity that relieved Greek-Americans of *any* identity beyond the vague memories of grandpa muttering to himself in a foreign tongue about a civilization long gone.

"If anything," Nikos wrote, "Greeks are a victim of bad marketing. Like joie de vivre? WE invented it. Like democracy—or at least the idea of it, in a form far more effective than the representatives you're used to? You're welcome. My father's hair-trigger defenses of our national character—which embarrassed me no end growing up—wasn't nostalgia for lost greatness, but rather the knowledge that our world was *their* world, that almost every concept we cherish was created by the ancient Greeks and the credit dispersed among every other 'civilized' country around the globe. No wonder he was pissed."

"My publisher called the other day," Nikos says now, rolling out the dough for the crust. "He read my new manuscript and he says he wants me to rant more. I said I *am* ranting and he says 'For *you*, this might be ranting. No one else would know.'"

Nikos was writing *The Angry Son* when I studied with him at Sarah Lawrence in the mid-70's. The book was a weird cycle of rants, rebellious episodes and apologies for them, the safety valve of a man who looked around a world in upheaval and found no place to fit. The irony was that even at the time he could barely manage to raise his voice. The man was so unfailingly polite to his students that it took us half a year to see how effective a teacher he was.

At first, he seemed totally ineffectual—this is the trap modern cynical life sets for nice people. Condescension is a withering tool. "He's very *nice*," we curse. Nikos would find something *interesting* in every piece his poor students brought to class. Kids who had no place in a writing course were given encouragement and a sincere appreciation of the one thing they did well. And, once everyone inevitably relaxed—how easy could this writing thing be?—Nikos managed to get his points in about the parts of your story that didn't work *quite* so well, and about other ways to approach those elements.

And as I realized in later years, as my classes became far more exacting and developed far less successful writing: by relaxing everyone, he got us to *write* a lot, and at that stage of our lives, that was the best way to force-feed growth.

Unfortunately, that approach didn't help his work. In print, he was always softening the blow, never *really* certain he belonged at the party, a man so grateful for being there that he worked much too hard to avoid offending. He would make angry, valid points about America and apologize in the next breath. Somehow, in his fiction, he couldn't break through the happy veil, at a time the audience only wanted recklessness.

"I've tried to rewrite the stories, to get more worked up," he says now, spreading out the sauce lightly, a thin layer evenly spread from a ladle in an even smooth movement. "I'm stymied," he admits. "I can't write a damn thing. I don't even have any ideas. I spent my whole life afraid of the anger in me and I finally did it—I conquered it. And nobody wants me this way."

"Well, if angry is selling," I tell him, "I should go back to the book I was working on last month. I had ten rants a chapter."

"Sounds promising," he says, spreading cheese over the sauce and popping a slice of cholesterol-free sausage in his mouth. "Book of the Month Club, for sure."

"Yeah, but I can't write a damn either anymore. I don't see the point. I get so angry every time I sit at the keyboard that I just go inert."

"It doesn't work either way, does it?" he says. The TV continues shuffling images, as always: Fuzzy combat footage of our aerial campaign in Afghanistan accompanies the news that after three days, we have air superiority and can bomb pretty much anyone we want. Pentagon sources say we have thousands of troops massing in Uzbekistan, right across the border, ready for invasion. In response to the Al Qaeda press spokesman praising the terrorists who destroyed the Towers, the Secretary-General of NATO says, "These are evil criminals and, by their words, we shall judge them. I think they are now speaking the truth, and we know who's doing these evil atrocities, and we know where to get them."

"Boy, rage sure works for everyone else, though, doesn't it?" Nikos says.

"Yeah," I nod. "We're the only ones left out. You're too evolved to get angry and I'm too angry to express anything."

"The perfect comedy team," he muses. "Laurel and Godzilla. Costello and...Abbott? Which one of them was the calm one?"

"Neither," I say. "They were both angry."

Late that afternoon, Nikos says, "I guess we should make some plans. Are you going to stay here or shall I come down to you?" Then he pauses for a moment and stares at me. "You know, you really do worry me. You've been down since the Towers, but not like this. What happened?"

"I did something very very stupid the other day," I tell him. "I sent out ten more resumes Monday and got no response. I got three more rejection letters for the book. And then, out of nowhere, I got an email from one of the women I wrote the book about. You remember I told you about the Canadian girl? She wrote me. And I had this huge surge of adrenaline and immediately wrote an insanely enthusiastic reply—and I haven't heard a thing back. Two days. Obviously, I scared her off." I shake my head. "I'm so stupid. The damnedest part is, I'm not even surprised. I know better. But I saw her name in my inbox and it just blew my mind. It was like a sign."

"What kind of sign?" Nikos asks. He's wouldn't dispute the existence of signs and omens—another ancient element of life passed on to the world, if not invented, by the Greeks. But Nikos is also my dear friend, and he worries for my sanity, with reason.

"I don't know," I say, "it was just so bizarre, so out-of-left-field. How many years did I think about her with nothing happening? Then I finally finish the book and bang! She writes! It was just such a bolt from the blue, like proof of some benevolent force in the universe looking down on me. And with the way I've been feeling lately, it was like, for a moment, something reminded me what it was like to have hope—and then it all fell apart again. And now I feel like an idiot for letting myself get so excited."

"The hell with benevolent force in the universe," Nikos says immediately. "Call her up."

"And what do I say? Sorry I was a psycho on email?"

"She remembered you 25 years later," he says sensibly, sliding the pizza into the oven. "She wants to like you."

"I already sent her an apologetic message. I go any further with this and I'm gutterwash."

"Women don't really care what excuses we make," he tells me, "as long as we understand we're always supposed to apologize." He watches me for a moment—I am unmoved by this wisdom.

"*I'll* tell her," he says and I shake my head at his hallucinations. "I'll be a nice old man, I'll shuffle up to her and say 'You know, my friend Ted is a very nice guy and I happen to know he's really good in bed—he just doesn't know how to get off on the right foot sometimes."

I find myself laughing. It creeps up on me, such an unfamiliar experience that I don't even recognize it at first. Heaving chest, eyes narrowed, shoulders shaking, coughing —yes, it's laughter. Another old friend I've missed.

"I can *see* you doing that," I tell him. "I can see you walking up to her and saying that word for word. That is the most frightening thing I've ever heard."

We laugh together for a couple of minutes.

"It's good to see you do that," he says. "Maybe that's the medicine you need. You remember Norman Cousins, *Saturday Review*?"

"Yeah yeah I know—he cured his cancer with Marx Brothers movies. I remember reading the articles."

"Well, please God you don't have cancer," Nikos says. "Though it would be helpful if you knew. But you certainly suffer from a defeated attitude at least."

"And you think that humiliating myself for a woman in Ontario will help cure a defeated attitude? With the odds against this match, aren't you more likely to drive me to suicide?" I'm laughing again and I can't help noticing how good it feels. I also see that Nikos notices.

"Defeat doesn't spring from failure," he says. "It springs from not trying."

"Well, it also springs from failure," I said, "but at least with trying you get some exercise."

"It would work," he insists, a gleam in his eye. "I've got this little old man shtick honed to a tee."

"C'mon Nikos, get real. She's in *Ontario*."

"So?" he says, throwing his arms up with that Mediterranean expansiveness we share—Jews are a Mediterranean people, as he constantly reminds me. "It's not California. We could be there Thursday afternoon if we leave tomorrow."

"Uh huh," I say slowly, my head nodding like the ball in a Pong game. "I can see that. 'Hi—I just drove 700 miles to try to revive our 25-year-old relationship, which lasted all of 12 days to begin with and we never even kissed. This is my 77-year-old friend who drove out here with me—in fact, it was his idea—*he's* going to vouch for my sanity.' Kara's going to *love* driving to Ontario to bail us out."

"She'll laugh," he says. "I can't make her come anymore, at least I can make her laugh."

"It's not like anything would come of it," I say and my whining is now beginning to annoy me. "I haven't seen this girl since she was 18. She's not a girl anymore—and I'm not the guy I was, either."

Nikos' smile is still on his face but it's fading fast. He pulls the pizza from the oven and goes to get the pizza-cutting utensil. I wait for a story about the Greek technician who invented the thing but he switches up on me.

"It's painful to live," he says. "I've had times when I wonder why I keep going. Not how—why. Whatever death is, I don't expect it to hurt—at least not for long. And in truth I don't know if I have much of a life to miss anyway. Kara and I started sleeping separately once I couldn't get it up anymore. It's too hard to lie next to each other and not be able to do anything. It aches if we're together and it aches if we're not. But somehow I keep getting up hoping I can live another day. I don't even know what that means—I don't quite know what I'm hoping for—but I hope anyway."

I sleep that night in Kara's bed, with fifty overstuffed pillows, a down comforter thick enough to stop nuclear explosions and pictures of her friends and family staring down at me. I've never felt so out of place.

Lying alone in this big puffy bed, I do a terrible thing to myself—I run down the list of my last five employers and how much money I made for them while managing their businesses. I figure out what they have left and what I have left. This is a very bad idea. I go to the bathroom and find I am no longer pissing blood. If I knew I really didn't have cancer, this would be encouraging—as it is, it's just another reminder that I remain in limbo. Is everyone in limbo all the time or is it me?

I scan the décor, the pictures on Kara's wall. Who is the woman in the ancient stock car with the big red helmet and goggles—a personal friend? Has Kara for years been buddies with the Queen of Demolition Derby racing? Is it a secret life? If Nikos never comes in here, maybe he doesn't know. They're lesbians in stock cars. Sounds like a Bravo miniseries. I enjoy this lovely image and drift toward sleep planning the pitch letter to the network. *Sappho in Nomex*—that should sell, or maybe there's an even more brilliant title lurking in the back of my mind.

And then I think of Nikos. I think back on the afternoon and only in replay do I realize how alive he became when he proposed our lunatic road trip, for those few minutes when he seemed to really think it could happen. Remembering the smile fading on his face in the kitchen, I see the light fade on my own. I shift on the pillows. The day drifts by without meaning or satisfaction and then I can't sleep at night. I stare at the light on the ceiling, the streetlights outside reflecting in. Soon the sun will be up and drown out the lights humans make. The sun rises and sets—some things are out of our control. But we have a say about the light inside ourselves. I drift to sleep seeking the light.

Four

The next morning, Nikos is reading the paper as I come into the living room. "That was a crazy conversation we had last night," I say, and hold my breath.

"Which one?" he asks.

"You'd drive up to Ontario if I said I wanted to?"

I'm drumming my fingers on the table. I'm biting my lip till it's about to split. If he takes more than a second to answer, I'll explode.

"Sure," he says, barely looking up from the paper. He's not exactly chomping at the bit. But, at the moment, it is enough.

"Okay, let's go," I tell him, jumping up from the table.

"What?"

"Pack your bag—we'll eat on the road," I say and lead him to his room. I fetch his things from drawers and closets—"Need this? No? How about this?"—until we have enough to cover a few days on the road. Nikos looks dazed as we head to the car. It may not be a lot of walking, but at the pace I'm pulling him, it's surely the most intense exercise he's had in months.

I drive to Brooklyn, pack my stuff and am back downstairs to the car in fifteen minutes. We motor halfway to Pennsylvania without much in the way of conversation.

I'm afraid to speak. There's something tugging at me here that frightens me to death. I'm totally unsettled and I don't know if it's really because of Nora Hill or some romanticized memory of the way I felt twenty-five years ago or just the experience of feeling something—*anything*—again. I don't want to discuss it but I don't want to lose it either. I have a feeling that right now, being unsettled is a lot better place than where I've been.

While I'm watching the traffic and juggling maps, Nikos progresses from breathing loudly to clearing his throat to that hacking noise older people make just before keeling over.

"Ted?" he says finally.

"Yeah?"

"You know, I really shouldn't go without meals. The doctor says it's bad for me."

Oh God. "Jesus, Nikos, I'm sorry. I can't believe I lost track of that."

"It's no big deal," he murmurs, white as a ghost and sweating.

We pull off Rte. 80 in Denville. Where now lurks a Starbucks, my grandfather once had a luncheonette. He let me sit behind the counter and mix myself Cokes. Now Nikos and I wander the block, passing a pancake house, a chain store, a McDonalds—all the local alternatives. It is our first crisis.

"Look at this," Nikos says. "I can't eat this."

"Not very inspiring," I agree.

"No, I mean I *can't* eat it. Ted, I've been a vegetarian for thirty years. There's nothing here."

"You're still a vegan? You just made me a pizza with sausage."

"That was a present from my butcher," he protests.

"Yes, but you *have* a butcher! I'm a meat eater; I don't have a butcher. Your butcher gives you *presents*, no less!"

"Well, I can't cheat all the time," he says, moaning.

"Okay," I say, trying to regroup. "This is New Jersey. We should be able to find a health food store or a veggie restaurant."

Nothing in Denville, nothing in Dover, or on the local highway between. An hour has ticked by on my precious schedule. We might be able to make up time on the highway if we find something soon, but what will we do for dinner?

"Oh, let's go here," Nikos says suddenly and I turn into the lot without even looking.

"Nikos, this is Nathans."

"So I'll cheat one more time," he says. "I love their French fries."

Lunch is an adventure. Nikos actually finds a veggie burger on the menu, though it looks just as dangerous as the regular ones. I get a chicken sandwich, take the chicken off the bun and pick at it with plastic fork and knife.

"No French fries?" Nikos asks.

I can't—I'm going to see Nora Hill. Last night, I was the living dead; today, I'm worried about losing weight. I have to look good. I need to work out. I need to run. I need to lose twenty pounds today. I need to shave. I *need*. To need is to live. As ridiculous as these concerns are, they are at least signs of life. For anyone else, vanity is superficiality, the triumph of the shallow; for me, it's a harbinger of mental health.

"As soon as I finish the French fries," Nikos says, stretching, "we should go for a walk. You promised Kara I'd get my exercise." He stands stiffly, throws out his cup and plates and heads toward the beckoning florescent-lit halls filled with Halloween displays. I follow dutifully. I am the oldest son in my family. Birth-order proponents say the oldest child is generally wracked with guilt and responsibility, so I can be had this way.

"Oh—what is that?" Nikos asks the instant we reach the mall, staring into the window of an electronics store.

"It's a personal organizer," I tell him. "You put your phone numbers and your schedule in it and take them with you in your pocket. One of my friends has a portable keyboard—it's the size of a wallet. You unfold it and it becomes an almost full-size keyboard. So he takes his Palm on trips and types whole speeches and memos on it."

That's what I tell him. What I am thinking is: Here's another thing you can buy at an inflated price to show other people you have expendable income. I, of course, am above all that or at least I would be if I *had* expendable income.

"That's so interesting," Nikos says, looking stunned. He stares at the shiny object as though waiting for it to speak. "Do you think when people start relying on electronics to take the place of their memory they're in some way diminishing their brain capacity?"

"The electronics companies will tell you it leaves you *more* capacity for complex thinking," I say. "On the other hand, it will surely offer more space for advertising."

"Hmm," he muses. "I used to have a little notepad I carried around in my pocket. But it wasn't a calendar, and I would still have to search the whole thing to find a note when I needed it. And I had to remember there was a note there. So, I guess there is a lot of mental overhead involved. I suppose this thing beeps or something when you have an appointment?"

"As long as you've got it on, yes."

"Wonderful," he purrs. "Yes, it could be a revolution in people's thought processes. How marvelous."

I don't want to do this. I liked it better when we were back at his house and I could politely listen to him or ignore him, the same way I have most of my elders my whole life long. I would really rather be cynical and Nikos won't let me. Watching him consider this $69.99 ON SALE NOW item, I realize how few thoughtful people there are in my world. Nothing is inconsequential or without implication once he becomes aware of it. He has less money than me and his health is failing but he harbors no resentment.

I used to admire this in him. Now, I'm tired of it. It's an impediment, an endless series of detours on the road to wherever the hell it is I'm going. It's phony—it's pretending the world is underneath a nice place if you only have the eyes to see it. The world isn't nice and it shows every sign of getting worse by the day. It's a marvel he can keep up the energy necessary to support this façade and come to think of it, it's the reason I agreed to do this with him—he might yet charm Nora Hill into speaking to me again—but I resent it all the same.

We walk another ten steps, each a separate activity. My normal walking pace beats most people's jogging—I'm a lifelong New Yorker, so my normal assumption is that I'm always behind the times or missing something every second. Nikos has almost no momentum at all. You can almost watch him command each leg muscle separately to move.

A woman walks by wearing a baby carrier, with the baby riding her chest, facing her. Nikos shuffles right up in front of her, pointing and smiling, and her headlong pace falters for just a moment.

"That's such a nice papoose," Nikos says in his most amiable, loving grandpa voice. "This way you can always see her face."

"Yes," the woman says, "I like it a lot."

"I see," Nikos remarks, "she seems to be talking to you already." The baby is making the usual baby coos and ahhs.

"She's talking a blue streak today," the mother answers.

"And she's not just making noises," Nikos says, making a big smile at the baby on Momma's chest. "She's really saying things, don't you think? She doesn't know the words, but if you listen to her voice, the tone keeps changing."

"Yes, I just noticed it the other day," Mom says. "When was it? Tuesday or Wednesday...All of a sudden, she had a completely different sound to the noises she's making."

"That's how it happens," Nikos confides. "The little changes mount up and suddenly they're grown. You're so lucky to be the kind of person who notices."

"I miss them, way too often," the woman answers. "I was just lucky to notice it this time."

"Well, that's part of the trick, to keep noticing," Nikos says. "It gets easier as you get older—everything becomes precious. But it's so important to do it while you're young, while the big events are still happening all around you."

It actually hurts to watch this. The rules of life don't apply to him. Maybe because he's got the old grandfather shtick down so well. Maybe because it's *genuine* in him. While most people respond to disease and age by drawing inward, Nikos continues to bloom, to embrace everything around him.

I walk away from Nikos and the happy new mother and the gurgling little baby and I want to strangle someone—anyone, for that matter. I've been in a state of walking anesthesia for a month now, a cotton ball world, isolated from everything outside and inside. All at once that seems like a positive. Because suddenly my isolation has broken down completely. I'm brimming with anger.

Nikos finds everything fascinating, so he has a fascinating life. The experience of living is still sweet for him despite the pains. I understand that this is real, but I don't know how to feel that way. I don't understand his total lack of resentment at the way old people are ignored and marginalized, about the fact that he can't get it up and his retirement money runs out the 18th of every month.

I feel like life is false advertising from birth to death and that at an advanced age I'm just catching on to this. I also feel that most of the people around me—including him?—haven't caught on to this yet and don't necessarily want to know. I have an image of myself as Kevin McCarty at the end of 'Bodysnatchers' running around the countryside warning people against the pods while all they want is a good snooze in a nice cocoon.

When I was younger, I charmed everyone. I was rude and headstrong, I knew nothing about anything. I have more regrets than pleasure looking back. Nonetheless, people wanted to know me, found me interesting. Now I've evolved, I've grown. I'm on the whole a much more considerate thoughtful person than I was. I understand other people's needs far better than I did and I take the time to find out about them. I'm nowhere near as tunnelvisioned after my own goals. And somehow my old friends have fallen out of touch and the new ones I make come and go. I seem unable to convince anyone to care about me.

I've gone on several dates in the last year or two and all they've done in push me deeper into hibernation. It's not that I've developed a hunchback or a cleft palate. It's not that they're all terminally damaged, though the disappointments show in all of us. It's simply that magic is hard to find.

Even when a woman is interesting and attractive, those things come across as consolation-prize emotions. I'm unable to push myself over the edge, to take the plunge and really believe this is a magical creature. Meanwhile, I met magical creatures every three days when I was twenty-five.

The fault lies not in the stars but in ourselves. I don't believe anymore. I've seen through love. I've recognized its transparent phoniness, and as much as I accept the reality—the fact that it simply isn't out there—I miss the hope it once gave me. So I hate everything and especially those pleasant heartwarming feelings

Nikos engenders in everyone he meets. Everyone but me. I don't even find something genuine in the genuine anymore.

As we hit the road, Nikos humming happily to himself in the passenger seat, I sink deeper and deeper. How can I meet Nora Hill in this frame of mind? How will this make anything better?

I check the messages on my cell phone.

"This is Doctor Speilman's office. It's very important that the doctor speak with you. Please call xxx-xxx-xxxx. Thank you."

Very important? Shit! I call.

"The doctor's left for the day. Can you call back tomorrow?"

"It's only 4 o'clock."

"He had an appointment. Can you call tomorrow?"

"Yeah sure I can call." I carefully place the phone back on the console, carefully so as to keep myself from slamming it so hard as to break it.

It rains as we split the shallow canyon of the Delaware Water Gap, running along the swollen river in violet-tinted light, beneath bare trees and ancient hills.

We spend the night in Central Pennsylvania. This is a bit scary—I'm unemployed, so the idea was to get to Canada fast and spend as little on hotel rooms as is humanly possible. Nonetheless, the town has a vegetarian restaurant to counteract Nathans' and I'm as tired as he is or so I think.

Nonetheless, I spend the evening staring out the rainy window while Nikos snores in his bed. Not for the first time, I feel like a massive fool.

As we get older, the feelings get riper, deeper. Closer to the surface, closer to the bone. The hurts resonate. It's one thing to write stories about them—doesn't take a lot of courage to pretend to love someone when you're plotting out their every move, or most of them (characters have a way of getting on about their own business after a while and if you're a smart writer, you don't get in the way)—but it's another to actually let yourself take that chance with another person. I've evolved into a cautious, cynical-about-love adult.

Nora is probably one of the only people on earth who could have unlocked this Pandora's box in me. When I heard from her, it was like time travel—the feelings that poured out of me at that moment came full-blown from the earnest, impossibly innocent 20-year-old me. I am carrying the photo I took of her, her parents, sister and brother on the cruise ship all those years ago. When I see it, when I look at her open smiling face, I respond as I did then. I feel the way I did then and anything is possible.

And that's the problem, ain't it? Everything doesn't seem possible anymore. The world isn't ours to command. We aren't going to write our own script, nor are we necessarily our own best friends, nor is everything—or even anything—going to go the way we want. And we can't possibly have grown in the same direction over all those intervening years. Most people who've followed paths like mine are confined to little padded rooms for their own protection.

> Nora Hill? Do I remember you?
> Is this the Nora Hill that had
> me park the Porsche over by the
> high school so she could sit in
> the front seat and smoke
> cigarettes and look tough? (Did
> you smoke cigarettes really? I
> can't say if I actually
> remember that or if it's one of
> those painterly details that
> looks good in my mind's eye...)
> Is this the Nora Hill who had
> all the band members fighting
> over her in our little teen
> lounge at the back of the boat?
> I doubt I've thought of you
> more than ten or fifteen times
> a year since then...

To write her such an obviously desperate reply was stupid and typical of me. It's how I always drive women away—my heart is on my sleeve before we've even gotten to know each other. And to actually act on these feelings—to drive up to Canada to see her now—is insanity. She may have just seen my name on a webpage and wanted to say 'Hi' and here I am, ready to storm the castle, claim the maiden, slay the dragon and write a novel about it at the same time.

I'm a sad lonely motherfucker. I'm a pathetic fool who daydreams and hopes to make a living at it. But even if I reach *that* goal, it won't make this one any less crazy.

Tomorrow morning, I will take Nikos and go home and send another email to Nora. I'll forget about her if she doesn't respond. Or maybe I'll try her again in a month or two—I have her email address, after all—and see if she'll give me another shot. I'll grovel. A little gravel up the nostrils is a good thing now and then, in a good cause.

It's the taste of real life.

Five

When I awake, Nikos is already in the shower. I know this will take at least half an hour, so I dawdle packing up and figuring out what to wear on the drive home. I'm avoiding my own avoidance.

A memorial service is already starting at Ground Zero, the Mayor speaking and bagpipes droning. We're bombing the shit out of Kandahar in Afghanistan and they're making a fuss over anthrax being found in a supermarket tabloid publisher's offices in Florida. Excuse me... Anybody who could cook up flying airliners into the World Trade Center isn't looking for small-time revenge on some scandal sheet.

Eventually I give up on the news and do my duty. I call the doctor's office. At least it won't make me feel much worse than I do already.

I actually get the doctor, which is a shock. The receptionist takes my name and the actual doctor picks up. In this day and age, where medicine is just a fancy front for penny-pinching insurance companies, I start sweating. Do I have AIDS? Why else would the doctor talk to me on the phone? I only had sex once without a condom since my last physical and she *swore* it was okay.

"Hi Ted," Doctor Spielshit says. "I just want to head off a problem before it gets serious."

Now I get chills.

"Problem?"

"Well, you haven't been in for another biopsy."

"I finished pissing blood yesterday," I tell him. "Isn't there supposed to be a cooling-off period?"

"Well, I'm sorry, that is one of the temporary complications of this procedure. It might actually have been preferable if we'd run the test again immediately, which would only have held up the healing process a few days. Now, of course, you'll have to go through the whole thing again. Can you hold a minute?"

Now I'm fuming. I listen to the on-hold music—cool jazz, perfect for the anesthesiologists' lounge.

"Yes, I'm back," the doctor says.

"OK," I say. "What is the purpose of this 'important' call?"

"I'm sorry?"

"Your office said it was important I call you. Why?"

"Oh, well they may have overstated that a bit," he says. Professionals are always so comfortable judging other people's performance. "It's just that it's been two months."

"I thought prostate cancer was slow."

"It can be. It isn't always."

"Well, okay—that brings up an interesting point. Let's say I come in and we do another set of clippings from my innards. Let's say you find some cancer, okay?"

"Well," he hedges, "we're a long way from there." I am sure doctors are told how soothing this dismissive approach is in med school. At the moment, it just reads like another way to hold off responsibility.

"But for argument's sake, let's just say you find I have a cancer of the prostate. Does your test tell you if I've got 1% cancer or 20% cancer?"

"The test simply reads positive or negative," he answers. "But we can get some information about the spread from the result of the multiple samples."

"Okay, but if you only had one sample that came back positive, you'd still recommend treatment, right?"

"Again," he laughs nervously, transparently trying to end the call now, "we're many many steps from this discussion."

"No, we're not—we're actually having it right now," I tell him firmly, "but it won't take long." I'm banking a head of steam here and I know where I'm going. "If you had one sample come back positive, you'd recommend treatment—right?"

"Well, of course," he answers. "You're young. If you were in your seventies, there wouldn't be much need, as most prostate cancer is very slow-moving. The saying is, 'people don't die of prostate cancer—"

"—they die *with* it', yes I've read that a lot lately. And maybe I heard it from you--maybe more than once. But again, if I've got a cancer, the treatment options at that point would be—"

"Well," he huffs, making sure I know just how inconvenient this discussion is now, before he's ready for it, "there is the radiation and chemotherapy route or the surgical solution. But there are several variations on each of these, and that discussion makes no sense until we know if you actually have a cancer, and if so, in how many samples, etc."

Let's just make everything as disembodied as possible, why don't we? Nikos comes out of the bathroom now, singing. *If you can use some exotic booze, there's a bar in old Bombay—come fly with me come fly let's fly away.* I feel a smile on my face as all my anger comes bubbling up inside. For once, somehow, it doesn't overwhelm me. It doesn't lead me out of control, beyond control. It doesn't make me stupid. For once, I focus on a solution, at least a temporary one: if I'm looking at a potential future of feeling bad, for the moment let's do whatever feels good.

"OK, fine doc. Let me boil down my question: with a surgical solution, there's always a risk—small or large—that I will come out of it unable to have sex and wearing a diaper for the rest of my life, yes?"

"There is a risk of impotence and incontinence," the doctor recites.

"Which is what I just said but not as ugly, right?" There is a very noisy speechless pause. I can hear him breathing—his teeth must be gritted right against the mouthpiece.

"Yes," he says. I'm pretty sure I should never allow this guy near me with sharp objects again.

"Okay, and as far as I'm concerned, radiation and chemotherapy are the modern equivalent of leeches and bloodletting. So now we know where we stand. Thank you Doc—I'll get back to you."

"So, do you want to schedule an appointment?" he persists. God, he's stubborn, thick-skinned and doesn't care when you insult him. He'll probably end up *owning* the insurance company.

"After I get back," I tell him, "from my trip to Canada."

Six

And so we're off. I make real good time—the only traffic problems are near shopping malls and we hit several of them at off-peak times. Nikos eats a diner salad for lunch and we walk around the parking lot for ten minutes for his exercise.

Once we get to Canada, we'll figure out something a little more meaningful," I tell him.

"I'm sorry I'm such a burden," he says.

"You're not a burden," I answer and feel properly ashamed of myself for the things I've been thinking the last twenty-four hours.

"Yes I am. You'd be up there already if it wasn't for my food and my exercise and all my maladies."

"That's alright—you just charm this girl to death when we get up there."

"Well," he smiles, "I can't do too good a job or she'll dump you for me. What's her mother doing?"

"Her mother's gorgeous but her father's a media mogul or something if I remember correctly—the Rupert Murdoch of eastern Ontario or at least the local couple of towns."

"Money—and handsome, I assume."

"Ronald Coleman," I tell him solemnly.

"No, that's no good," he murmurs. "How's her grandmother?"

"If she's still around, she should be something like ninety-two," I say. "Too old for you."

"I can't get it up," he laughs again. "What's the difference? Maybe she's a good kisser."

By early afternoon, we're rapidly approaching the border. The radio warns of new attacks in coming days. The Government announces that nine of the nineteen Sept 11 hijackers were in the United States legally that day, and four others had visas that had expired. This is a real consolation—wouldn't want them to murder thousands of people and be guilty of immigration crimes on top of it.

"Shit," I say.

"What's the matter?" says Nikos.

"It's the one month anniversary of September 11 and we're approaching a border crossing."

"Yes?"

"Is your passport in your pocket?"

"Oh." He gets that thoughtful look again as though that will help.

"No, mine neither. I've always crossed this border without thinking twice, but that's not going to work anymore. We need to be creative," I say. I'm not ready to back down. We've come this far—I want to find a way through. If we get turned back, at least I tried.

"Pull off on the scenic overlook there," Nikos says. I obey, though I can't imagine what he has in mind. I can't find anything that qualifies as 'scenic' either—maybe it's a patronage thing or maybe there has to be a scenic overlook every so-many miles. What do you mean our county isn't scenic?

But it appears Nikos actually has a plan. He has me pull into the spot next to the pay phones, pulls a little black book from his pocket and makes a call. When he comes back to the car, he starts reading me very explicit and complex directions he's scribbled on the back page.

"Isn't this taking us way out of our way?" I ask.

"He says it's only twenty minutes drive."

"Who says?"

"Billy Hassun. Was he at Sarah Lawrence when you were there? I don't think so—he was mid-80's I think."

"I wish I was that young. No such luck. Hassun? Is he Muslim? Must be having a hard time..."

"No, actually he's Native American. Hassun is Algonquin for stone. He wrote some really interesting stories about what it's like to assimilate into the culture that destroyed your own. But he hasn't sent me anything to read in several years. He lives around here somewhere—he's always telling me to come visit him."

"Well, this isn't really what I had in mind. I do want to try to make the border tonight, even if we have to try to talk our way across."

"This isn't a visit," Nikos says. "I told him it wasn't. Billy's a very smart kid—very shrewd. If he lives here, he knows everybody I'll bet." He nods, pleased with himself for this idea. "Yes, I'll bet on Billy over the US Government."

We meet Billy at a diner that actually is twenty minutes drive off the highway. He is a hulking man, well over six feet, broad-shouldered and barrel-chested and dressed very nattily in flannel and corduroy. A country gentleman with a face that reminds me that Native Americans are supposed to have been Asians who wandered over the landbridge.

"Nikos!" he cries with delight and folds our old professor into a deep hug. "Nice to meet you Ted," he says and nearly crushes my hand while shaking it.

The diner has a spinach salad with garlic and nuts for Nikos. I order trout and spend my whole meal coveting his salad. Billy eats bean curd and brown rice with Budweiser.

"So what are you doing now? Are you still writing?" These are Nikos' unending concerns. The two questions are inescapably joined when he sees a student after a gap. It is of no importance to him *what* you're writing—Nikos' former students include several celebrated novelists, a popular film reviewer on the Web, a major press spokesperson for the Republican party, the editor of a notorious New York show biz insider publication and two famously-ruthless press agents—the concern is simply that you maintain the love affair with words. Nikos asks the question and Billy grins and looks around before answering.

"I'm making a damn good living writing," he says, "or at least I was. I was writing erotica, churning stories out by the dozens a year. It's amazing how good the imagination can be if properly stimulated," he says and laughs again, a deep growl of a laugh like an animal hiding down his throat. "But that's over—Internet is killing all the magazines and nobody reads stories over the Internet. At least, no one will *pay* for them over the Internet. So I may have to go back to writing something serious. I've got the money for it now." He looks at me and winks. "Never hurts to sell out young. You can always start over. Don't believe 'em if they tell you different."

"This is beautiful country," Nikos says admiringly. "There must be some interesting stories up here."

"You're the one that taught me there are stories everywhere," Billy says, his eyes opening up a bit. "When I got back here, years later, after New York and LA and Bogota, I started rediscovering the old legends, the spirits in the land and the shamans who communicated with them and told their stories. Storytelling is a respected tradition among my culture. Unfortunately, there aren't that many that respect the old culture anymore."

"Well, *that's* a subject," Nikos insists. "Don't think about it, just *write*."

The look in Billy's eyes says this is easier said than done. And while Nikos offers this as a panacea, he isn't writing himself. Billy fixes his gaze on me. "You're with Nikos so I assume you're a writer. What kind of stuff?"

I find myself rubbing my forehead and looking at all the interesting details of the room for several minutes.

"Don't know anymore," I tell him. "Humor. That's what I used to write." The napkins are in rough wood enclosures on the tables. A tractor-trailer with sixteen American flags flapping on plastic arms rolls by on the highway. Billy continues to stare at me, sizing me up while I frantically try to fix my attention somewhere—anywhere—else.

"So what's funny these days?" he asks me.

"That's what I don't know, I guess."

He shrugs and goes back to his beans. Sure, be like that. If this was a movie, he'd have some mystical-sounding primitive Native American wisdom to share with me and I'd feel all healed up and ready to go. But no, not me—I get the hulking Native American macrobiotic erotica writer.

"So Nikos says you have to get across the border and for some reason he thinks I will know how to do this." He looks at the two of us as though sizing us up. "I'm not a smuggler. And though he knows I have my own funny attitudes toward America, I certainly don't want to compromise anyone's security when times are tough."

"You still owe me twenty-seven dollars over a pair of eights," Nikos tells him, his expression comically serious. Billy's laugh bubbles up again.

"Nikos, that's twenty years ago."

"I'm not asking for the interest," Nikos says, "though twenty years at even 18% would be pretty substantial. Just get us across. You know how harmless I am."

Now Billy laughs out loud. "Yeah, I know how harmless you are—that's why I'm thinking about it so hard." He turns his gaze to me. "You play poker?" he asks.

"No—never learned to play cards," I say.

"Too bad," he says. "Good source of humor. Many opportunities there to learn to read a man." He looks back at Nikos. "He seems too serious to be a funny writer."

"Oh, he's very funny when it's in him," Nikos defends me. "Most of the really funny writers are very serious people, almost morose."

"Oh, well then you must be a *bundle* of laughs," Billy says and cackles again, this time laughing *at* me. For some reason, I find myself joining in. If morose equals humor, yes, I'm pretty comical at the moment.

Half an hour later, we find ourselves at a flimsy shack on a curve in a dirt road eleven miles from nowhere.

"Ralph, take them," Billy says.

"I did my last run twenty minutes ago."

"So untie the damned thing and take them," Billy repeats. Ralph sits at his dinner table staring at the Big Mac and Fries he's just set down there. He is lean and grizzled like only an old single man can be. Mean from neglect and resentment. Argumentative from loneliness. Paralyzed by habit and the memory of failure, which he nurses every night before going to sleep. I know this guy. I see him in the mirror every once in a while when I'm not looking.

"The boat's tied up, Danny's gone home. I got nobody to work the ramps and tie up," he says. "I can't do everything."

"I'll do it," Billy says. "I used to do it for you in the summer."

"That was twenty-five years ago Billy."

"How hard is it Ralph? It's a couple ropes and putting my foot out when we get near the dock. Once I've tied up, you can help me with the ramp."

Ralph maintains his stubborn look. He pulls the Big Mac out of its wrapper and takes a bite.

"You know, you haven't asked us why we need you," Nikos says, though there's no evidence at all that Ralph cares about this in the least.

"Why?" Ralph asks without conviction. "Is it dope? You can't smoke that stuff on my boat."

"It's for love," Nikos says with a smile. "There's a girl on the other side waiting for this guy. He hasn't seen her in twenty-five years."

Ralph looks over at me. "What of it?" he says.

"Well, I just thought you'd want to know," Nikos answers in a soft voice. "I'm sure you take a good deal of responsibility in your job. I wanted you to know it's for a good cause. I'm sure there's somebody from twenty-five years ago you'd like to see again if you had the chance." Ralph looks up at Nikos as though trying to imagine what planet he's come down from, but he puts the Big Mac back on the table for a moment.

"There was a Greek river god," Nikos continues, "Alpheus, I think it was, a tributary of the Tiber. He loved a huntress but she wouldn't marry him. She turned into a spring in order to avoid any further problems, but Alpheus mingled his waters with hers."

"Well of course he did," Ralph says. "If she didn't want him, why'd she turn herself into a spring? That makes no sense."

"It's an ancient legend," Nikos says. "Sometimes they don't translate well to a modern sensibility."

"Sensibility?" Ralph bellows. "It's just stupid. If she stayed a huntress, all he could do is get her *wet!*" He takes another bite of his burger. It's cold, evidently—he throws it on the table and stands, hitching up his pants. "I'm gonna take a leak," he announces, "and then we'll go across the river." He walks up to Billy and points at Nikos. "Just keep him quiet—and away from me." Then he trudges off to the john.

"You see?" Nikos says as the door closes. "Love convinces people to do all kinds of things."

"Nikos, I think he just wants to shut you up," I tell him.

Nikos shakes his head. "No, he's sentimental. He just doesn't show it well."

Ralph comes out of the bathroom and walks up to me. "You're the one in love," he says. "That'll be a hundred bucks."

Ten minutes later, we're on a ferry. I call it a ferry because its purpose is to ferry us across the St. Lawrence River, a body of water whose size I never properly appreciated before. Facing it with only the protection of this pipsqueak of a boat, with its rattling coughing motor and barely room for my Honda Civic and the four of us, the river seems a giant monster. The ferry is bouncing on the little waves and there's more to come—the purple clouds are sweeping across the sky as we untie and set to our business.

We head out around an island. I keep my eyes open for patrol boats and, sure enough, see one as soon as we come clear into the main channel.

"I think that's the Feds," I say, using up all my smuggler lingo at once. "Do you make a run for it? Do we hang near the coast for a while until they go away? I can't afford to pay them off—unless you're willing to split your fee with them," I call to Ralph. The wind is picking up severely—I have to yell at full throat to have a chance of being heard.

"This thing only has one speed," Ralph says and tends to his tiller. He appears to be making no effort at all to stay hidden. Does he *want* them to catch us? The son-of-a-bitch! We spoil his Big Mac so now he's going to have us jailed as terrorists? Maybe he gets some kind of reward?

Billy walks up and leans over me. "We don't have to hide," he whispers. "They know Ralph's boat. This place is a self-governing reservation. We're technically not part of the United States—they can't touch us. Besides which, they know this boat is so small, you couldn't carry very much of anything on it."

I look at him carefully. His gaze is not entirely transparent. And why is he whispering? "That's fine for smuggling," I say. "You'll only have enough dope for a local dealer. But what if it's a small atomic bomb?"

"They're not that small," he says. "Even a small bomb would be too heavy for this tub." How does *he* know? As soon as we hit the main channel, it starts to rain—hard. Ralph and Billy immediately throw plastic buckets at Nikos and me. I'm about to ask what they're for, but instantly I see the answer—the ferry is filling with water at an alarming rate.

"The drains is all clogged," Ralph says. "I keep meaning to fix 'em."

"In the meantime," Billy orders, "bail!"

I bail. It's amazing how much motivated you can be when your largest piece of personal property is sinking into the St. Lawrence River.

"Are you okay?" I yell to Nikos. Looking at him, I'm instantly stricken with guilt. He's bailing very slowly and he has to keep bending over, which can't be good in his condition. He's drenched already—the man is here because of my insanity and now he's going to end up with pneumonia.

"I'm getting my exercise," he says, laughing, the rain running down his face.

"I'm so sorry," I tell him.

"Why?" he says. "I could be sitting in my house complaining about the tightness in my chest. Now I'll either have a heart attack or drown." He takes another scoop with his bucket and tosses the water in my direction. "I was so looking forward to a Viking funeral," he yells.

I look around. The patrol boats are near and watching us, but apparently they really can't interfere. I can't help imagine, however, what a picture we must make. Ralph is kicking the engine in the back of the boat, Billy is running around preparing ropes and cursing a blue streak. The boat is flopping from one side to the other in the wind and the waves, Nikos is bailing with surprising vigor and I am soaked to the skin.

As I look out at the back of the ferry, I see a ratty old pirate flag—skull and crossbones—whipping in the wind. All of a sudden, I start giggling and can't stop. I keep bailing but I'm hanging over the rail from lightheadedness. I feel positively goofy.

Nikos looks over at me, clearly alarmed at this sudden breakdown of my moroseness. I glance over the front of the boat and order him, "Get in the car."

"We're not there yet," he yells back.

"It's okay," I tell him. "Get in the car. Start her up. Get it warm inside."

I can see the far shore approaching quickly. Even without bailing, the ferry will make shore before it sinks.

As soon as we hit the shoreline, I help Billy pull out the ramp. "Thanks guys," I yell and get in the car.

"We're gonna be stuck here for hours bailing," Ralph complains, staring at me. "I should have something extra."

"We're even," I say. "You didn't tell me we were going to have to row across." And I gun the car up the ramp and away.

Seven

We make Waterline around 8PM and stop for a local roadmap. When I come out of the gas station, Nikos is hobbling around the parking lot like someone shot him in both knees.

"What happened to you?"

He immediately straightens up and walks the rest of the way back to the car in a completely normal fashion for him—still slow as molasses, but normal.

"Just practicing," he says. "She's not going to know what hit her. I'll shamble up her driveway and she'll feel guilty just for being able to walk—and then I'll tell her about you."

"You probably should omit the line about me being good in bed," I remind him.

"Thanks for reminding me," he says. "I would have forgotten to say that."

I get in and give him the address and the map. I drive ten feet and have to stop, since the map's unfolded so big I can't see the windshield. The two of us wrestle the thing down to size and then he starts barking commands, like the old combat sarge he is.

"Left here. Two blocks down—make a right. Now there's a...a squiggly thing, where you bear right. Oh, hell—this street doesn't go through. We have to go back."

We take a few adventurous routes through town—there are some nice houses and a lovely view of the inlet—but he seems no more certain of our direction than when he picked up the map.

"This is a very interesting town," he says. "You always get such interesting layouts where you have rivers and inlets like this."

"Yes, it's lovely," I say. "And I'm blessed to have had such a thorough introduction to the area. Are we any closer to where she lives?"

"Well, I think it's *here,*" he says, holding up the map, which doesn't help me while I'm driving. I pull into a parking lot and consider.

"That's the right road," I say, "but it doesn't look right. I remember there being water nearby—right nearby."

I look at the map. Apparently, Canada's roadbuilders aren't any more brilliant than those of the United States. A road with the same name appears across the inlet, running along the water.

"We're going *there,*" I say, pointing and driving at the same time.

When we get across, I can tell which house it is immediately—a little newer than the others, a little more rustic taste than the ranches and split-levels built in the 50's and 60's.

There's a car in the driveway. I pull up across the street and Nikos gets out.

"You know," I say to him, "now that we're actually here, I'm wondering if this is such a good idea. I mean, maybe I should just go to the door and talk to her. The worst she can do is slam it in my face."

"That's true," he says, "but you know she wouldn't slam it in *my* face—my nice Greek-American grandpa face. I've been rehearsing this since my shower yesterday. I'm going to give an Academy Award performance." I must still look skeptical—he reaches a hand in and pats me on the shoulder. "Relax," he says, "you're in good hands."

And now he moves across the road, peering tremulously in both directions for traffic—and if they are a mile away when he starts, they still have a good shot at him before he gets across. Every movement is painful to watch—I can imagine Lon Chaney Sr. giving him a run for his money but no one else.

I'm trying so hard to keep from laughing that my neck cramps. I turn my head to the other side of the street, the one I'm parked on. I look down the row of houses and realize that the second one up is Nora's parents old house, the one I visited her in back in 1973.

And as I stare at it, Nora comes out the door with some guy, who opens an SUV door for her and stomps on the accelerator, backing out of the short driveway with a screech.

"Nikos!" I yell. "Come back!"

"I'll get there," he says over his shoulder.

"Wrong house," I yell. "That's *her!*"

I'm pointing at the car as it goes by. He stands stock-still, staring at it as though it might lift off the ground at any moment.

When it goes by, he looks at me and says, "She's very pretty."

"Thanks," I say. "Get in the *car!!*"

I wrestle the car around into the driveway of the wrong house, Nikos gets in as quickly as he can, and then I tear down the road doing 60 in a 30 zone (no kids in sight, thank God) after the speeding SUV.

"What was she doing *there*?" he asks.

"If I remember right, that's her parent's house. Either they still live there or I got the wrong address."

"Where's she going?"

"How do I know?" I keep the pedal down till we hit the bridge. There's traffic and I can see them just a few cars ahead. At one point, she turns to get something from the back seat and I instinctively duck my head. I realize instantly what a bad idea this is and look up, but then I have to hit the brakes hard to avoid hitting the car in front of me, who's come to a dead stop for traffic. My brakes screech hard, and the car even swerves a little. I can see her look back from the SUV. Shit—did she see me?

"I'm busted," I say.

"What do you mean?"

"I think she saw me."

"No, she saw a green Honda Civic being driven very badly — not you," he says. "If you're lucky, they'll go to dinner and by the time you talk to her, she'll have forgotten the car."

The SUV stops at the same gas station at which we bought the map what seems like hours ago. I pull into a spot along the side street and wait, idling, craning my neck till it hurts to make sure I don't miss them when they pull out.

Nikos has been looking at me for some time now. I only notice when I straighten my neck out momentarily.

"Um, Ted--?"

"Yeah?"

His lips are pursed—he looks as concerned as he'll ever let himself show. "What do you plan to do?" he asks.

"What do you mean?"

"Well, are we—are we going to follow them around? What if they go to dinner and a show?"

I realize all at once what he's saying: Ted, are you stalking this girl? Oops...

I hold my hands up. "I just want to see where they're going. Then I'll find us a hotel, okay?"

Which is a little like saying, I just want to shoot the gun once to see if it's loaded. Nonetheless, I can't stop now. I could find a hotel and come back in the morning, but I can't. I just can't. I want to see her tonight. I've driven a long way.

No, none of that is the answer why I'm following her and I'm not going to answer that question—not even to myself. Besides, what if it's just a casual male friend taking her to the drug store and she'll be home in five minutes? Why she needs a casual male friend to take her to the drug store is irrelevant—all I need is the flimsiest excuse to keep going at this point.

Shortly, the SUV pulls out of the driveway and hurtles past us. This guy must drive NASCAR on off-weekends. I follow as fast as I can, but I'm in a 4-cylinder Honda Civic and he's in a dual-turbocharger Behemoth with the Super-size Fries and a Coke. I begin weaving between lanes, using any tiny space to pass and zip ahead, to gain on the speeding SUV.

"I'm sorry," Nikos says at one point, pulled up fetal in his seat and a bit green. "I get really uncomfortable when I can read the stenciling on the taillights as we go by."

"There's no *close* here," I say. "If we don't actually hit them, we have enough space."

But I know the toll my driving takes on more timid souls. And soon enough, the road thins out and only a smattering of cars stand between us and the SUV.

He's still a distance ahead, but the exits are widely placed (NEXT EXIT 22 MILES) so I can creep up on him—if doing 90 can be called creeping—and make sure I get into good stalking distance before we reach the next town.

Over the next several miles we close the gap. They'll remain in sight if they turn onto local streets but we're still far enough away not to be conspicuous. Jeff Gordon seems to have it on cruise control. I'm feeling more comfortable.

This comfort level erodes, slowly but steadily, as we continue barreling down this highway another hour. By this point, there are very few other cars on the road—I actually let the gap widen between us, so as not to be too obvious.

Nikos appeared to be dozing, but at one point his eyes flicker and he says, "Have we found out where they're going yet?"

"They haven't got there yet," I answer, but that's not answering the question he's really asking. I know we're over the line now. I know it. I do. That knowledge doesn't help somehow. I came to see her and I can't head back to town while she might be going away. I mean, maybe they're just speeding off to a restaurant and will be back in a couple hours but what if they aren't? I can't drive to Canada and risk my life and freedom and citizenship to get across the border just to glimpse her speeding by and call it quits.

"Whatever hotel we find, I hope they keep the polar bears away from the dumpsters," Nikos says, laughing his little wheezy laugh. Then he goes back to dozing. It's a comfort he's not telling me to stop, but that's not his way. He'll just lightly remind me—as he has—that I'm now into obsession territory, and that the psychosis is growing, evidenced by every mile we drive further into the Canadian North Woods.

Eight

It's another hour and a half before the SUV slows for an exit ramp, making a long sliding turn toward an arterial highway. Not a house in sight—been a long time since I've seen a house. Whole lot of trees, though. Nikos is asleep but that hasn't kept me from keeping score. All told, we've followed Nora and the Guy 235 miles into the wilderness. I'm that many points over the deep end and haven't even spoken to her yet.

I can't imagine they haven't noticed us by now. There are only four cars in sight the length of the highway. But I'm actually feeling more comfortable, more like I can size up our situation a bit. It's been at least thirty or forty miles since the last town—well, maybe not what I'd usually consider a town, but at least a cluster of buildings—well, maybe just a house and a barn but that makes two man-made things in the same general vicinity. Out here, that makes a town.

And suddenly, we turn off onto another four-lane, well-maintained highway shooting down a valley between mountain ranges—and not a driveway or cross-street in sight. Government construction money isn't spent *that* capriciously. If some bureaucratic agency agreed to build a road this size this far from the nearest house, there's a lake or ski resort or *something* at the end of it. Owned by investors offering big campaign contributions—hell, Canada isn't *that* different from the US. So if they're going to a resort, it's a good thing I followed. We could have sat at Waterline all weekend until they got back—or even a week if she's on vacation! Two weeks maybe!

Yes, this was good thinking. Nikos will see that when he comes to. Maybe. Anyway, all I have to do is blend in wherever they stop, drive on to the next lodge or something and then I can find out—find out what? What am I after—what did I drive two hours into the Yukon for?

I want to know if she's going to a business meeting or if she's sleeping with this guy. If she's staying with him, then that's that, I guess. Hell, maybe they're even married and she's just kept her maiden name. She was just being friendly with her email and I over-reacted.

Or, on the other hand, maybe she's just up here for a business meeting, a conference or something. I don't even know what she does for a living. She could be the chairman of the board or a masseuse. I might not even like her. Somehow, that would be okay—if I don't like her, I can walk away disappointed and survive. But if we don't even meet, it'll drive me crazy.

Finally, I see his blinker go on. There's a turnoff coming up and not another road in sight. The highway continues straight through this canyon for miles. So I slow, not that there's much point in hiding. There's nowhere else to go.

As soon as we make the turn, I see trouble. This isn't a road. It's a rutted, boulder-strewn path barely as wide as their truck. I have no problem with width—if you can't fit a Honda Civic down it, it's either a bridal path or you've detoured to Liechtenstein. But some of the rocks here are huge—I have to plan really carefully every hundred yards of progress, while he just barrels over them with those elephant tires of his. If there are several turnoffs ahead, I've lost him for sure.

Happily, the road ends after a half-mile in a large parking lot full of SUV's and trucks. I pull to the far end of the lot, away from Nora's friends' Behemoth. I idle in a space, watching in the mirror. They're going to get out in a moment and go someplace. No one stays in a parking lot.

I'm spending a lot of time repeating really obvious information to myself right now—it's a sign of disorientation. That's it—I blame the whole thing on disorientation, your honor. Nonetheless, they're going to get out of that thing in a moment and I'm going to have to follow them, just to know where they're going. Not being obtrusive in any way. Just necessary information so I can continue stalking her.

I'm uncertain whether to rouse Nikos or not. I don't want him to wake up here alone—he might be alarmed. It might be a bit upsetting, waking in the middle of a Yukon Jack Bigtire Convention.

But in truth, I'm not ready for his softspoken moral authority. Self-righteous people drive me crazy, but they don't make me as guilty as he does. My friend! Sure—let me do whatever I want. Encourage me in my delusions. Throw a few soft-spoken reminders my way but let me make my own mistakes like an adult. While he's slept peacefully, I've fashioned the noose and tightened it around my neck.

But once they've fingered you for the Brinks' job, you might as well go on holding up the local candy store. I get out of the car and move up, shivering, behind a truck watching Nora and the Guy pull their bags out of the back of the SUV and start up a barely visible path through the woods.

He doesn't have his arm around her or anything—but then, he is carrying a backpack the size of the Alamo. And they're Canadians, genetically bred to avoid public displays of emotion, so who the hell knows?

Once they pass into the trees, I follow, walking as carefully as I can, because we're a long way from anything and any sound might give me away. I start to walk sideways, which, according to *The Last of the Mohicans*, will keep you from crunching leaves and sticks. I crunch them anyway. Damn! That's what I get for reading the Classics Illustrated version.

I look for something I can duck behind, in case they turn back to see who's tailing them. Then I realize they had to know I was right behind them—they saw my car pull into the lot, the only thing there without six-foot high tires, a towing package and getting more than 6 miles to the gallon. So they won't be surprised by the sound of me behind them.

I'm pulled from my self-absorption by a sound not unlike that of an Apollo rocket going off a hundred yards from my left ear. I jump forward, inadvertently and all at once, the whole place opens up in front of me.

The path winds around a lake, just as I thought. Bingo—Ten Points!! The lake is surrounded on the opposite side by a group of cottages, log cabin affairs with a really quaint, convincing rustic air. A group of rowdies is down by the shoreline, playing with some kind of motor. It looks like a regular outboard motor, but in this incredible solitude surrounded on all sides by mountains, the sound is magnified a thousand times. They're shrieking and heckling each other loud enough to be heard over this mechanized noise machine.

Nora and the Guy have made it halfway around the lake already, not looking back, oblivious even to the incredible shriek coming from the dock. They walk to a cabin—I'm watching carefully—and walk in through two different doors. So they're staying separately! But then, they're also at very least in adjoining cabins in the same building, so who knows? So I came here to find out absolutely *nothing*? This is no good.

It wouldn't take much information to make me feel like I'd done what I came for—and then we could go home. I'm exhausted and weighed down by my foolishness—I can only ignore it for so long and I'm long since past my expiration date here. But I can't go home with *nothing*. I at least need enough information to be able to feel sorry for myself later, over a good merlot.

The office to this Daniel Boone housing project is the first cabin. I don't even think about it—I just walk to the door. I understand I'm about to compound my stupidity but it's late and I just don't have it in me to drive home without knowing more than I knew when I left.

"How much is a cabin?" I ask.

"Geez, this is really authentic," Nikos enthuses, rubbing his hands together and huddling under a wool comforter in the corner. The cabins have no heat other than firewood, no electricity of any kind and no running water. The ownership has kindly provided firewood, kerosene lamps and blankets.

A poster on the wall suggests the best place in the lake for washing your clothes and recommends against skinnydipping. In sub-zero temperatures—which is the only thing you're likely to find in this neighborhood till late May—skinnydipping is not a big concern. It also sternly advises putting out your kerosene lamp before going to sleep.

If this isn't forbidding enough, the crowd of nuts on the beach have finished with their power saw—that was the motor we heard. They have lashed several old trees together to create a bonfire the size of Rhode Island and are happily dancing around the flames, chanting loudly, their breath smoking in the night air. All this and beer at a reasonable price, cases of it stacked by the pyre. No wonder everyone drives so far to get here.

No sign of Nora—or the Guy, for that matter. All the windows are bright in the cabin, so either they like to do it with the lights on or they are living separate and respectable lives in their two halves of the place. But what business would bring you up *here*?

This reverie is broken by Nikos, who sits next to me at the window, staring silently until I can't ignore him.

"Hi," I say cheerily.

"What do you plan to do next?" he asks, a smile on his face but he isn't fooling me.

"Nikos, all I want to know is if she's involved with him. If she's sleeping with him, we're gone. We'll leave first thing in the morning."

He sits, taking small glimpses away and then jumping back to me, as though there's something essential I must have said and he just missed hearing it.

"How do you plan on finding that out?" he asks.

"Well, I figured as soon as they get really worked up out there on the beach and no one's paying attention to anything, I'll head over to Nora's cabin and check it out."

He looks at me with deep tenderness, the way you'd look at your favorite cat or your first grandchild.

"Which means, you're going to sneak through the woods and peek in the windows?" he asks.

I shrug. "I don't know any other way to do it," I say. Seems perfectly reasonable to me.

He closes his eyes and tilts his head back. He takes a long breath. Finally, he looks at me with an intensity I can't ever remember seeing on his face before. His hand springs into the air between us, index finger pointed toward the ceiling.

"Love makes us crazy," he says, wagging the finger at me. "Even the possibility of love, which is all you've got."

"Well, that's it. That's the point," I say. "I have to know if there's the possibility. If we met and didn't hit it off, then I could at least go home and know it just wasn't there. But to have her contact me after all this time and then disappear without giving me a chance to find out is going to put me over the edge."

"Too late!" he chimes. "You're there already. If you're going to go over there because you're hoping to see her naked in the window, that's one thing. In that case, just make sure you leave me the car keys. And remember my pension money usually runs out by the 18th of the month, so I can't do expensive bail. But if you're going over there to find out if they're together — and you aren't even getting an erection out of it — that's too much of a risk to take."

"Well, what else can we do? If we're here in the morning, she'll see us."

"Better she sees you standing here in the morning — she might take that as a nice thing, women sometimes like these long-distance seeking things, it seems noble somehow — better that than she sees you being dragged away from her shuttered window by the police as a peeping tom. I would think that would kill the relationship right quick."

Nine

The next morning, 20 or so members of the boy's club are all outside, hale and hearty, chanting around the steaming pyre of last night's festivities, having eaten a massive breakfast—through the stout walls of the cabin, I can smell eggs, bacon, sausage, hash browns, pancakes or waffles or something with batter, oatmeal and coffee. It's amazing how specific your nose can be when you're hungry.

And there's probably other stuff out there, right nearby, that you just *can't* smell, like orange juice and maybe even bagels—scratch that, we're in Canada. We have none of these things in our cabin, of course, since we didn't drive up here expecting the outdoorsman's version of solitary confinement. This place has no store, no restaurant and we have no provisions.

Nikos keeps kicking my bed. I stay under the covers, my teeth chattering from the cold.

"C'mon," he says, "you know you've got to face her. Might as well be now."

"What happened to my nice accommodating professor?"

"He slept in a real bed in a room with heat and food and without a bunch of Indians chanting outside the window at 6 am."

"I'm sorry," I say. "I don't know where the food comes from. Do you think there's a store here somewhere, hidden in the trees?"

"No—I think they brought everything with them from home," Nikos says. "I can't quite figure out what they're doing. They're all gathered around where the bonfire was without jackets, as though it was still generating heat. They don't seem to be nature lovers…"

"No," I agree. "A little too much beer and shouting and power tools for that."

"It does sound pretty militant. But they don't have guns—at least, I haven't seen any—and they're friendly to each other. They're just so *noisy*."

"Have you seen Nora?"

"No. I think she'd stick out in the crowd."

"Well, whoever they are, I wanted to face them washed and looking decent, instead of smelly and needing a shave."

"I understand," Nikos says vacantly, as though still half-asleep. "The washing area of the lake is clearly marked. Bring an axe to break through the ice. I personally don't mind a little body odor, given the choices."

"You're not trying to get a girl to fall in love with you."

"From what I can see, if she's up here, she has a choice of stinky men. Nobody was crazy enough to go in there this morning. Several of them wandered around the beach, and one or two put toes in—but that was that. So you'll all be at the same disadvantage. And, given time, she might get a bit rank herself. Besides, I don't think that's our biggest concern."

He pulls the shade away from the panes so as to keep an eye on the gathering, which is getting louder by the minute. It sounds like they're chanting, but the voices are too disorganized and each to his own meter, so it's just a jumble.

"What *is* our biggest concern?" I ask.

"Well, *my* biggest concern is starvation," he says. "The doctor said I need my meals, you know. I don't remember eating dinner, though I'm having trouble remembering. My second concern would be that all these guys seem to be here on some kind of mission, and we're going to stick out if we're not on it." He draws the shades an inch further from the window, looking out carefully. "But *your* main concern, I guess, would be the guy in the ceremonial headdress with the axe."

Huh?

I come over to the window—we're both huddled in the corner staring through a narrow crack of light. Out by the remains of last night's fire, the members of the Flies have come to a state of general attention.

The tall guy in the black robe and red cape and the African ceremonial headpiece—a facemask with bulbous protrusions over the eyes and a long narrow nose that extends half a foot out—is addressing the crowd. I can't make out a word he's saying, but he's loud and quite vehement, waving his arms in the air and shouting. Periodically the rest of the group sends up a roar.

"Jesus! Where did *he* come from?" I say.

"The second cabin up," Nikos says, pointing to Nora's cabin. It's the Guy. She came with the Lord of the Flies. Great.

"What the hell is this? Some kind of cult worship thing? Is she a virgin sacrifice?" I mumble out loud.

"If she's a virgin 25 years after you met her, I don't think she's for you," Nikos says.

I step away from the window—Nikos lets the shades go and sits on his bed.

"I still can't figure this out," Nikos muses, nodding his head. "It looks like terrorist training camp but something just doesn't feel right."

"Any terrorists they train here specialize in taking over breweries and drinking them out of their inventory. This is impossible," I say, dropping my face in my hands. "How am I going to find out what they're up to without making a complete idiot of myself? What if they really *are* dangerous?"

The whole situation is loopy. I go back to my tiny room and lay on the bed, swooning from the extent of my own stupidity. I close my eyes to make it all go away. I'm hungry. Maybe the only answer is to just get back in the car and give up. But if Nora is watching from her cabin—and what else is there to *do* up here?—then I won't even be able to email her once I step out this door. I'll be too embarrassed.

I sit up, feeling helpless and hopeless and useless. I open my eyes and Nikos is gone.

I blunder to the door, not thinking, and throw it open. He is standing in the field, surrounded by the group of devil worshipers or whatever they are. I stagger down the two wooden steps. I'm a little woozy. I glance at my watch—an hour has gone by since I last looked. I must have fallen asleep in that moment of closing my eyes and am now stomping around, groggy and off-balance.

As I focus, I can see they're not hurting him. He's not so much surrounded as at the center of the gathering. The bellowy guy in the facemask has gone, nowhere to be seen.

"Oh, here's my friend Ted," Nikos tells the Braveheart clan. Their expression is not unfriendly but there is something uncomfortable about it I can't quite place. They simultaneously decide to ignore me and turn back to Nikos with total enthusiasm and respect. He's become their sage while I closed my eyes.

"So the first principle of the Trapper," Nikos says, "is to respect your surroundings. I remember my grandfather Nestor—he came from Corfu—taking me through these woods when I was a little boy. This was when there were still roving packs of grizzlies all over the place. Oh, the stories I could tell you."

"Why don't you take us?" says one man.

"That would be so cool," says another.

"Well, Ted and I have to work on the cure a bit," he says, and the heads turn toward me again with that same mixture of pity and discomfort I saw a few moments ago. "And we have a few quick errands to run. But I could probably take you on a hike at—" he glances at his watch, "oh, let's say 2. How's that?"

"Yes, yes," they're chanting and the group breaks up.

"Get your laptop," Nikos whispers to me, taking me by the arm and leading me. "We can talk on our way to the store." I throw my coat on and grab my laptop case.

As soon as we get to the car, he whips open the laptop while I try to warm the poor Civic up from its frozen slumber. He's banging away at the keys in a frenzy.

"What are you doing?" I finally ask. I haven't seen this much activity from him since college.

"I'm writing down the bullshit I told those guys. Some of it is pretty good," he says, laughing his little wheezy laugh.

"What the hell were you talking about?" I ask.

"Well, I came outside and they were just finishing their little tribal gathering," he tells me. "The chief was feeding them this mumbo-jumbo about the mountain-god spirit and the Power of Mondo, the Man-God."

"Who?"

"Don't ask me—I'm just a tourist. So after he finished whipping them into a frenzy, he takes off and they're getting ready to tear trees out of the ground by the roots and eat them raw, you know how it is when you stick a bunch of real men out in the woods all by themselves without women. And somebody turns to me and says, 'What are you looking at, pop?' And I hate being called 'pop' or 'grandpa' or any of that stuff, you know."

"So I just opened my mouth and said, 'I am just thinking of what pleasure the Great Trappers would have had, seeing you men up here feeding your manliness.' I don't know what got into me, except it felt like the old days where I was making things up— you know that feeling—and it had control of me and I couldn't stop. And I was thinking of Billy and his spirits in the woods and the shamans and so forth. I had to have an answer and I opened my mouth and there it was.

"And someone said, 'The Great Trappers?' and I started talking about the Great Trappers who founded Canada and all the great cities up here. And I heard myself tell them I was the descendant of those trappers—I made them all Greek, of course, out of habit. Thank God there's not a historian among the crowd, though that didn't seem like a big gamble with this group. I said I'd studied here—at this very lake—with the last of them when I was a child. And after I told them about Stavros the Bold and Dimitris of the Black Hand, they decided they wanted me to show them the Great North Woods through the eyes of the Great Trappers. So I'm going to take them later."

"Stavros the Bold? Dimitris of the Black Hand?"

He's typing wildly. "I told you—I made them up. Weird guys though. That's why I'm writing it all down before I forget. Have to keep things straight if they ask questions on the hike."

"Nikos, with all due respect, it took you 15 minutes to go from the front door to the parking lot here. You're taking them on a nature hike?"

"Yes I am," Nikos insists. "We don't have to go far—just out of sight of the cabins. This way, I'll have most of them out of your way and you can have your talk with Nora. I'm sorry I won't be able to smooth your introduction, but I can only do so much, even for you."

The car is warmed up now but I have no idea why. "Are we going somewhere or did you just want to sit in the car?" I ask him. Not that it's a bad idea—it's actually getting warm in here. I'd forgotten what warm really felt like.

"I found out there *is* a store just two miles down the main road. They have food, which would be really good—even vegetarian food, I'm told—and showers and gas." I begin to move around the boulders, heading for the main road.

"And what are we going to do when they find out you're bullshitting them and they decide to take out their manly energy on us?" I ask him.

"I just have to talk fast," he says, looking up from his typing, "and make sure they don't catch on. It's wonderful — I'm having such fun."

We hit the local highway and head farther down valley.

"Great — but it could be dangerous. You don't know who these guys are."

"Sure I do. They're mostly stockbrokers or shipbuilders or lawyers during the rest of the year. Professionals mostly — harmless. In fact, they're here, by and large, because their lives are too dull."

"Let them move to New York and drive around with a bullseye on their backs all the time," I say. I didn't even know I felt that way until I hear the words coming from my mouth.

"That's funny," Nikos says. "I had that same thought. They're complaining of no tension or danger in their lives and we just want the stress to go away. None of us is ever happy with what we're given. Anyway, they come out here twice a year for a week. It's a national organization, they have a couple hundred members or something. They come out on a schedule every six months and worship Mondo and get in touch with their male energy.

"Besides," he reminds me, "writing is only a safe profession in America," and I remember him telling me this in college. "If you lived in Colombia or China or Zimbabwe, you'd always have to keep an eye out the window. So just pretend that, for a second there, you were getting a taste of how the other half lives."

We motor down valley slowly and finally I can see the store—just a little woodframe set off the road near a bend in the river, an old house that's had wings added over the years.

"Why were the guys looking at me like that?" I ask.

"Oh, well they wanted to know why I was here," he answers, his voice a bit hesitant now. "So I told them the Trappers used to come here to dry out, to get over their alcohol binges. I told them—I'm sorry, but you know once you start telling stories, how things just happen—I told them you were an alcoholic and you'd come off a really bad bender so I brought you up here to sober up and get back on your feet."

I can't help feeling his description isn't far off the mark. "And then they saw me stumbling down the steps when I came out—that'll give me loads of credibility."

"You don't *want* credibility with them," Nikos says, cannily. "Then they'd pay attention to you. You want to sit quietly in the house until they all go away and then you can talk to your Nora."

"Well, we'll see if she's my Nora," I say. "She's shacked up with Mondo the Man-God—or at least his tribal spokesman. I don't know how I stack up in that company—or in the eyes of someone who'd be attracted to such a person."

"Well, let it play itself out," Nikos says. "We've come this far. At least you'll *smell* better than him."

Ten

When we return to the campground, it's almost 2. We've both showered and Nikos has had a fine meal of something green and mushy that the owner swears is cultivated locally (which sounds like another way to say it's mulch from the backyard, but I'm not eating it so I don't care—I have a nice safe hamburger from hormonally-injected force-fed cows).

As we come around the lake, we see the boys are ready for Nikos. They're all wearing their backpacks and hiking boots—I'm relieved to see they've actually got winter coats. I bring our bags of provisions into the cabin and Nikos goes off to encounter Nature in all its wild glory. I watch him say a few words to the group and then begin to shuffle, in his halting one-step-at-a-time fashion, towards the edge of the clearing. I can see some of the boys exchanging skeptical glances at him before they all take off, like the Cub Scout troop on their first campout.

I wait the ten minutes it takes them to finally clear the area. I spend that time trying to summon my nerve and focus my imagination, to try and find a productive way to approach Nora.

The problem with this is that the ideas that come to mind are stupefying. Like:

Nora (opening door): Ted?

Ted: Nora

(Fall into each others arms, music swells, fadeout...)

This is obviously idiotic, but it's the only thing that comes to mind, no matter how many times I try. The reason I'm a fiction writer is that I always know exactly what to say—nine months after I need to say it. Which doesn't help me a bit here.

Nora: (opening door) Ted?

Ted: Hi.

(We stand in the doorway staring at each other for a moment)

Ted: I've waited 25 years to kiss you. I think it's time.

(We kiss. Music swells...)

Unless I actually *hire* a string quartet, there's no music here and we can't fadeout, so this scenario is useless.

I've driven all this way to talk to her and now find myself incapable of thinking a single sensible thing to say. And even feeling sentimental; she's *Canadian*—how much sentimentality can possibly issue from a culture that centers on ginger ale and ice hockey? Isn't there *another* way?

Nora: (opening door) Yes, I saw you skulking about this morning. What the hell are you doing here?

Ted: (shrugging sheepishly) I wanted to counteract whatever bad impression I may have made in that email.

Nora: So you drove 350 miles and claimed to be an alcoholic taking a cure used by the ancient Greek Trappers who founded Canada? *That* makes me feel much better, thanks.

I'm totally lost. And I don't have lots of time to play with either—if Nikos spends twenty minutes in the woods, I'll have to put him on an EKG. So I open my door, walk resolutely to her cabin and knock.

First, there's nothing at all. Unless she snuck out while we were at the store, she has to be here.

Finally I see a fluttering at the window shades, just a flicker of movement, and then the door cracks open. I can see her eye and then—door opening a little wider—the eyes the nose the mouth that chin the bright blonde hair now cut short around her ears—it's her. She looks glorious. Jesus, she's prettier than she was when she was 17.

"Hi," she says, as though she's not surprised to see me. But she doesn't sound angry either. I'm a little off-balance, trying to read the signs before responding.

"Hi," I answer. "Can we talk a little?"

"I don't know," she says, not moving, not opening the door, just watching me through the slit. "I'm surprised to see you."

"Well, I realize I must have made a bad impression with that first email. I just got so excited hearing from you."

"I was very excited hearing from you," she says. Her tone of voice is very disengaged though, like she's carrying on a game of ping-pong behind the door while talking to me.

"You were? Why didn't you answer?"

"I did—I sent you an email back a day or two after I got your reply. I was busy."

Shit! She probably sent it right after I left with Nikos. I *did* over-react.

"But what," she says carefully, very precisely, "are you doing *here*?"

Oh God, how sharply the stakes have raised. She was 'very excited'—I'll remember those words to my grave—to hear from me. I *was* off to a good start. The only danger of my being exposed as a psycho will be my answer to *this* question.

"Um, I'm here for my friend Nikos. He's a terrible alcoholic and he's taking the Cure." Turnabout is fair play, after all, and this answer is at least familiar. It's been tried once this weekend already and went over okay.

"Out here?" She's not bothering to hide her skepticism. Oh God, I hate lying and I'm a shitty liar. I don't know if I'm a shitty liar because I hate lying or if I hate lying because I'm no good at it, but at the moment, the difference isn't going to buy me much.

"This place is famous for the Cure—best place in North America," I say, with as straight a face as I can muster. And then, all at once, I realize that that's why I'm a lousy liar. When I tell a lie, I put everything I have into trying to look sincere. Meanwhile, when I'm talking about facts, I always have a comment, a little ironic or cynical touch or something. "I guess we're supposed to be impressed with the Spartan conditions," I add, stressing the sarcasm.

"I didn't realize this place was that well known," she says, but somehow the suspicion lessens. God help me for going after love by lying, but if it works, I'll never tell the truth again.

"Well, I can't say this is the best place for him, but I heard it was good and he's got a bad case."

"Gee, that's really sad," she says and the doorway opens a bit more. She's still slim, but the curves have filled in from the skinny girl I remember. Wow! She's amazing. Just a second more and I should be inside with her, talking and laughing and trying to get into her pants and her life. Not necessarily in that order but...well, any order would work.

"Where is he?" she asks. "Shouldn't you be watching him?"

"He's taking a little nature hike," I say.

"The old man?" she says immediately, and the door almost shuts from her flinching. "That's your friend—the Ancient Trapper who's stolen all my guys?"

"All your guys?"

"They were supposed to be making *teepees* now!" she says, voice almost cracking under some strain I don't even come close to understanding. Then she slams the door shut in my face.

Eleven

The moon has been grounded for the evening. It sits inches above the horizon, just on the other side of the lake. Without doubt, if I could climb the tallest SUV in the lot without getting sued, I could jump onto its surface—but Nikos reminds me the place is thick with lawyers. The moonlight totally overwhelms the puny yellow glow produced by the kerosene lamps in the cabins.

I am staring out the window, the shades thrown open. No sense hiding now; she knows I'm here and doesn't care. Or she's mad at me. Or she's mad at Nikos, which makes no sense—she doesn't even know the man. Is she mad because he bullshitted the boys about the Trappers? While she's here with some guy in an African headpiece? I can't unravel the threads at the moment.

I can see my breath inside the cabin. The fireplace is rustic and very pretty, but it only warms if you're sitting *in* it. I turn to Nikos. "Personally," I tell him, "I can't *wait* for global warming." He ignores me.

He's banging away at the keyboard like he has a deadline. He made me go warm up the car so he could charge the laptop again. I purchased this machine last summer to write my first great novel, but so far Nikos is the only one getting any mileage out of the thing. That isn't surprising—it's the way this entire trip has gone. In contrast to my debacle with Nora, Nikos had a triumph with the Boys.

They took a nature hike. They were gone four hours, during which they traveled a mile and a half out and back and they were all raving about him when they returned.

"Listen to this," he says, pushing his chair back from the table. "'The jocinda bush has a leaf that summons the Woodland Wraiths if rubbed against the skin between the fingers. It was used by the Natives locally first, then adapted by the Great Trappers to control their enemies. '"

"What's a jocinda bush?" I ask.

"I don't know," he answers. "I just pointed to the first bush I saw and out it came. I had them rub it on their hands and they were convinced they were seeing giant grizzlies in the hills. I even convinced myself."

"Nikos, there *are* grizzlies out here. Remember the sign in the store listing what was legal for hunting and what wasn't? Grizzlies are out of season, but they're definitely here."

"Oh—wow," he says, looking concerned all at once. "I shouldn't have thrown those rocks at it then, should I?"

"You threw rocks at a grizzly bear?"

"Well, you know I don't see distances well. So they all saw it but I didn't, I guess. I thought they were just buying my Woodlands Wraith story. So I started yelling at it to go away and threw a couple of rocks in the direction they were staring."

"Jesus," I say, "what happened?"

"Oh--lots," he smiles at the memory. "Once I threw the rocks, the whole lot of them began to run and you know I can't run so I started walking after them calling out, "It's just a hallucination." And after a while one of them came back to get me—he was panicked, but he wasn't going to leave me out there. And I don't know, I guess I was still there and the grizzly wasn't, you know. So he said, 'you're a brave man.' "

Now, with a fuller understanding of what happened dawning on him, the tears start to stream from Nikos' eyes again and the laughter begins pouring out of him around the words. "And I said to him, as seriously as I know how, 'I'm a Trapper—I know how to handle the Woodland Wraith. *You're* the brave man.'

And when we reached the others, I built him up bigtime for coming back for me. So now he's like the Eagle Trapper. And I explained to them that throwing rocks was the lowest level of Trapper self-defense—there are eleven other levels that are more ecologically friendly and spiritually uplifting."

"That's good to know—what are they?"

"I haven't the slightest idea," he says, still laughing. "I wish I'd made it *four* more." He finishes typing. "OK," he says. "It's here when you need it."

"What do you mean when *I* need it?" I ask.

He turns in his chair to look at me. "Here's how I see it," he says. "I can't really write a book about the Great Trappers of the North, because it isn't *that* funny all by itself. We might sell a few copies to these guys outside, but not enough to even interest a real publisher. But if you tell the story of us coming up here and me bullshitting these guys and then you include some of this stuff, *that'll* be pretty funny."

"And what do *you* get out of it?" I say. I don't like this — there's a little too much of a graveyard ring to it.

"Oh, I'm having a *wonderful* time," he says, and he starts to laugh again, his face lighting up. "I've been sitting around in White Plains worrying about my exercise and what idiotic medicine they're going to give me next and whether I had enough legumes this week. And now I'm creating again — I've created this alternate state of Canada, this wonderful Greek-Canadian republic. It's the first conquest the Greeks have had in a thousand years."

I smile at this thought. "Obviously, I'll take whatever you give me," I say. "It's not like I'm writing worth a damn now anyway. But you may want to hold onto it — maybe you can start a franchise with it if they tell their buddies about you."

"Oh yes," Nikos stammers, "I can see me in my ceremonial headpiece shouting Greek phrases for the guys to use worshipping the Great Trapper Gods."

"Be sure to face North when you do," I say, laughing too.

It's a sweet moment, but then our attention is stolen by the noise building outside. Nikos wanders slowly over from the table to watch.

The entire group has filed out for the evening's ritual logburning, or so I assume. But there is no pyre ready and no one is cutting telephone poles. They're all just waiting and staring across the water. As I watch, I can see—and hear—why.

A mist grows over the icy lake. And grows and grows, until it's clear there's nothing natural at work here. Someone's got a case of dry ice or something and the whole area is overrun with smoke. Above the chants of the crowd comes the banging of drums followed by weird atonal music filtering across the surface. Either someone bought batteries for a really huge boombox or it's that string quartet I meant to hire this afternoon. Odd, 12-tone screeching, just eerie enough to shut up this crowd.

And then through the fog comes Mondo, in his cape and fertility-God headpiece with that phallic nose, struggling into view pulling a chain...pulling the skeleton of a boat. A *big* boat! How the hell is he moving that thing—it looks massive! He drags the ponderous weight through the dry ice smoke and as the music rises to crescendo, pulls it hard onto the beach and throws the chain into the air, to the cheers of his guys. Hell, this guy *is* strong. I crack the window slightly so we can hear the priceless dialogue sure to follow this exhibition.

"ALL HAIL MONDO THE MAN-GOD!" yells Mondo, throwing modesty to the wind. He's got some kind of echo effect built into a microphone in his headpiece—it lends his voice that Darth Vaderish echo. I wonder if he uses it with Nora in bed.

"ALL HAIL MONDO THE MAN-GOD!" echo the Lost Boys. They're exchanging looks like they're taken by surprise.

"Did he have that echo thing going when you heard him this morning?" I ask Nikos.

"No, that's new," he laughs. "Gives it that good ol' down-home Roman Coliseum touch, don't you think?"

"THERE IS NOTHING WE CANNOT DO!" yells Mondo.

"THERE IS NOTHING WE CANNOT DO!" they return.

"THERE IS NO MOUNTAIN WE CANNOT CLIMB!"

"THERE IS NO MOUNTAIN WE CANNOT CLIMB!"

Okay, I get it. This is Jesse Jackson (*I Am—Somebody!*) for the pale of complexion, Tony Robbins with hunting and fishing, EST but they let you go to the bathroom in the woods whenever you want.

Whoever this guy is Nora's hanging out with, he's got a pretty good scam going. Wear the mask, shout a few slogans with the boys, make sure they stay properly lubricated with Molsons and Labatts for the weekend and make sure the checks clear before they get their cabins.

"THERE IS NO CHALLENGE THAT CAN BEAT US !"

"THERE IS NO CHALLENGE THAT CAN BEAT US!"

"NO ENEMY CAN DEFEAT US!"

"NO ENEMY CAN DEFEAT US!"

Nikos pulls up a chair and the two of us sit around the window like it's a big-screen television tuned to the Super Bowl. I even bought nuts at the store. We open the nuts and I grab a couple cans of beer sitting in the snow outside.

"Not real imaginative, is it?" I say, trying not to laugh.

"Actually, I was thinking how much it sounds like the news," he says.

The chanting goes on for ten more minutes. I guess if you're a middle-level manager at some big company, trying to convince yourself you're not just a cog, it's helpful to scream for Mondo twice a year and get it out of your system. I've been that manager—I know just how helpless you feel. Maybe it'll convince a few of them to tell their boss to go fuck himself.

Then the boys begin taking two-by-fours from a pile by the dockside and filling in the hull of the ship, chanting ceremonial slogans as they hammer and carry.

There is no caulking going on, so this barge would go straight to the bottom the instant it tasted water, but it turns out that's not part of the plan. When they've got the planks mostly hammered in place—not necessarily aligned very tidily, but you get the idea it's supposed to be a boat, at least—Mondo addresses the crowd again.

"Tomorrow when the moon is full, we will unite ourselves in brotherhood with Mondo the Man-God. Here beneath his sacred mountain on his sacred lake, we will place the ceremonial figure of Mondo in his Viking ship, push the ship onto the middle of the lake and give it the fiery funeral a God deserves—ARE YOU READY TO WORSHIP MONDO?"

"Yes!" They yell.

"Okay, let me play this one back," I say. "Mondo, the god with the African headpiece, is about to get a Viking funeral?"

"That's right," Nikos says, nodding slowly, "I heard it too. They're going to worship him by burning him to a crisp."

"What kind of a God needs a funeral?"

"Maybe all of them," Nikos muses. "To think of all the time I wasted going to church."

"ARE YOU READY TO SACRIFICE THIS SHIP?"

"Yes!"

But this cracked logic is clearly beside the point. When you've gotten away from the women and you get permission from a guy in an African tribal headmask to burn something really big and impressive that took you a good couple hours to build, well, it's a satisfying weekend. I obviously don't understand much about WASP culture.

"WHAT MORE" continues Mondo's press spokesman, "CAN MONDO DO TO SHOW US OUR WORTHINESS, TO GET US IN TOUCH WITH OUR MANLINESS? IS THERE ANYTHING ELSE MONDO COULD DO?"

"Well," one voice cuts through the crowd, "he could shout down a grizzly bear."

The whole place goes dead silent. I can't even hear the music anymore, though I'm not certain whether they've turned it off or I'm simply suffering a stroke. Nikos is staring at the floor, shaking his head and muttering to himself—in Greek I think, though I may simply have lost my capacity for language. Surely the feeling will go out of my legs next.

"He could put us in touch with the wilderness all around us," the voice continues. "He could teach us the twelve evolving levels of self-defense in the world."

"Tell me—please," I beg Nikos, sounding as pitiful as I can remember since I stopped begging my ex-wife for sex, "that that's not our Eagle Trapper."

"That's him," says Nikos, nodding his head slowly and biting his lip, trying to keep from laughing.

"We're fucked," I say.

"Oh yeah," he agrees.

I can't exactly say what happens next. I may have actually blanked out for a few minutes. All I know is, the next thing I see is one group of campers pushing the Viking ship towards the middle of the frozen lake while another group tries to stop them.

There is a scuffle and arms begin to fly around, hands in other guys' faces, falling and rolling around on the ice. Men in the real world never throw fists at each other—you're simply trying to figure out what damage you can do to the other guy without messing yourself up for work on Monday.

Somehow in the middle of this—and thank God Nikos and I are clearly visible in our window so no one can fairly accuse us of anything—the Whigs attach a motorized sleigh to the back of the Viking ship just as the Tories are setting fire to the front of the boat.

Seconds later, the whole huge mass is sliding rapidly across the surface of the lake, fighting campers scrambling in all directions to get out of the way. It jumps the bank and careens headlong up the incline, coming to a sickening halt against the cabin right next to us.

Flaming planks scatter all over the yard and the sleigh flies up over the roof and into the woods, revving uncontrollably until it tangles with a tree. There is a loud thud and silence reigns for a moment.

The whole group of us—with the exception of Mondo's ambassador who is nowhere to be seen—spend the next few hours on a bucket brigade. Water is funneled from a section of beach (hole opened with an axe, as Nikos suggested earlier) to the smoldering cabin and the flaming timbers scattered around the yard.

The owner of the campsite is hopping mad, finally disappearing into the Mondo cabin for at least half an hour before he leaves, check in hand.

Nikos is helpful organizing the brigade and directing traffic, though I make him promise not to lift any buckets himself. I spend a good deal of time wetting down the outside of our cabin, just in case—hey, we're right next door.

When every ember is out and the whole crew is exhausted, we file back to our cabins. Nikos heads directly to bed, leaving his door open. I can see him from my chair in the small central room, as I stare out at the skeleton of the Viking ship, which sits smoldering against the cabin next door.

"What's the matter?" says Nikos.

"If Nora's involved with Mondo," I say, " I don't think I did my cause much good tonight."

"I know," Nikos says. "I spoke to Clint on the bucket line— he's the Eagle Trapper. I told him I didn't want any publicity for the Trappers. He didn't need to challenge Mondo. I just wanted to pass on my knowledge of the Old Ways."

I look over at him, bundled up in the covers, just his head and hands visible over the blankets.

"Nikos," I say, "you know there are no Old Ways. There are no Trappers—right?"

"Of course," he says. "I just didn't want to take that away from him too. After what he did to Mondo tonight, it would be like telling your grandson there's no Santa Claus."

"There's no Santa Claus?" I ask, but he rolls over, determined to avoid unpleasant truths. After staring at the smoky hulk on the lawn for another moment, I decide it's a good plan and head into my bedroom to hide as well.

Twelve

I wake to the sound of the door creaking open. I roll over—Nikos is sneaking out the door with the laptop.

"I just want to charge it up," he says. "I have some thoughts to write down, and I think you should probably make some notes on last night—you have to use that scene *somewhere*."

I wave goodbye and roll over, pulling the sheets over my head. The only thing I could write at the moment are funeral dirges.

I have a dream. I am taking a drive with Jean-Pierre Aumont. We park by some apartment complex and walk over to a hill, overlooking a new and very overbuilt cookie cutter housing development. The sun is going down and in the light, despite the tract housing, everything looks beautiful at a distance.

And I say to him, "How about this? Cary Grant and JD Salinger driving cross-country in a convertible DeSoto in 1952."

"Ah," he says. "Two gifted people, closed to their Left. We should strew rose petals in their path."

"I don't feel that way," I say. "I just admire their talent. I don't care about their politics."

"Of course," he muses. "You don't care about their politics. Let us bow to their talent to amuse."

I look down on the town, which looks glorious as the sun settles over the hill. And then I wake up, ready to argue with somebody, anybody.

Someone's knocking at the door. Nikos probably forgot his key. I stumble out of the tiny bedroom and open it.

The Guy is standing there. Somehow, in a parka and a blue flannel shirt, he still manages to give the impression he's wearing a business suit—or a uniform. Military bearing will out, I suppose.

"Hi—Art Marshall," he says, thrusting his hand at me. I suddenly remember the last time someone thrust their hand at me—the doctor, after fingering me up the ass. I feel the same way taking this guy's hand—not because I have anything against Mondo the Man-God, of course; simply because his expression is not noticeably friendly.

"Hi," I say.

"Can I come in?" he asks, and I get out of the way.

He hurries in and sits in one of the chairs arrayed in front of the window, left over from last night's Super Bowl half-time show. I take the other.

"I hope you understand that disruptions like last night cost our organization money and credibility," he says with the air of a State Department spokesman.

"Well, I wouldn't want to hurt Mondo the Man-God's credibility," I snicker. I'm still pissed off at Jean-Pierre Aumont for being a French leftie snot, but he's not in the room right now, so I'm taking it out on Art.

"I don't think this is funny," he says, with the conviction of the humorless. "Organizations have a right to preserve themselves, and clearly, your friend the Trapper has been disruptive to our process."

I don't know what's more idiotic—his proto-legal syntax or the fact that he's taking my friend the Trapper seriously.

Even *I* can hear the intimidation behind this garble-de-gook. He's *threatening* me—the asshole with the penis mask is fucking *threatening* me in the privacy of my own (rented) log cabin!

I haven't gotten mad in a long time—I haven't felt *anything* in a month, but it's coming back to me now. Not just the anger he's earned either—I find myself ticking off a list including insensitive urologists, bosses who've made money off my labor without paying me what I deserved, bank tellers who treat me as though it's *their* money, voice mail systems that don't care if I ever reach anyone to complain about their company's lousy service and every person who ever acted like the world owed them something it hasn't granted *me*.

As I've seen—not always to my benefit—anger can focus your attention and I find myself reading the subtext here real clearly. All at once I understand why Mondo came out of dry ice last night squawking through a Darth Vader voice module. He's unnerved! Nikos shows up with his Ancient Trapper routine (which didn't even exist before yesterday) and scares the shit out of ol' Mondo here, so he starts overcompensating with Viking funerals and Alice Cooper theatrics. I look out the window at the wreck of the Mary Deare on the lawn. Now *that* didn't turn out very well, did it? He's not in a strong negotiating position at the moment.

"As I say, we have a responsibility to preserve ourselves," he continues now, "and we will take whatever steps are necessary to fulfill that responsibility."

I worked in television for fifteen years, much of it overseeing kids just out of journalism school. We would hire them as producers and after their third show getting paid pumpkin seeds, they'd want to know why they couldn't get a raise. And I had to explain to them that you didn't get a raise in the real world because of merit—you got it because of *leverage*. I always hated that speech, because it symbolized all the things I'd learned in fifteen years of working, all those truths about the world that I hate. I promised myself that if I ever got leverage myself, I'd remember to use it. And now, in this tiny corner of a shrinking world, I have a lever the size of Miami.

"Well, I'll tell you one thing ol' Mondo ol' buddy," I say. "I'm not threatenable. The Ancient Trappers used to wipe their shoes on the faces of guys like you, so back off or eat shit. We're going to have every single one of your boys ready to jump ship and hike into the sunset with us unless you negotiate right quick—and I don't mean in a court of law. Nikos will have them charmed to death by tonight, and they'll tell their friends who'll tell *their* friends and soon you'll be able to chop up your little ceremonial headdress and use it for kindling."

Not Sam Spade, but not a bad bluff. Maybe I *can* learn to lie productively sometime before I croak—it's a goal to work on, anyway.

And Mondo blinks. At least, he gulps. His eyes have gone blank. He gulps again, trying to keep it quiet. Finally, he looks at me and says, "What do you want?"

"I want to talk to your assistant," I say.

"Who?" he stammers.

"The blonde," I tell him. "I'm not negotiating with you anymore. I'll talk to *her*. When she's ready to talk, she can send a note over here and we'll set up a time and a place. Otherwise," I say, looking him deeply in the eye, "Mondo goes the way of his Viking ship." I stick my thumb out towards the window. He doesn't even bother looking.

By the time Nikos gets back, I've already commandeered the yellow pages from the cabin office.

"What are you looking for?" he asks.

"A nice restaurant," I tell him, "for my date with Nora."

Thirteen

The note arrives an hour later:

'Meet you in the parking lot, 10 minutes. Nora' is all it says.

When I get to the lot, I can hear the SUV idling. I take a quick look inside—she's alone unless someone's lurking behind the seats. I decide to take the chance and the passenger seat.

She looks lovely. Her hair has gone lighter—there's some silver in it that she hasn't bothered to touch up. I like that. But her smile hasn't changed from the photo in my pocket—open, direct, no trace of guile. The only addition is the wistfulness any grownup develops, because we know so well the many wrong paths down which a smile can lead us.

"I have a feeling I'm a better memory than reality," I begin. She looks at me quizzically. I shrug. "You remembered me 25 years later, so I must have been a pretty decent memory. But you contact me and I manage to get off on the wrong foot twice in 4 days."

I have spent the whole afternoon working this out. I consider it appropriately modest—the right degree of apology without actually groveling.

She smiles. Her eyes light up and her mouth only moves a fraction, but it's as though everything around me changes in an instant. One way or another, no matter what happens between us, it was not a mistake to drive up here. If nothing else, all of a sudden I feel *alive*. I want this woman.

This is not just sex but desire—don't ask me the difference but there definitely is one; I'll figure it out later. I want her now or as soon as can be arranged and if I don't get her I want to find someone else who'll make me feel like this again. It's magic and it's real and it's an overwhelming immediate intense shock to my weary jaded worn-out half-dead psyche. God, I didn't overestimate this woman.

"Your friend caused me some trouble," she says in that half-Canadian lockjaw, half Midwestern drawl I'd totally forgotten. She's so white this country-western accent is almost exoticism, as close to ethnicity as she comes. It's beside the point but very very cute. God, I'm over the edge.

"Did he?" I ask. "I thought *I* caused the trouble."

"You?"

"Yeah—I'm the one who said I'd only negotiate with you, instead of your boss. I hope that didn't make it too uncomfortable for you."

She clearly finds this amusing, but she's not responding as though it was a joke. Instead, she looks around the inside of the SUV a little, gathering her thoughts. Maybe he is her lover— damn!—and I can't get her in trouble with him. If she was mine, nobody could get her in trouble with me, that's for damn sure. At least not until after we'd had sex the first 600 times.

"Well, first of all," she says, "you've got it backwards—I'm *his* boss. It's my company—he's just the mouthpiece."

I blurt out a laugh—I can't help it. I feel so stupid for not knowing it immediately.

"Of course," I say. "Because you certainly aren't going to convince anyone you're Mondo the Man-God."

"I'd like to think not," she says, and the smile opens up and I'm bathing in it. Omigod when this woman smiles, all you want to do is dive in and swim around for a while.

Physical beauty gets such a bad rap. It doesn't fit with the whole rational bent of Western science and philosophy and it grates against the whole Calvinist Christian we're-so-sorry-we're-rich-and-beautiful-please-beat-us-so-we-can-repent   ethic—the adherents of which promptly amassed 99% of the worlds wealth not located in Kuwait, so go figure. But the reality is, beauty is its own justification and a real force, both physical and spiritual, that needs to be reckoned with, and by denying its existence, we leave ourselves defenseless against it.

Social nuance didn't come easily to me. My nature is to be totally transparent, to wear my heart and all other internal organs on my sleeve. It took years and great effort for me to learn distance and finesse, the telling glance and the soothing reassurance. To learn *cool*.

And now, in the face of Nora Hill's goddamn *smile*—not even the sight of her naked body or the experience of coming in her or anything really life-enhancing—just from a goddamn smile, I'm ready to tell her everything I know (though it takes a full tank of gas just to listen to me tell a single funny story) and give her everything I own (*that* wouldn't take much time at all). All in hopes that I can see her smile again at me sometime.

"So," she continues, "I don't know whether to take your threat seriously or not." Does she realize I'm already stunned and bleeding, incapable of resistance?

"My threat?"

"You told Art you'd bury Mondo with the Great Trappers if we didn't negotiate. Which sounds like you're planning to open a competitive business and are up here stealing my customers. And that confuses me. First of all, it seems like a long way to go—and I thought you were in the TV business. And then you told me you were only here to help your friend with his alcohol problem."

Like I say, my nature and history is to be totally transparent, to admit my feelings and tell the truth and return the toilet seat to the lowered position. It took me several years of dating and getting dumped to realize women didn't really want guys who were trustworthy and decent, not as long as they could get guys who would mistreat them and leave quickly.

So as much as I want to surrender here, to just explain the misunderstanding that brought me here—I could blame it all on Nikos, he would cop a plea without complaint—nonetheless, I'm cautious.

And at the same time, I'm still vividly aware of my leverage. It's a bit different dealing with Nora than ol' Mondo or Art or whatever his name is, but if anything the stakes are higher. I want to know if she's interested in me. If she is, there's a point in laying everything out. If she's only interested in protecting her business, then I'm not going to give up my bargaining chips so fast. And she hasn't made her interests clear yet, and I'm not sure how calculated that caution of hers is.

"Well, I may have overstated things a bit," I say. "I wanted to make sure you'd meet me. You seemed taken by surprise yesterday. And I wasn't sure Art would like the idea either, so I put it a bit strongly."

Now she's smiling. "You mean you didn't think Art would want me to meet you?" she asks.

"Well, you came up together—you're staying together—I don't know what the situation is," I answer. Nor do I have any reason to know, of course, but I'm sure hoping she'll tell me nonetheless.

She does a masterful job of controlling the smile, of keeping it from growing and I can't blame her for feeling a little smug. Damn! "Art is Kate's husband," she tells me. Kate's her sister, the auburn-haired younger sister. She was on the cruise too, always hovering nearby, one of the reasons I never got Nora alone.

"But don't you think you're being a bit mysterious here?" she continues, the smile diminishing pretty fast. "I haven't seen you in 25 years and now we not only exchange emails, but here you are at this little place so far from New York. Wouldn't *you* be surprised?"

I'd be so suspicious you couldn't convince me I was telling the truth, sweetie. But then again, that's such a non-answer to the question I really want answered — is she glad to see me — and she's too smart not to understand that. God, this is such a mess.

"It's quite a coincidence," I admit, trumping her non-answer with a truism.

"You know, it's so funny," she says. "I actually brought a box with me — a box I had of stuff from back then. I brought it with me to look for our stuff and I found it, the other night just before I saw you here. I found your letters to me and some pictures and I even found some Super-8 movies of the cruise."

"You're kidding!"

"No," she erupts in a boisterous cackle, and suddenly she's talking like a teenager again — like the girl she was the last time I knew her. "I have no idea what's on that film! Aaugggh!"

We both sit laughing for a moment, contemplating the horrors of remembering yourself starting out once you've rounded the far turn.

"So what's the price of admission?" I ask.

She cackles again. "Admission to *what*? I don't have a Super-8 projector. And I'm not sure I want to share such potentially embarrassing film footage with a potential competitor."

"How'd you find it?" I ask. "Did you keep your whole life? Everything?"

She turns bright red—it's shocking as her pale face flushes all at once. "Remember who I am," she says. "I'm the girl who came back home. I've lived in the same town my whole life. Everything I ever had was in my parent's house until I transferred it to my own."

"Yeah, but you haven't always stayed home," I say. How do I know this? I know somehow.

"Well no," she says. "But I haven't traveled like you have."

"How do you know?"

"Remember you wrote me for years," she says and I'm shocked and discomfited to realize I *don't* remember. "You moved to Colorado and California and you sent me letters. Not as many as the years went by, but for several years."

My radar has now shut down for the duration. If she's still talking about business, she's got me fooled. This feels like flirting and I like it. I *want* it. And more than that: Somehow this feels like a conversation with an old friend, and that's something I could never have expected. I just feel comfortable, natural, at home with her in a way I haven't felt with anyone in years.

"Tell you what," I offer, "how about I find a Super-8 projector around here somewhere and we have dinner someplace nice tonight—would you agree to that? And then I'll answer all your questions. I think you'll be satisfied with the answers."

"There's no really nice place around here," she says, laughing and shaking her head. "Like Gertrude Stein said, 'There's no there there.' But there's a decent restaurant—it's got a tremendous reputation but it's not *that* good—about fifty miles away in Sharpton. It would be nice to have dinner—and if you can find a Super-8 projector around here, we'll watch the movies afterward. Okay?"

"Okay," I say.

Fourteen

It takes several phone calls, but I find a camera store with a Super-8 projector for rent fifteen minutes from Nora's restaurant.

"Are you staying locally?" the owner asks. My radar goes off so I answer cautiously.

"What do you mean by locally?"

"In Sharpton—in town here? I can't have my equipment traipsing around the country, you know."

"Yes," I tell him, "I'm staying at a local motel."

"Which one?" he asks.

"I can't remember the name—it's on the highway," I say—how can I go wrong with that? "It's got the green roof."

"Which--? Alright, well, just have your receipt with you when you pick it up."

This is certainly an added expense, but, even unemployed, it isn't hard for me to imagine the benefits of a local motel room after dinner with Nora.

Unfortunately, this is exactly the way she sees it too. She is wearing heels and a practical winter coat—certain pneumonia being the other available option—with the skirt of a distinctly impractical cocktail dress fluttering beneath. But she pulls the coat tightly around her when I mention that getting a Super-8 projector necessitates us stopping to pick up a motel room.

"Well, it was kind of inevitable anyway..." I say.

"Oh—and how is *that*?" she asks, distinctly chilly. God, is there any way I can screw this up in which I haven't indulged already?

"There's no electricity at the cabins. How were we going to run a movie projector?"

"There's a generator at the boathouse," she says.

"Oh—I didn't know that," I admit and then wonder why I'm feeling guilty. Maybe all the enjoyment I was getting at the thought of that motel room ... I wag a finger at her.

"You've gone out with too many men—you've gotten cynical," I accuse her.

"It doesn't take many to be too many sometimes," she replies. "Besides, the hotel room with an innocent justification is sort of Female Puberty 101—you learn that one before you've even been hurt very much."

We sit in the car for a long uncomfortable moment—and then I burst out laughing. She looks at me in wonderment—if I'm on the make, I should certainly be more sheepish than this.

"I'm sorry," I finally say. "I'm just imagining you displaying yourself at 17, me with my Allman Brothers haircut, your sister and brothers and parents from 1975 on the wall of the boathouse for the Lost Sons of Mondo the Man-God." I can see from the expression on her face that this thought has taken root. "Pretty grisly, isn't it?" I say and we both laugh together.

I give her my most piercing earnest look. "Nora, of course I'm on the make—I'm a man; it's inevitable and no woman ever appealed to me more. But if I was on the make for a night in a cheap motel, I could have found that much closer to New York."

It takes a nanosecond for her to accept this and instantly everything's fine. We start joking about the types of comments the Boys would have made about our clothes and hair and what innocent children we were at the time.

"And we *were* innocent," she says, "By the way, I *wasn't* 17."

"What do you mean? You were a senior in high school."

"I jumped three grades going into high school—I thought I told you that."

"You were *14?*" I shriek, horrified and a little thrilled at the same time.

"It was January, so I was 15 by then," she says.

I let out a long breath. "I suppose I should be grateful I was such a doofus with women at that age."

"Oh yeah?" she says, arching an eyebrow.

"I could have been jailed without a single regret," is all I can say. I hear her cackle but I don't dare look her in the face.

We stop at the first motel off the highway—it even has a green roof. It takes two minutes to get the room—I notice the owner eyeing the blond in the car outside. Then we pick up the projector—I give my credit card and show him the hotel receipt and we're clear.

"God, *look* at that thing," she says, as I bring the projector box out to the car. It is a mess—battered and dented.

"What do they say? 'It's not the age, it's the mileage'—this guy's done the marathon a few times."

"Do they still *make* Super-8 anymore?" she asks.

"I don't know," I say. "Maybe that's why the guy was so cautious about letting me rent it. That didn't even occur to me. You'd better get those movies transferred to video soon."

"Well, I have to make sure they're not pornographic first," she says.

"I'll be so pissed if I missed *that* party," I tell her and hear her cackle again as we pull into the parking lot of the restaurant.

"You don't think it's valuable, do you?" she asks, looking at the projector as she gets out of the car. We both stare at the battered box.

"It would be really anal if we carried it in with us," I tell her.

"I know," she says, but she shrugs while she says it. So, of course, I grab the handle and we go inside.

As soon as we walk in, I see what she was saying about the place. A lot of money has been showered on appearance—lots of etched glass and brushed aluminum in the visible kitchen, butcher-block surfaces on the tables and chairs, soft lighting and an actual dinner orchestra, with a few horns and a real string section. But the menu is steak or chicken, a little fish—nothing particularly memorable—and the food, when it comes, is mediocre.

I could care less. The only thing I want to eat is the woman sitting across the table from me. I want my tongue all over her as quickly as can be arranged. I also want little bites of her radiance, of the brilliance pouring out of her every time she smiles. It's like a physical assault sitting across the table from her when those eyes open up and that mouth widens. It's supernatural power.

"I married a man who was *so* wrong for me, so completely wrong! We have two kids in university—they've now had ten years to see us separately—they laugh at the thought that we could ever have been married.

"We're good friends now thankfully and he's a good father so it's all worked out in the end. But at one point, I could have killed him. We were both members of a local club and we hadn't told anyone we were splitting up—we had a lot of friends we'd made together and I was concerned they'd take sides—it would have been devastating to lose them. And we were both still living in the same house, because we didn't want to disrupt the kids until they'd gotten used to the idea. I moved into the guest bedroom. So no one else knew—I told my sister Kate but that was it."

"And one day, I showed up at the club and everyone's being just a little *too* nice, you know? The man who reserves the tennis courts is being way too helpful and the woman who always sits by the fireplace reading—who has never looked at me before—is now giving me a sad smile. And finally, the bartender says he's sorry to hear the news. I said, 'Excuse me?' and he said, 'I'm so sorry about Nick and you.' Nick had come in that morning to play, went into the main room and *announced* our separation."

"If I knew how to kill someone, I would have done it on the spot. And when I confronted him that afternoon, he told me, 'I'm the man—I *had* to make the announcement.'"

"So, three days later, I was reading an article about these men's groups that go back to nature and celebrate their maleness together. But there was nothing like it yet in Canada. I was sitting with Kate and her husband Art and actually, it was Art's idea. He said, "Nick would be a patsy for something like that. If anyone did a hundred sit-ups, Nick would do five hundred. If anyone else climbed a tree, Nick would wrestle the tree to the ground." So I decided to set up this tribal weekend and get Nick to go and make a big fool of him and we'd catch it on film or something. Frankly, I don't know what I was thinking and I'm amazed Art was willing to go through with it. He loves Kate so much—Kate gets flaky at times, you know Kate and Art just keeps things steady all the time—so maybe that's why.

"I made professional-looking fliers and applications and put them in all the places Nick went so he'd sign up. I was stunned when we got 32 applications—and 20 with cheques paid in full! We got up here and nothing happened the way I expected. The men went crazy over these silly competitive situations we made up! The more outrageous, the crazier the demands, the more they liked it. It's amazing men ever have families and work productively together. And Nick didn't excel. He didn't even like it much. He left early. When we got to the end, I saw how much the other guys got into Mondo and I just couldn't make them all feel stupid. So we juryrigged an award ceremony to send them all home happy. And as they were leaving, several of them wanted to know when the next session would be, because they wanted to bring their friends. One promised to bring every man in his office! So suddenly I had this business—a very lucrative business—helping men celebrate their maleness."

She laughs now like a torrent. It's musical cathartic laughter and I'm shocked at the freshness of the cut. I feel like I can feel everything inside her. I feel consumed with lust and at the same time more innocent than I have in decades. It's like she's a wormhole in time, sucking us right back to where we left off while we somehow retain everything we've learned since. If there's a more powerful fantasy in life, I haven't heard of it.

When she settles down again, she says, "I haven't told that story to *anyone*. It was such a plot, we just kept it to ourselves. My parents think I'm doing management consulting—they're really impressed I've built such a lucrative practice so fast. Little do they know," she says, arching an eyebrow in infectious mischief.

"But God, I haven't talked about myself like this in…I don't know, a long time. How are you? Where *were* you?" Without her saying another word, I know what she's asking about. I explain where I was when the towers came down. No details, just the basic rundown—all the information I want to deal with at the moment.

"It's an awful story," she says when I've finished.

"It's just another story," I tell her. "Everyone in New York has one."

"You're so brave," she says, shaking her head at me. "You're handling it so well." I'm old enough to know I should just accept this admiration. I want the girl in bed. I need that comfort more than I've never needed anything, need it in a way that just now begins to feel a bit scary. One way or the other, however, I have never been able to leave well enough alone and it's too late to start now.

"I'm not brave," I tell her. "I'm not handling it at all. I don't know what to feel. I'm not sure I know *how* to feel. I'm trying to, though."

"I've been reading my grandmother's journals," she says. "It's eerie, in a way. I thought I knew *her* so well, after all these years. We were such friends and I thought we were such confidantes. She passed away a year ago, age 92. I used to go over at lunch every day during the week and read to her, help her with her meals, you know, the sort of things you do for people."

"The sort of things *you* do," I say. "Most people talk about things like that, but very few actually do them."

Her cheeks color for a moment—Good Hit, Ted, you made her blush!—and she moves on.

"Well, to read the journals is such a revelation, and it's almost disturbing. I feel like I'm intruding—but, you know, I can't stop! It's fascinating, and yet it feels like someone else, another person. I don't know—is it possible I really didn't know her all this time?"

"I don't think that's it," I say. "I suspect it's the difference between talking to other people and talking to yourself."

"Maybe," she says, staring at her glass—and at me. "I'd love to know someone that well though someday."

Me too, I find myself thinking. And I know who.

My response to her is leaping over all my boundaries and suddenly I have a sense of why. She overwhelms all stereotypes. She is bright and funny and generous and caring and relentlessly nice. She shows no signs of neurosis and every indication of perspective, common sense and well-being.

My response, naturally, is to look for a hunchback, a hideous portrait in the attic, a nasty skin condition—something! To no avail. I can understand why Nick, if he had the slightest insecurity, might have felt a need to assert his manliness—she's so effortlessly competent it's scary. On the other hand, if I can just surmount my own cynicism, the fact that she's a wonderful person might also be a basis for hope, and I could use some of that at the moment.

So I spill. I abandon all efforts at guile and subterfuge. I grit my teeth and tell myself to forget the past and just let the chips fall.

"Nora—there are no Ancient Trappers. Nikos is my writing professor—he made it all up on the spot. We came up here because I was convinced I'd scared you off with my first note."

"You could have called me—you found my address, so you had to have my phone number," she points out, and there's a question attached, left unasked. And having come this far, I'm prepared to answer all her questions, as I promised this morning— even the ones she, typically, is too polite to ask.

"A phone call wouldn't have answered my questions," I tell her. "Nora, I didn't come up here to be your friend—we're both old enough to know how things work. I wanted to see if there was a spark. I might have convinced you to talk to me again with a good email—and we might have decided we liked each other by phone—but I needed to be in a room with you to see if there's a spark."

Both eyebrows go up and she levels that mischievous face at me again.

"And—?" she asks.

"Do you want to dance?" I answer.

We dance, but not for long. The music is slow and quiet and very romantic and as soon as we touch hands for the first time there' s a current so strong between us it almost knocks me over. And that can't only be happening to *me*. So I relax and take her in my arms and suddenly we're inside a forcefield that just shuts the whole world out. It's us and the music and the floor and a mountain of feeling churning around inside.

We make a few turns and I kiss her for the first time ever and then about ten or twenty more—kisses like breaths, soft sweet kisses with us quickly panting in each other's faces. And then I kiss her once or twice on the neck, because I've wanted to for twenty-five years and oh is it *sweet*.

And then she puts her head on my shoulder and kisses me once softly on the neck and says, "On the other hand, a cheap motel room with *no* innocent justification can be a very very nice thing."

Fifteen

The room itself isn't bad. I have images in my head the whole drive of rats and spiders and dingy sheets, but the first impression is decent generic hotel room.

We have to feel fortunate just making it back in one piece. Between all the flashing lights on the road—must be some sort of ambulance convention—and our hands all over each other in the car, just avoiding an accident is a major achievement. Finally, we open the door and lurch together through it, pawing each other like high school kids after the prom (or do they reach this stage now at age 12? How do they get hotel rooms?).

Somehow, we silently agree on a moment of serenity and fall onto the bed together, just staring into each other's eyes and smiling like rank idiots. What are you looking for when you gaze into the eyes of someone you're crazy about? All at once, I know the answer—you're looking for your own happiness reflected back at you, your own lust and excitement and that sentimentality we cling to and try so hard to deny. So far, both of us seem to like what we see.

More kisses. Oh, kisses are so much better at this age. So much more and so much less all at once. Half of it is just sharing breath, little gasps at the other person, sliding lip across lip, touching cheek, touching neck, touching shoulder. She has wonderful skin and a really soft dress that offers a preview of taste treasures to come. And then back to her mouth. No rush—we've got time.

"I'm not going to say I've never done this," she says, "but I'm not usually this easy."

"And I wouldn't be pushing this hard normally," I say.

"Oh sure you would," I hear her cackle. "I can already see you're a pusher."

"Well, I wouldn't expect to get here so fast, how's that?" I offer. "This is one of those barriers that just gets taller the longer you wait and we've waited 25 years. Time to push over the damn wall."

"Oh, it'll crumble," she assures me, each word a sigh. "Let's just enjoy the steps." And she kisses me really sweet, a swirling electric probe dancing around my lips and inside my mouth and both of us passing it back and forth between us as we keep dragging the covers around.

"I love the way you look at me," she says.

"You're more beautiful now than you were when I met you,"
I say. "And you were one of the most bewitching creatures on the
planet *then*."

She shakes her head. "I love that you feel this way about me. I
was always the little girl in school, since I started so young—they
made fun of me all the way through, even though I probably grew
a foot between 11 and 12. But I think it affected the way I thought
of myself ever since. I've never thought of myself as being pretty. I
feel pretty when I see you look at me."

"I understand the words you've said but they're never going
to mean anything to me. To me, you'll always be one of the most
beautiful women I've ever seen," I say, knowing better.

'Always' and 'never' are two words that should never (there I
go again) be used in a serious sentence. The question is whether
words spoken between crazed adults in bed should ever be
considered serious. They're always just statements of intent. 'I
intend to love and respect you for as long as you earn it'—that's
the truth, but it just doesn't have the ring of 'I'll love you forever,'
does it? And when you're caressing each other and pawing the
sheets off the bed, you're about the business of thrilling the other
person and secondarily of thrilling yourself and you don't look to
split hairs.

And then she just surrenders. The strap comes off her
shoulder and I'm kissing her breast, rolling my lips along the side
of it and my tongue over her sweet nipple and then I'm no longer

aware of where I am or what I'm doing anymore—pure instinct clicking in. It feels like I've been here for years, instead of waiting for years. It feels like we already know what the other person wants and when and how hard and all the other million-and-a-half details that you couldn't keep track of with a bank of supercomputers if instinct didn't somehow encompass all and transcend all.

It takes a few minutes to get down to her in panties and all the other clothes on the floor. She wouldn't object to being naked already, but I'm enjoying the process.

We're snuggled under the covers—it's still Canada in the middle of the winter, heated room or not. My hands are moving over her inner thighs, keeping away from the magic zone for just another moment, letting the anticipation build. She's making those little cries women make, mingling joy and some ancient sorrow. I reach for her panties.

BAM!!

There's light all over the room and shouting and I'm lifted off the bed and shoved very rudely against the wall. Whack! In my condition, that really hurts.

I look around real quick. Nora is sitting at the head of the bed, sheets pulled around her. The door is in pieces and the room is full of people in black flack suits. One of them has his hand against the back of my throat and is holding me against the wall, his other hand holding my arm behind my back, threatening to break it if I move. I'm not moving.

The person in the center of the room makes one of those ominous-sounding statements about the perimeter being secured into his walkie-talkie and then an agent takes off her helmet and offers to escort Nora to the bathroom to get dressed.

The guy with the walkie-talkie looks at the cop with his hand on my throat and says, "Okay, get him ready, James. I don't think you'll have to frisk him."

Twenty minutes later, we're in the basement of the local police station in separate interrogation rooms. A few officers enter Nora's room first, but I don't hear any screams so I assume this is Canada and there's due process and we'll probably be offered tea and some kind of little English cakes or something to make our brief stay with the constabulary more pleasant. At least, that's how I used to feel about Canadian justice before the experience of a Canadian cop's fingers pressing my throat into a wall.

Eventually, two men come into the room and take seats. Well put together, neat, trim, wholesome-looking. The antithesis of the New York doughnut cop stereotype. Blonde crewcut next to me, balding sandy hair across the table. Good cop bad cop—one to confront and the other to sympathize. And, I suppose, to make sure I don't leap the table and throttle my accuser for pulling me away from a moment I've dreamed of my whole life.

"What is your business in Canada?" Bald Cop asks.

"Can I ask what I'm being accused of?" I respond. I try to sound polite, but I'm not stupid enough to answer questions until I know what I'm trying to weasel out of.

"You haven't been accused of anything," he says. "This is a simple interrogation and maybe we can get it done quickly if you'll cooperate with us."

"I'll cooperate as long as you get the US Ambassador or someone from the consulate on the phone. I'm an American citizen."

Baldie says something like 'get him' and the other cop steps to the door and calls down the hall. He returns to his seat and they both turn back to me.

"Did you cross the border without a passport?"

"Yes." Not much point in denying it—they won't find a passport on me.

"How did you accomplish that?"

I don't even think about this. From the moment we met Billy Hassin, I knew I'd have to lie to *someone* about the border crossing. Now that it's actually come up, I find that same storytelling impulse Nikos has been riding the past couple days kicks in for me as well.

"I told the man at the station I'd been crossing back and forth between the US and Canada for thirty years without a passport and I'd bring it next time but I don't *have* a passport now and I showed him a 25-year-old photograph of this absolutely gorgeous

Canadian girl I knew when I was a kid who was now just waiting for me to jump into bed with her and I was just about *there* when you broke down the door of my fucking hotel room which I paid for fair and square and you could have at least waited till *morning* and arrested me *while I was happy*!!!!"

I have never regarded yelling at police officers as a desirable thing to do. They have their very disagreeable jobs and they're necessary and sometimes really comforting guys to have around — although never when you're alone in an interrogation room with them. Nonetheless, at this moment, several things are bubbling out of me, ebbing away so to speak, some of which I can't discuss in polite company. So I go off.

"Can I please understand what is going *on* here?" I demand. "We were certainly well over the age of consent!"

"What was your plan for this evening?" Blondie asks politely. At least I haven't offended him with my tirade. Maybe I can with the next one.

"What do you *think* my plan was?" I shriek. "You found me naked and her in panties, which were almost *gone*." It's a wonder I don't dissolve in sobs on the spot.

"Now, now," the sandy-haired cop next to me says, patting me on the shoulder. "There'll be other days."

"Pretty girl," says Blondie.

"Thanks," I say, dabbing my eyes with a handkerchief I pull from his jacket pocket. "She doesn't think she is—you wouldn't believe how insecure she is."

"Really?" says the cop. "Wouldn't have believed it, looking at her."

Then the door opens and a tall distinguished-looking man in very expensive skipants and parka walks into the room—there are several other similarly-attired personages with him.

"Alright gentlemen," he says, "why don't you let us do our consult?" No Canadian accent. "And no surveille, please?" he says as they get up to go.

He sits down opposite me and waves the rest of his party out of the room. He's not exactly angry, but his expression isn't real friendly either.

"So—I understand you wanted to speak with me?" he says.

"I did? Who are you?"

"I'm the United States Ambassador to Canada."

I look him over twice, blinking repeatedly. Finally he pulls a little billfold-type thing from his pocket and flashes it in my face. They even give them little ID cards and State Department laminated badges and such—not much better-looking than what I could get in Times Square, though.

"Okay," I say, feeling a bit goofy. "I'll admit it—this is *service.* I'll never complain about my taxes again."

I see a wisp of a smile around the edge of his mouth, but he doesn't seem to have a lot of difficulty repressing it.

"I was at dinner with the Prime Minister, so naturally I'm here," he says. "We had to make a statement."

I'm now in way over my head. I'm getting some information here, which is more than I got from the cops, but I can't make head or tail of it.

"What *happened*?" I ask with total ingenuousness. I feel like a child, yet I also fear that, once he tells me what happened, any childhood I have left in me will be gone.

"You don't know?" he gasps.

"No—they just keep asking me what my plan was tonight. I wanted to make the girl—that was my plan, *en toto*."

That little smile dances around his lips again and lingers a little longer this time.

"Okay, I think we can get this over with fairly quickly. I doubt any charges will be filed. I doubt they will even prohibit you from entering Canada again."

"I would hate that—it would really cut into my love life," I say. "Although the way things are going, that might be over too."

"Okay," he stands up. "I'll see what I can arrange."

"Wait a minute," I insist, standing across from him. "Before anyone else comes in here, at least tell me what I did."

He sits. I sit. He seems to be searching his mind, to try to figure out how to tell me. Is it that horrible or that confusing?

"Did you rent a Super8 projector tonight?"

Ohhh yeah—I forgot all about the projector. "Yes," I admit guiltily. "But it wasn't due back till tomorrow morning."

"I'm sure that's fine," he says. "Do you know where it is?"

"Oh shit," I moan. "We left it under the table at the restaurant." I feel like the kid in the principal's office. Then I shake my head.

"Okay," I tell him, "so I get that we left the Super-8 projector in the restaurant and it was the personal property of the camera store and we really should have returned it. But why are you and the Prime Minister of Canada making statements to the police? Is there really *that* little crime in this country?"

"The Prime Minister and I are on a skiing trip up here," he explains. "We must have come in just after you left and sat at a table near the one you'd just vacated. Somewhere during the appetizer, someone noticed the metal box under your table. They notified the maitre'd, who did the appropriate thing—he evacuated the restaurant and called the bomb squad, who helicoptered in from Ottawa. The man in the big lead blast suit went into the restaurant with the robot bomb disposer and placed your Super8 projector in a blast container and very gingerly took it out to their truck outside. In the truck, they X-rayed the box. However, because there is a motor inside a Super8 projector, they couldn't X-ray all the way through. Therefore," he concludes, "they took it out behind the County Court House and detonated it with a small charge."

I hear this twice in my head, on replay, before it really registers, and then I replay it several more times before I can speak.

"You *detonated* it?"

"The Canadian authorities did," he says. "They had to—couldn't take the chance it was a bomb."

"It wasn't a bomb."

"We know that now."

"What's left?"

"You don't want it."

"Can I have the pieces?"

"It's gravel."

"But—but—I rented it from the camera store," I say pathetically. "It was the guy's prized possession."

"I know—he took down your hotel on the slip as security—that's how we found you. I'm sorry," the United States Ambassador tells me. "You'll have to explain it to him."

"I'm really going to get in trouble with that guy," I continue to whine, all the air coming out of me at once. "Isn't there a State Department spokesman or someone who can come with me to make this right?"

He stands over me, making the most of his height and that very expensive ski suit for persuasion. "The United States

Government has already agreed to compensate the Canadian Government for the use of a military helicopter, a bomb truck, robot bomb disposer, explosives, personnel and equipment, compensating the restaurant for an evacuation in the busiest time of day and your motel for a busted door, because you, an American citizen, were responsible for this damage. Don't you think you can handle the camera rental?" he asks, and the brusque expression is very clear on his face.

"Sure—give millions to friendly governments and begrudge five or six hundred bucks to help out one of your own unemployed citizens," I growse.

"Well, maybe we should look into how you're traveling to Canada on unemployment," he says, standing up again. "I'll get you out of here in one piece. Find your way back across the border as soon as you can, alright?" And then he's gone.

Sixteen

At the front desk, they hand us back our personal belongings. They emptied and catalogued her purse, so naturally that takes some time to put back together. She has condoms inside, the naughty wench. Just throw the near-miss in my face, why don't you?

I managed to weasel a note out of the police captain describing the projector's destruction as an 'issue of national security' in hopes this will sooth the camera store owner, but that concern fades instantly as I experience Nora sitting silently in the back seat next to me the whole way back to the motel.

Once we reach the parking lot, we get in the car and wait for the engine to heat up. It is 2 in the morning and we are the only ones in the lot.

Finally I look at her as forthrightly as I can bear to and say, "I'm sorry."

She stares out the window a long time before saying, "What are you apologizing for?"

Ah-HAH! Think you've got me, eh? I didn't go through 15 years of marriage without learning that this is a just a TRAP! You're checking to see if I *know* why I'm apologizing or if I'm just a good trained monkey who knows he's supposed to apologize but has no idea why.

The problem is, I *am* just a trained monkey who has no idea why he should be apologizing—except that I'm a man and that's our role when something goes wrong. And so far, this definitely fits my definition of a date gone wrong. But I also know that hesitation is surrender, and I'm not going down without a fight.

"I'm sorry this happened," I say first, probing at the boundaries, testing to see if she'll accept that as an answer and I don't have to go further. Of course, she doesn't. She continues to stare out the windshield vacantly.

Do they teach this in women's boarding school or something—is there a mail order course in how to torture men? Did they cover this subject one day on *Oprah* while I wasn't watching? Since unemployment, I've gotten hooked—I know all about Steadman and Dr. Phil but clearly I don't know everything.

And then, against my better judgment, I get a little annoyed. I've been thinking about this just long enough for it to bubble up from underneath. And with me, nothing ever simmers for long.

"And I'm apologizing," I continue, "for bringing this entire episode down on us." *Now* she looks over. Maybe there's even a little hint on her face that I'm being unnecessarily rough on myself, but it's too late for that now—I'm off and running.

"I mean, let's face it," I spout, "if you're crazy enough to leave a Super8 projector under your table at a nice local restaurant, you're inevitably going to end up accused of attempting to assassinate the Prime Minister of Canada! *Forget rental projector— meet the SWAT team.* This is why people feel *safe* when they go skiing in Canada!"

She's trying to maintain the stern look on her face. She's trying *really* hard. But I see those little cracks around the eyes, sweetie—you're straining. You're just not ready to let me off the hook, and I can't really blame you, wrong or not.

"But if you think you're going to punish me," I continue, "by not talking to me or ignoring me for the rest of my life or whatever's in your head at the moment, forget it. After 25 years, I was ten seconds from heaven and they pulled me away—*nothing* you can do will hurt me more than that."

It takes about four seconds but then I see that little switch go off behind those incredible blue eyes—that switch all women have—the 'Awwwww' switch. Her expression completely changes—I can see her melt.

And thirty seconds later, we're back in the lobby of the hotel and the manager is frantically trying to find a reason not to rent us another room—one with a door intact —for what's left of this night.

"I don't know if we take Mastercard, sir."

"There's a decal on your door."

"Our machine is out of order."

"Call it in."

This guy isn't even making an effort to appear convincing. He's busy cataloguing every item on his desk, searching for some excuse to keep us out of this quiet little backwater.

"You don't have a passport," he tries next.

"I didn't have one when you took my money earlier tonight."

"Here," Nora says, "take *my* card. I'm a Canadian citizen." All of a sudden, she is not the same person I had dinner with. She shoves her credit card across the counter at him. He tries to shove it back but she clamps her hand down over his and refuses to let it up off the counter. The two of them are virtually arm-wrestling, both their arms tense to the point of vein-popping.

"I'm afraid we may be full up," he says, glancing at the room catalog just enough to pretend he's checking. Meanwhile, his hand is still clamped under Nora's. But not for long.

"Okay, I've had it," she says, reaching across the counter and grabbing him by both lapels. "Either you are going to give us a room or we're going to park our car in the front doorway of this building and hump in the back seat with the windows open until noon. Now which is it going to be?"

And so I get to heaven.

At first we both make really loud noises to annoy management. But after a little while, nature kicks in and we just get lost in each other.

We duck out of the room about thirty seconds before the 11 am deadline. I think I may even have gotten a couple hours sleep in there somewhere, but I could be hallucinating—which would only be fitting. The whole thing feels like a hallucination anyway.

The camera store man is happy as a clam when we stop by. "I've already called my insurance guy," he says, brandishing the morning newspaper. "I only rented that thing out about four times a year anyway—now I can tell those cheapskates to transfer those films to *video*."

"May I see the paper?" Nora says and he hands it over.

The headline reads 'Bomb Scare Musses PM.' The article notes that 'briefly held were Nora Hill of Waterline, President of Gimmick Enterprises and Ted Krever, an unemployed transient from the US.' Transient? *Transient*? Where's the dignity of the foreign traveler? I'm a tourist between jobs, for Christ's sake.

"Oh dear," Nora says while continuing to read. From other people, this is the mildest of exclamations. Coming from Nora, this is serious distress.

"What's the matter?"

"Well, Gimmick Enterprises is the proprietor of the Mondo The Man-God Self-Actualization Weeks," she explains. "We're a publicly traded company—my name is buried in the paperwork, along with Art. He's listed as CEO. But *someone* reads those things—I have plenty of lawyers who are avid members. It would be a problem if those guys realize a *girl* owns the Man-God."

"You mean it'll remind them too much of real life?" I say and she slaps me on the shoulder. We get back in the car and head North, to camp and the next crisis.

Seventeen

Nora sits, quiet and preoccupied, for most of the drive back, worrying—I suppose—about her name in the paper. I hate this fact of adult life—we allow just about everything to interfere with our happiness. We tell ourselves we are here on this planet searching for contentment and peace, yet when it's right in front of us we worry about whether our hair looks right and if the Dodgers are ever going to move back to Brooklyn. But this news, at very least, shouldn't affect this week's crew—I can't imagine the papers ever make it to Frozen Lake.

"So—one thing worries me," I say, breaking the silence.

"What's that?" she says. I can see the nervousness all over her. Has she really had so little go wrong in her life, or is she so used to managing everything perfectly that she can't handle the in-betweens?

"What do we do for an encore?" I ask.

She smiles and returns to me. She reaches for my hand and holds it to her cheek. These moments don't promise forever but forever is in them anyway. At least forever is in them for the moment and that's enough for now.

"Yeah," she says, her voice throatily sexy, "sure beats going to the movies."

"You'll collect Nikos and take off," she tells me. "I'll finish out the week here. I'll be back in Waterline Saturday, take care of the books and such and then I'll see when I can fly into New York."

"Uh-huh," I nod. "When do you think that'll be?"

"Oh, sometime in the next several weeks," she says.

Next several *weeks*? That's it? I appreciate independence in a woman but this is Nora Hill. She found me on the Internet and I drove all the way up here to see if there was a spark. And we started a forest fire. So now she's talking about several *weeks*? I want to be with her, period, and I want her to want to be with me. Why is several weeks okay with her? What am I missing here?

We pull off the highway, heading for the lake. We've gone less than half a mile down the local road when I see flashing lights behind me.

"License and registration?" the officer asks. I hand them over. It's really hard to keep a straight face while he's wearing those Sergeant Preston of the Yukon hats and those pants that go all puffy at the hips—it looks like the pants would float if his canoe ever capsized.

"Thought you were heading for the border," he says after perusing my documentation. Okay, I see—I'm an all-points bulletin, granted the freedom to leave on my own through the influence of the much bigger, richer, nicer climate, more profligate country a few hours South.

"I have clothes and a friend up here at Frozen Lake," I tell him. "I'm picking them up and then heading home, believe me."

"So I should see you heading back this way in an hour or two?" he inquires. God, I get the hint, okay?

"With my tail between my legs, yes," I answer. I figure they're not going to begin prosecuting for sarcasm, hopefully.

"And you?" he says, looking at Nora.

"Bonny Parker here is a Canadian citizen," I tell him. "She's staying." She hands him her drivers license.

"Okay," he says, looking uncertain. Maybe he doesn't have specific instructions for her—or maybe he memorized the bulletin and doesn't remember anything about Bonny Parker.

He returns our paperwork, nonetheless, and takes off in a hail of scattered dust.

We drive silently the rest of the way to the lake.

As soon as we reach the parking lot, it's obvious something's wrong. There are only half as many cars in the lot as there were when we left yesterday (is it really possible that was only yesterday?). As soon as we start up the path to the cabins, we hear a silence that's eerie. The beach is torn up and full of debris— scattered logs, charcoal remnants of old fires, what look like old car parts and tires in piles all over.

Art, the brother-in-law, comes tearing out of the cabin they shared (how proper was that? I wonder).

"We need to talk," he says to Nora, throwing a not-very-subtle look at me.

"Talk," she says. "We're all friends here."

"Well, there's been a coup," he tells her.

"A coup?" we both say simultaneously, with different notes of pain.

"Well, maybe not a coup, but at least a rebellion. Sorry," he says with a really sincere tone I make a note to emulate. "A group of our guys were going on another nature walk this morning, while we were supposed to be having the blood-mingling."

"Blood-mingling?" I groan. Just the image makes me queasy.

"It's a wine-tasting," Nora says. "We call it that to make it sound more Mondo-ish."

"Don't you worry that mixing wine with the beer they had for breakfast will have a negative effect?" I say, and she flashes me a look that says, 'not the time.'

"So I felt I had to do something," Art continues, looking right past me at Nora. "You know I always have your interests at heart, even if I don't always end up with the greatest results. I told them that if they went, they were violating the sacred pact they made with Mondo. And Shrader the lawyer said the pact had no legal standing and that the Trappers were a more viable role model, or something like that."

"Oh *wonderful*," Nora moans. She turns to me. "Shrader's one of the biggest litigation attorneys in Canada. He's the one who came to the first session and brought back every guy in his firm."

"And this is his idea of a vacation—fomenting revolution in the North Woods," I say. She shrugs.

"So what did you do?" Nora asks Art.

"I told him he had to decide," Art says.

"No," Nora shakes her head. "He had already decided— that's what he was telling you."

"Well, I think I made my *big* mistake right after that," Art continues. "The guys behind me who were ready for the blood-mingling started yelling at the Trappers and I didn't stop them right away. And a minute later, they were all trying to punch and kick and knock each other over. It got ugly really fast."

I find myself trying to count every individual blade of grass on the ground beneath me. Nora gazes skyward. Actually, the number of clouds should be easier to pin down. Practical thinking on her part, as usual.

"Great," she mutters. "And what happened?"

"Well, the Trappers had weapons, so they beat us."

"*Weapons?*" I hear myself shrieking.

"Tomahawks," he says. "Not real ones, but they beat us back with them. And then a whole bunch of guys just got in their cars and took off. They left a couple of hours ago, after the battle. And the rest of them are on the Wilderness Trail."

The Wilderness Trail—such a majestic name for a dirt path. I wonder if they called it that before Nikos showed up or if it's another invention of the New Order of Ancient Canadian Trappers.

"I'm sorry," I say to Nora and this time I have no trouble at all sounding absolutely sincere.

"It's nobody's fault," she says. "They came up here looking to bond on man-type stuff, and they found something more genuine than Mondo."

"What's more genuine?" I say. "He's making it all up."

"The Ancient Trappers aren't *real*?" Art stammers.

"You thought Canada was settled by the *Greeks*?" I respond. He looks crestfallen.

I can't tell if he's developed a very inappropriate (considering his position) affection for the story or if he's frustrated at being beaten by something just as fictitious as Mondo.

"Well, let's just say more convincing then," Nora says. She turns back to Art. "We're going to have to do damage control," she says. "If they left two hours ago, some of them are home already. Call around, get a sense of what they're feeling—will they ever come back again? Did they like the Ancient Trapper thing? Get me some impressions, okay?" Then she turns back to me.

"We'd better find your friend Nikos," she says, turning to me. "We've got to stomp this thing down before it gets worse." We start heading for the trail.

"What do we do when we find him?" I ask. I'm alarmed by this turn of events, although I'm also a bit amazed that *anything* could alarm me after the last 24 hours. "Do we have to kill the Ancient Trappers?"

"How?" she says. "They're *winning*," and we head off up the hill looking for Nikos and his wandering Band of Gypsies.

Eighteen

Nikos' pace guarantees they can't be *too* far away, of course. Though in truth, they've gone much farther than I expected—at least a mile up the path when we find them, and marching back at a pace I wouldn't have thought possible.

Nikos sees us coming and I see both delight—at our being together—and real concern—he has to know the tomahawk battle was a problem—on his face.

"Can we talk?" I ask and he says, "You guys head back— we'll catch up."

"How's it going?" I ask when they've all marched out of earshot.

"It's amazing," he says, pausing and leaning on a tree to catch his breath. "The stories are still pouring out of me. I've figured out all seven of them."

"Seven of who?"

"The Ancient Trappers. There were seven who started the Order, and each of them has a distinct set of personality traits. I've managed to work it all out, but you have to recharge the laptop, so I can finish writing it all down. The guys are dividing up into groups, based on the Trapper they most admire. And the groups are sharing their skills to work together. It's really wonderful, watching this happen."

Nora looks like she's swallowed a fly. Nikos begins to walk down the hill, slowly, but certainly with a much brisker pace than he'd had when we arrived.

"Nikos, where did the tomahawks come from?" I ask.

"Well, it was supposed to be a symbolic thing," he says. "They were just cardboard on a stick. I figured we'd meet the Mountain Wraiths again, and tools like tomohawks would be the next level of self-defense after rocks. I was very specific that they could throw them at Mountain Wraiths, but not at real grizzly bears—and that knowing the difference was one of the major things that distinguished a pathfinder from a trapper."

"A pathfinder?" I asked.

"It's like a junior grade trapper," Nikos answers. "I need some method of distinguishing between the guys that really get it and the ones that are just along for the ride, right? Some way to encourage the lazy ones to learn?"

"Well, sure," I say. "That would be right if we were *really building an organization* here."

He pauses for a moment, soaking up my point.

"Well, it seems to be building now, whether we want it to or not," he says in his usual thoughtful way. "You know, it's like when you've started writing a book and characters begin doing things all on their own. The thing has its own life now. I don't know how to stop it."

I look at Nora—from her expression, I don't think she sees any easier way out than I do.

"So how did the battle happen?" I say.

"They *attacked* us," he says, and turns to Nora. "You have to understand—men just have a different hormonal approach than women. When confronted, the first impulse is to confront back. It's a very ancient impulse and regardless of all the work we've done to progress, it somehow remains. I've always found it so interesting, because men can create such wonderful art, music, architecture and so forth, yet so many of those same men can be so brutish at almost the same moment. I can't make up my mind if I should be disappointed at the persistence of this behavior or terribly impressed with the broad range of experiences we can encompass at one time."

Nora's smiling now, staring at this apparition—this old man so determined to be thoughtful about the absurd world around him. If things had gone the way we'd planned, he would have charmed the pants off her. Figuratively speaking, of course.

"I mean," he continues, "who would have thought I could ever be part of killing a moose and eating it, right out in the wild?"

I replay this one several times, but it doesn't help.

"Run that one by me again?" I ask, piteously.

"We were out here and this animal *attacked* us," Nikos explains, saying the words as though they actually have meaning, while my eyes begin to water. "He was charging us, horns down—it was an amazing sight. You know, you never really understand the power of animal intelligence until you see them when they feel threatened."

"Nikos—what *happened*?"

"Well, the men just rallied," he continues. "One guy threw a rock, which seemed to stun it, and another guy pulls this knife out of his belt and slits its throat." He looks at me quizzically. "Does that make it kosher?" he asks.

"It's the right manner of killing," I reply, "but I doubt you had a rabbi among the group to say the blessings."

"Well, and then somebody said 'Let's eat it right here.' So we built a fire out in the clearing over the rise there and roasted and ate it. Not bad meat, actually. They did all this dancing around the fire, chanting and taking the hooves and ears and stuff and throwing them into the fire."

Nora looks like she's going to pass out at any minute.

"That's a Mondo ritual," she tells us. "We would bring them an animal—it was usually the culmination of the week—and they would take the extra pieces and throw them in the fire while we were roasting the meat. We made it into a big ritual, where each guy got a piece and he had to chant something before throwing it in the fire."

I must be staring at her open-mouthed; she blushes at me as she's explaining. "It just seemed like the right note to finish up a week of rampant maleness—sort of 'Lord of the Flies' meets 'Apocalypse Now.'"

"Yes, that's what they were doing," Nikos says. "No wonder they knew how to kill the animal—they learned it here."

"They didn't learn it from *us*," Nora says. "We got the meat all cut up from a butcher."

Nikos walks up to her and takes her by the hand.

"Well, you've created something here that's really got some resonance. I mean—this kind of life is clearly not what I was raised for. I come from the school of 'if it breaks, call the plumber.' My idea of exercise is to stand on a treadmill for twenty minutes three days a week with my walkman on—and here I am, wandering in the middle of the Canadian mountains, yelling at grizzlies and telling these guys made-up stories about every thing we pass, and I feel *wonderful*. It's so liberating, just the air and the space here. I've got so much energy now, it's better than 20 visits to the doctor."

Then he stops.

"Although," he says, "my stomach seems to be a bit upset all of a sudden."

Nineteen

After half an hour in the bushes on the ridge, Nikos finally emerges.

"I should be okay for a little while now," he says.

I say, "Okay—we should get going then" and turn to head back to the cabin. Nikos immediately says 'Uh-oh' and rushes headlong into the undergrowth.

"What is going on?" I ask him, trying to maintain some equanimity.

"I guess moose just doesn't agree with my system," he says. "I guess I got a little giddy, being an Ancient Trapper and all that, and forgot how tied up I am at ground level."

"Yeah," I breath. There can't be much left in his system after half an hour in the bushes, I tell myself. We'll come back next year—if I can get across the border—and there'll be a grove of trees thriving on this spot.

"Okay," he says, coming out again. His teeth are chattering and his hands are shaking from the cold and I'm not surprised. "I think I should sit down inside for a little while."

I nod and we walk down the little rise to our cabin. Nora is inside, stalking back and forth with her long strides. She pauses for a moment as Nikos pulls a chair virtually into the fireplace and sits.

"Are you okay?" she asks.

"I won't know until I thaw out," he says. "That could take several hours."

"Would outhouses be considered a really bad civic improvement here?" I ask her. "Would anyone miss the rustic joy of squatting in the snow?"

"How do you think *I* feel?" she says. "We started the program here because it was Nick's favorite place—he used to drag me here when I was pregnant. God knows how I managed not to deliver in one of these cabins—or on that rise, for that matter."

"How's Art doing?" I ask.

"He's still making phone calls—the guys are just getting home—and I can't bear to listen." She comes over and puts her arms around me—I enfold her in mine and we stand there for a few minutes. I love the hug, but it's a bad sign—she's really in need of consoling.

"I'm dead," she whispers in my ear. "I called Kate—the story made the Toronto papers and someone there found the connection with the company. It got mentioned in a *humor* column on the Op-Ed page of the Star. So now it'll be everywhere."

"Well, it doesn't necessarily mean the end of the program — it just means you need a cover story," I breath back, remembering my days in big business.

"If you can find a cover story for this, you're a genius," she whispers.

"I'm on a pretty good roll with stories lately," Nikos says. "Maybe I can help."

"You heard that?" Nora says.

"Ears like a hawk," I say and they both look at me cross-eyed. "Okay," I shrug, "you know what I mean."

I lead Nora to Nikos. "Nikos, meet Mondo the Man-God. It's *her* company."

Nikos shakes hands, laughing his little laugh. "Yes, I figured it was you."

"You did?" I say. Why didn't he share his insight with me? I could have looked brilliant, although looking brilliant on the last trip would have taken a recent Nobel Prize in Physics.

"Well, what else is a woman doing up here? And how come she never leaves the cabin? I kind of figured it was her program," he explains, making it all sound easy, dammit.

"Well, there's not going to be a program after this," she says. "You can't have a woman owning the Man-God, the celebration of maleness. It's already a joke in the Toronto papers."

Now Art bursts through the door. What happened to Canadian decorum?

"I called about ten of them," he hiccups. "They were very strange conversations. As best as I can piece things together, they left because everything felt out of control."

"I don't wonder," Nora mutters.

"The funny thing is, several of them really enjoyed the fighting—they were just uncomfortable because it felt real to them."

"Real?" I say. "Cardboard tomahawks?"

"You had to see these guys," Art says, shaking his head at the memory. "They were really angry at each other. Our guys felt betrayed by the Trappers, the Trappers felt our guys were blocking them from the Next Step. The weapons weren't real but the *feelings* were." He looks apologetically at Nora—he doesn't like the message but he's a faithful messenger. "All but one of them were real impressed with the Ancient Trapper over here."

"Who wasn't?"

"Shrader." The Instigator. Art begins reading from notes on a yellow legal pad. "He's offended at our lack of security. He says he doesn't understand how a rival program could infiltrate our space so easily. He says that proves us incompetent as a warrior organization."

"Wonderful," Nora muses.

"I get the feeling they're *all* calling other members," Art continues, "guys who weren't here this week but guys we usually get, and they're telling them all the story. And it's all over the email group."

"We have an email group?" Nora asks.

"Oh yeah," Art says. "I started it a few months ago. Seemed like a good idea at the time." He looks absolutely defeated.

"Don't worry about it," Nora says. " I hear myself saying that more and more often as I get older. Did anyone mention the Toronto article?"

"So far, only one."

"Yeah, but it's still early," she says. She starts stalking again in front of the fireplace. "So let me recap for the home audience — half of our clients have left and are telling their friends about the Ancient Trappers and the chaos up here. The other half are still here, but they're going on hikes with the Ancient Trapper himself over here and generally ignoring any Mondo activities we have for them. And I have been outed as the girl who owns the company and a suspect in an attempt to blow up the Prime Minister."

"What?" says Art.

"We had a really interesting first date," I tell him.

Nora actually manages a smile and says, "Yes, it *was* interesting. But now, like all women, I've got to figure out how to handle the aftermath."

We all turn to Nikos now, who sounds like he's swallowed a bellows. But he's fine — he's laughing so hard he can barely contain the air.

"I took my wife on a ride on a hot-air balloon for our first date," he tells us. "We ended up getting stranded and had to slide down those long ropes they have to get down onto the ground again. And then we got married. Ted's my spiritual heir. So blowing up the Prime Minister probably seemed much more interesting than finding a place with good sushi."

Nora smiles wistfully, despite everything. Her even-temperedness is amazing—I couldn't blame her if she had her hands around my throat at this point.

"I've got some amazing stuff here," Nikos continues, pulling out the laptop. "I've basically created a whole societal structure with these Trappers. Some are builders, some ne'er-do-wells, but I think I've got the whole range of personalities covered. And it came just like my books when I was younger—I didn't even think about it, whatever I needed just appeared at the right time."

"That's great," I say, without much conviction. Doesn't he see how difficult this is at the moment? Nora, somehow, seems more interested than I am. She pulls up a chair next to Nikos.

"Do you have enough to publish?"

"Oh yes," he says. "I came up with some real hum-dingers on our walk today. I think I've got elements of Robin Hood, Davey Crockett, Les Miserables and the Bhaggavad Gita—or is it the Kama Sutra?—in there."

"So," Nora says, "if we published this thing, it could be almost a handbook for a program of Ancient Trapper initiations and activities—?"

"Sure," Nikos enthuses. "Every time I see a plant, I come up with another story about its magical properties and place in the Trappers' world. I already have three hierarchies of Woodland Wraiths, and spells to protect against them."

"We could merge the two programs—incorporate the Ancient Trappers into the Mondo program," Nora says. "Or just dump Mondo altogether."

"This could be fun," Nikos says, beaming. "I love these guys—they hunt, they trap animal pelts, they are competitive friends with the Indians, they live in dung hollows in the winter—"

"Dung hollows?"

"They burrow into the piles of shit left by the buffalo when it freezes," Nikos says, laughing his silent laugh again. "They hang beaver pelts over the door to keep the wind out. Makes a really cozy place away from the snow."

"Is there *any* basis for this?" I ask.

"No, of course not. I just say the first thing that comes into my mind—but it sounds gross, right? So they loved it."

"And," Nora says, "there aren't that enough buffalo loose for anyone to try this at home. So we're okay." The business mind at work.

"Says you," Art interrupts. "If Shrader finds one guy in Saskatchewan with his own herd, your insurance premiums will—"

"Wait a minute," Nora says, stopping dead, serious as the grave all at once. "It still won't work."

"Why not?" I ask.

"Because we still have the same basic problem. I'm still a *girl*," she moans and slumps back in the chair. I feel myself slumping as well. The room goes dead quiet.

"Why is that a problem?" Nikos says.

"Well, it makes it all inauthentic if a girl owns the company promoting Mondo the Man-God," she tells him, slowly, as though he's had a stroke or developed Alzheimers or something. "And the same with the Ancient Trappers."

"Why?" he says. "Three of the seven trappers were women."

"*Women?*" Nora yelps.

"You forget—he was a professor at Sarah Lawrence," I tell her, relief flooding over me.

"You just say you're the great-grandaughter of Hera," Nikos tells her. "The lead female trapper. She taught all the others."

"I've heard that name," Nora says. "How do I know it?"

"In Greek mythology, Hera was the wife of Zeus," Nikos explains. "The goddess Hera was raped on her first date by Zeus, the head God. She married her rapist out of shame, and then plotted with the other Gods to kill and overthrow him. When he escaped the assassination attempt, he found he cared about her enough that he couldn't kill her. So she promised not to try to overthrow him anymore and he let her live. She then spends the rest of eternity trying to get revenge on him for his constant infidelities."

Nora takes this in and considers it. "Boy," she says after a moment, "there are a lot of women who could relate to *that*."

"It's virtually a blueprint of a modern marriage," Nikos agrees. "I told you—I tried to put a Trapper in for *everybody*. I wasn't excluding women."

Nora claps her hands together. "How did the guys take it when you told them there were women trappers?"

"Frankly, I think most of them loved the idea. I think they're sick of each other, really. And your wife always looks a lot more attractive once you've seen her out skinning a buffalo or burning a couple of tent stakes half-naked in the cold. But," he pauses, looking distinctly uncomfortable, all at once, "I think you'd at least have to add plumbing." And he rushes outside, making a beeline for the bushes. I haven't seen him move this fast since he was playing tennis every day.

"Okay," Nora says, clasping her hands together in front of her. "So I buy you guys out. I put out a press release and a newsletter that the Ancient Trappers program has taken over and that Nikos, the Ancient Trapper himself, has agreed to be chief instructor. I hire Nikos to keep writing additions to the history and lore of the Ancient Trappers. He comes up here once or twice a year if he wants to address a gathering. He could be the Trapper Emeritus, presiding at graduation. He can lead nature walks for the ones that pay extra."

"If he agrees to all this, you should have him speak at graduation this week," Art says. "Then word'll get around to the others when they get home, and it'll look almost like we planned this."

"Except for the fist fights," I point out. He shrugs.

Now Nikos comes *running* back into the house. If there's not a bear on his tail, his energy level has quadrupled in three days.

"I have an idea," he says. "The Ancient Trappers could have been *worshipers* of Mondo the Man-God."

"Which would explain why we came up here in the first place," I say.

"And why the organizations are merging," Nora says, almost jumping up and down. "We've got a plan."

At that moment, there's a knock at the door. Art leans into the window and peers at the front of the cabin.

"It's got a Mountie uniform on," he says.

Twenty

Nora goes to the door. When dealing with the police, it doesn't hurt to be a pretty girl. This is corroborated by the fact that, when we left the motel this morning and I asked her how bad the interrogation was at the police station, she said, "*What* interrogation?"

"Yes, officer?" she says.

"Sorry to disturb you, ma'am, but we have a report of a moose being killed here. Since we haven't issued any non-resident tags to this camp this year, I have to check that the person who killed the moose does have a valid Ontario hunting license."

This is the guy I've always thought of as Canadian justice. Tall, thin, slightly lantern-jawed, respectful and courteous, probably never cracked a smile in his life. Oh, that's right—I'm thinking of Dudley Do-Right. It must be the uniform. Actually, you've got to be a pretty decent-looking guy to look manly in that shade of red...

"Were any of you present when the moose was killed?" he continues.

And here we learn Lesson Number One in the difference between professional criminals and the general population. Each of us in the room wants to protect Nikos from the Mountie—we're all dredging the recesses of our minds for some excuse to send him packing. However, since Nikos is the center of our concerns, we have all instinctively turned toward him, to make sure he's not sweating badly or fainting dead away from the tension.

The officer might wear a silly uniform but he's not stupid. He looks from Nora to me to Art—bingo! Triangulation! The center point of all eyes in the room is: Nikos! This honesty thing better pay off in the afterlife, because so far it's not doing a thing for anyone here on Earth.

Nikos, however, steps forward cool as a cucumber. "I was there," he says. Art gasps as though it's Bruce Wayne announcing he's Batman. We all turn on Art, he blushes and the officer turns back to Nikos.

"Did the person who killed the moose hold a valid Ontario license?" the Mountie asks. "There is a substantial fine for hunting moose without one." Surely if Nikos says the guy has a license, the officer will ask for it. Nikos, however, seems entirely unconcerned.

"Well, I'm not sure who actually killed him," he says. "It could be the guy who threw the rock at him or the guy who slit his throat with the pocket knife."

"Rock?" the officer gulps. "Pocket knife?"

"And in truth, you can't really call what we did *hunting*," Nikos continues. "We weren't looking for him; *he* attacked *us*."

The officer has that fragmented look I get when I have to put money in the meter. "Where is the body?" the cop says. "I'll need to examine the evidence."

"I don't know how you're going to do that," Nikos says. "We ate him."

This seems to really throw the Cop, though why this seems strange after hearing they bagged the thing with a rock and a pocketknife is beyond me.

Nikos has now turned to Nora. "The whole thing was very primal, actually. I don't know if you realize what a strong emotional basis this maleness worship has. I was very surprised how affected I was by the ritual they learned here."

"Ritual?" says the Mountie, getting that authority-figure look around the eyes and mouth. "Maleness worship?"

"Well, it's just the way they cut him up," Nikos continues, oblivious to the gathering storm cloud. "You'd think it would be really hard to dismember a moose with a pocketknife, but they did a really expert job. And the dancing as they threw the body parts in the flames was very poetic." He looks at me. "You said it was kosher, right?"

"Not without the rabbi," I answer without thinking. "It ain't kosher unless the rabbi gets paid."

"When was all this?" The Mountie asks.

"Right after we killed him. We kind of had a celebration," Nikos says.

"Whatever is left," I tell the officer, "you'll find on the ridge up there. If you keep coming back over the next couple days, there should be a growing pile of evidence." Do-Right looks out the window and I guess the ridge is visible because he begins to look sick. The idea of spending a week kneedeep in shit looking for clues doesn't seem to agree with him.

"This is all just a business venture," Nora assures him. "Everyone here is either working for or going through a Mondo the Man-God Maleness Breakthrough Week—we're a registered Ontario corporation out of Waterline. No religious affiliation whatever."

"Mondo the Man-God?" says the Mountie and stands several inches taller immediately. "My brother did that two years ago. Doubled his income in six months."

"Really?" says Nora, suddenly looking very seductive at the Mountie. Hey, that's *my* look dammit! "What does your brother do?"

"Chief entymologist for the Province of New Brunswick," Do-Right barks the answer, almost coming to attention. "He's the gypsy moth man."

"Oh, how interesting," Nora says. "What does he do with gypsy moths?"

"Kills 'em," the Mountie answers with real conviction, as though there was some nuance to this. His voice drops to almost a whisper. "My brother says no one cares a darnn about gypsy moths until they want 'em killed. But when the time comes, BAM!!—he's The Man."

"Well," says Art, carefully picking every word, "we at the Mondo Weeks are really proud to have put him in touch with the moth killer inside." This is actually pretty funny—the first trace of humor I've ever seen in this guy. Didn't think he had it in him.

The Mountie seems to appreciate this. "Yes," he says, looking us all over, "you are all doing good work here. I'm sure there's a way I can slide this through the paper chain."

He looks at Nikos, who exhibits the beatific smile he practiced all the way up here and never got to use on Nora. "That was obviously," Nikos tells him in his most sincere voice, "a rogue moose."

"A rogue moose *up to no good*," the Mountie adds, writing it down simultaneously on a pad he pulls from his jacket. "Obviously you did a service to the citizens of Ontario," he tells Nikos, "ridding us of this threat to people and property."

"Thank you," Nikos stammers, struggling to hold back tears and his wheezing laugh. "I've always thought of that *as my mission*," he sputters, and then he can't control it anymore and a sound like an air conditioner exhaust issues from him. He doubles over holding his stomach. I rush over to him immediately and start pushing him toward the door.

"What's wrong with him?" asks the Mountie.

"Asthma," I say, pounding Nikos on the back and pushing him outside. "Breath, man, breath!!"

Nora follows us to the door, leading the Mountie. "Is that the right therapy for asthma? Shouldn't he have an inhaler?" he asks.

"New holistic approach," Nora says. "We're very big on holistic health."

"Wow," says the Mountie, "my brother's got asthma. I'll tell him about this."

He walks off toward the parking lot. Nikos finally stops holding it in and starts howling like an animal, the laughter pouring out of him. I find myself holding him so he doesn't simply fall over and hurt himself.

"Rogue moose *up to no good*," Nikos yowls. "This is the funniest man since John Erlichman."

"Well," says Nora, "at least we got rid of him."

"What do you mean?" I say. "In six months, his brother will be dead from untreated asthma and we'll all be wanted for murder."

Twenty-One

A minute later, the Mountie is back, standing across the lake by the parking lot. "Who owns the Honda Civic in the lot?"

"That would be me." I raise my hand—I'm already convicted, why fight it?

"Aren't you supposed to be gone by now?" he yells.

"Any minute," I tell him. "His stomach was upset by moose, so we're having trouble getting started."

"I would get started soon," the Mountie says. "I understand the deal was 24 hours."

"Oh," I say. "Nobody told me that."

"Consider yourself told," he says. Then he marches off to find his horse, Horse.

"We should get going, whenever your stomach feels better," I tell Nikos.

"Going?" Nikos says. "I have a nature walk with the guys at 2."

"Look, my pal the US Ambassador to Canada negotiated a deal for me personally," I tell him. He gives me an odd look, which I ignore. "We have to be back in the US by tonight, and I think with your stomach in that kind of shape, it's going to take us a while to reach the border." Not to mention stopping for water to take pills with and to walk around a parking lot and get the blood flowing in his legs and breaks to talk to the waitress with the beautiful tits—in other words, the usual Nikos distractions. Not that I don't love them—I just love them less with prison hanging over my head.

"Well, wait a minute," Art says. "You can't leave yet—we have a business deal to conclude."

"Excuse me?" I say.

"Well, we all agreed Mr. Papandreou is to address the troops and tell them about the merger between the Mondo the Man-God Breakthrough Weeks and the Order of Ancient Trappers of Canada. He has to make them understand that one mission leads to the other. He has to rebuild the loyalty he took from us this week."

This guy annoys me. He walks around in a penis mask on odd weekends but underneath, there's no abandon, not even much of a sense of humor. He's a tense piece of meat and now he's insisting on everyone else joining him in the locker.

"Excuse me Babbit," I answer, "he didn't cost you anything you hadn't already lost. If Mondo was so wonderful, they wouldn't have listened to anything he had to say. You just didn't convince them anymore."

"You're excused," he returns—again, that's more humor than I expected. *Anything* would be.

"Boys, boys—" I hear Nora's voice approaching.

"No, hold on here a moment," Art says, holding up a hand to stop her talking. He's not going to be silenced. In fact, there's something a bit commanding about the way he does this. If I was her, I might be offended, but at the same time I'm surprised by the power in the gesture. Maybe he has hidden depth? It's either hidden or nonexistent but I just saw a flash of something.

"We are a business with a legal right to protect our assets. If necessary, we could be in court tomorrow morning enjoining the state from removing these two from Ontario until our business is protected. And enjoining you two from leaving until you restore the good will you took."

"You're a *lawyer*," I whoop. I don't know why I'm so pleased by this—when is it ever good to meet another lawyer?—except it fills in some of the gaps in my understanding, which always pleases me. "No wonder you're such a stiff. Are you actually threatening us—and the State of Ontario—with *lawsuits*?"

"Loss of business is legitimate grounds for legal proceedings," he says in that calm tone of voice they must teach in law schools—Menacing Behavior 101. Sorry, not buying any fish today.

"You go right ahead," I tell him. This poor guy absolutely raises the middle-manager-strikes-back impulse in me with almost every word he says. "I will absolutely refuse to settle this –I'm going to *court*. I can't wait for this!! You spend how many years building up Mondo the Man-God and doubling the income of lepidopterists everywhere—"

"Entymologists," he corrects.

"Whatever. And then my 77-year-old business partner here, suffering from congestive heart failure and prostate cancer—you just ask him a tough question in court and watch him clutch his chest and wheeze; see what *that* does for your sympathy in the courtroom—anyway, he makes up a couple of stories off the top of his head in 36 hours for fun and steals away your whole group. I'll demand to see the entire legend of Mondo the Man-God in court— I'll read it out loud for the jury and then we'll read Nikos' stuff and see who the jury thinks the money should go to."

"Okay, let's break it up, boys," says Nora's calm, sensible voice. I feel her hands grip me from behind, rubbing my shoulder muscles, attempting to sooth me. There are other types of soothing that would work better, but this will do for the moment. Why did she wait so long? Does she really listen to Art?

"We're not interested in lawsuits," she says, pointedly I feel, to Art. "We want Mr. Papandreou's—"

"Nikos, please," Nikos says. Smiling, pleasant, always-wanting-to-please Nikos. Threaten him with a lawsuit and he still asks you to call him by his first name.

"Pardon me, Nikos," Nora says, flashing that dazzling smile of hers. "We want Nikos' cooperation here. We want to merge the Ancient Trappers with Mondo before there's any real damage done. We want him to address the boys before we break up, and we want his book of lore to support our work as we move forward and create a new family movement with men, women and maybe even children involved in our Breakthrough Weeks. Doesn't that make sense?" she says, looking at Art again. He shuffles a little, not happy but not really possessing much of an argument. Although I have to admit he does have a legal argument. Maybe he just knows the tone of voice that says Nora has taken control. Or maybe there's more here than meets the eye.

"Well, but just a minute," Nikos says, his soft voice exposing just how biting Nora's tone was, one second earlier. "Now we're dealing with publishing rights. I have an agent for that."

"You're telling us you have an agent for publishing stories of the Ancient Trappers of Canada?" Art explodes.

"It's fiction," Nikos says. "I am a fiction writer. I have a contract with an agent that says he handles all sales of my fiction, unless he opts out of a transaction at his sole discretion." Now we've hit the core—fair play, the thing that matters even more to Nikos than being polite and a nice guy.

"Surely you of all people must understand the importance of bowing to all that legalese bullshit, Art," I say. Just my luck he ends up my brother-in-law, but right now, I don't care.

"Can't we negotiate something today that would make you feel comfortable?" Nora asks Nikos. "We will agree to negotiate in good faith with your agent for publishing rights to your book on the Ancient Trappers with an advance...not in excess...of what you were paid on average for your last two books." She's figuring this out, phrase by phrase, as she goes along. You'd think *she* was the lawyer. Every time I turn around, I find another impressive side to her. Is there *anything* she can't do?

"Well, it's been a while since my last contract," says Nikos. Honest to a fault.

"Okay—not in excess of the price of your last two books, taking inflation into account since their publication," Nora says.

"And exchange rates, of course," I add.

"Of course," she says, digging her knuckles into my back at the same time.

"Pardon me but I don't see where you become involved in any of this," Art says, staring at me so hard he's sure to go cross-eyed any second. Is there any end to his belligerence? Is there any *reason* to it—doesn't Nora giving me a backrub signal that he should leave me alone? "What are your assets here?"

"He's my Muse, for the moment," Nikos says, "and my partner for these stories. If he hadn't been willing to drive me up here, I never would have thought of the Ancient Trappers. If he wasn't so obsessed with *you*," he says, looking at Nora, "that he completely ignored how dangerous this was for me, I wouldn't have gotten my energy back and come up with these stories."

"Don't help me so much," I say. I can feel Nora tittering behind me.

"And if *you* hadn't pissed him off so much," he turns to Art now, "he never would have thought of the Ancient Trappers as competition for Mondo. At that moment, he took my stories and turned them into a business, a business that now has assets—the affection of your customers. So actually, we owe that all to *you*. I should make you a partner too."

"Thanks," says Art glumly.

"But I don't like you, so I'm not gonna," Nikos finishes. Pa-Ching! He smiles his little ol' professor smile and turns to Nora. They beam at each other for a moment, and he turns to me.

"God, she is beautiful," he says. "And smart. Nice tits?"

"Let's talk about that later," I say, as Nora starts hacking.

"No," she demands, smacking me in the back again. "You *stick up* for my girls—I'm proud of them."

"You should be," I insist. "They're *spectacular*."

"I thought so," says Nikos, nodding, staring at her like a schoolchild eyeing cupcakes in a bakery window.

"So," she says, taking a long breath and bending over to force eye contact with Nikos, "can we come to a working agreement? We'll work out the price for the book later, and I'll further compensate you to come up here once or twice a year to give a talk and a nature walk to the highest-ranking members of the Order of Ancient Trappers. And we'll agree on an advance, to be no more than 50% of the cost of the original book, for any further installments to the Lore of the Ancient Trappers. Those books would only be 50 pages or so, so you could do them in your sleep."

"And if I want to do other stories on the Ancient Trappers?" Nikos asks. "They're my characters, right?"

"Well, wait a minute," Art says. "They would be our brands, trademarks of the corporation."

"Forget that," I say immediately. It is Nora's company and I did come up here to find the spark with her, but if it's a choice between her—or anyone else—and the Muse, Muse wins, period, hands down, no contest.

"That's not necessarily a problem," Nora says. "As long as we get the chance to read the stories first and they don't conflict with our image, I don't think it's a problem."

Art doesn't look happy with this approach. But then, neither does Nikos.

"I don't know if I can do that," Nikos says. "The stories are just coming to me. I don't control them. How do I know if they're going to conflict with your image?"

"Well, what are you going to do? They're not going to be raping and pillaging, I assume?" Nora says.

"Sally Hemmings," I say to Nikos.

"Right," he says. "What if Damian the Hairless decided to have an affair with a Native Woman? What if there was discrimination among some of the Trappers? I can't explore that, because they have to be faultless characters now?"

"We're building a multi-million-dollar business here that you're disrupting" Art fumes. "You think your stupid stories would be worth anything on the market if not for us?"

"At the moment, you're worth nothing without him," I remind Art. "'When you've got them by the balls, their hearts and minds will follow.'"

"John Erlichman," Nikos adds the citation.

"Greatest humorist since Twain," I add, looking hard at Art. We've got *cards* on the table buddy—go fuck yourself.

Nora walks to the window for a moment, staring out. Somehow, there is an authority to her manner that stills all of us.

"Okay," she says finally. "This is not going to get resolved immediately."

"What?" sputters Art. "It *has* to."

"No," Nora tells him. "It has to be resolved before Sunday morning, so Nikos can come address the troops before they leave. That gives us a day or two to come to agreement. However, every police officer in this area is watching out for *you*," she says, staring at me with some amusement.

"And I go where he goes," says Nikos.

"Yes, I got that," Nora says. "So I suggest you two leave here now—and travel as far as Waterline. I figure once you get that far south, they're probably not going to be actively looking for you. Here's the key to my house," she says, handing it to me. "You can use alarm code 2255. Let yourself in and stay out of sight. The guest bedrooms are to the left as you come in. I'll be there in the morning and we can figure out whatever we need to figure out in time for Nikos to come back up and help us smooth the transition—okay?"

"Sounds like a sensible plan," I say. Nikos nods.

We leave Art fuming like Vesuvius between eruptions, and head for the car. As I unlock the door, I say to Nikos, "You certainly know how to perk up my sex life."

Twenty~Two

The ride South is relatively uneventful. No Mountie hats and we do the last hour in one chunk. This makes a big improvement over the first half of the trip, which is filled with Nikos' bathroom breaks—and this naturally is the wilderness half, with far fewer actual bathrooms. Luckily, he's become hugely familiar with bushes, thanks to me.

The thing that's astonishing, now that I see him in a slightly more normal context, is his rejuvenation. In the past two days he's lost about twenty years of age. He moves at a normal pace, his joints seem fluid, he's more alert and even in better spirits. I certainly can't take credit for any of it—if I'd thought about what I was doing unselfishly, I'd have turned around and gone home when I saw the ferry. Nonetheless, he seems a new man.

By nightfall, we are on the outskirts of Waterline. We stop at a market to pick up some food, just enough to hold us over while we hide out at Nora's. The money I allocated for this trip is close to gone. They have ATM's up here, of course, but removing money is always a bit scary when you've no prospects of adding any back in the near future.

We find Nora's house easily this time and the alarm code works fine. Then we contend with the dog alarms. Two big black-and-white spotted dogs—setters? I don't know dog brands. Big howling for twenty seconds, then lots of licking and slobbering. Very affectionate, but I think they'd get voted out of the watchdog union. I expect to see Nikos clutching his chest, but he seems to know they're all bark from the outset.

I pull the car inside the garage, out of sight. Then I take the dogs for a walk along the river, staying within the trees so as not to be visible from the other side. I'm not exactly sure how paranoid to be, but 'as much as possible' seems a sensible choice for the moment.

Then we luxuriate. Heat. Running water. Sitting on a toilet in a warm room with no subsequent leaf removal process. I wonder what Osama's life is like, sitting in his cave—I turned the TV on, of course, so there's no escaping him. Anyone who doesn't think civilization has taken us in a useful direction hasn't tried to go in the bushes lately. I'll bet they don't even have those wonderful big fleshy Canadian leaves in the Afghan mountains. Of course, if he's really smart, Osama is probably sitting on a beach in Rio. He can shave his beard, sit around in Bermuda shorts, drink pina coladas and call Al Jazeera on his cellphone: "This is Osama. Kill the Infidels. Okay—did my job for the month."

This idyll lasts half an hour before Nikos drifts off to his bedroom to sleep. I'm not ready—I have this foolish desire to catch up on the world. I also don't want to go to bed too early—if I do, I'll be wide-awake at 3am.

This concern lasts only a few minutes. I start watching the news, which is overflowing with anthrax information—how to avoid it, what to do if you get it in the mail, how to recognize mail with it, how to get the right drugs to fight it and fifteen differing opinions on whether this has anything to do with Osama, who has to be enjoying the hubbub regardless. By the time I decide to watch only musical comedies for the rest of the night, it's too late—I'll be lucky if I can get to sleep at all. I start longing for my cabin in the woods.

Around 10, the doorbell rings. I peek out a window near the door. I can't make out the person on the other side, but I can see the car in the driveway, a white Mercedes coupe, one of the $110,000 ones with the air suspension and V-12. I read my Car and Driver religiously, so I can keep up with all the really neat cars I can't afford.

This concerns me for just a second. The truth is, I've never known a single even slightly threatening human being who drove a top-of-the-line Mercedes. So I open the front door.

My first reaction is, it's got to be the Mountie's older brother. Silver-gray hair—and a very nice haircut, too; one of those haircuts that comes with a manicure—but the same lantern jaw and big

white teeth. Very expensive Northern Face Parka with fur collar —
does PETA operate in Canada? I already don't like this guy, just
for conspicuous consumption—Abercrombie and Fitch corduroy
shirt and khakis, LL Bean boots, I'll bet. Only buys the most
expensive item of its kind, and pays retail. A Martian with teeth.
He's obviously not expecting to see *me*. For me, he wouldn't need
to bring roses—white roses, the wrong color if you're trying to get
into her pants, and even moreso if you already have, buddy.

"Can I help you?" I ask.

"Oh," he says, going blank all of a sudden. "I was looking for
Nora?" I resist the temptation to tell him she's repaired to the
cloister.

"She's out of town," I say. "Might be in and out, but won't
really be back till Sunday night."

"Oh," he says again, with that same dull look. God, do they
sell 'glazed vacancy' pills up here? I know a whole bunch of
people in New York who could really benefit from a little of that.
"Another of her business trips, I suppose."

"I suppose," I say. Has she kept Mondo the Man-God from
her boyfriends? Maybe they'd find him intimidating. Maybe
they'd find him ridiculous, though it's hard to believe, based on
the presentation this one's making, that he has any sense of the
ridiculous. He looks like the kind of guy for whom everything just
goes right all the time. More reason to hate him.

"Uh—I'm Derek," he says, holding out his hand. *Derek*? There are real people on this planet, other than Yankee shortstops, named *Derek*? And Jeter's at least Latino so it's okay. Calling a WASPy son Derek is sort of like naming your dog Rex or your horse Champion—it's proof that you're just way too comfortable on this planet.

What's worse is, I recognize his game. He tells me his name and gets me to tell him mine, and pretty soon the cops are at the door and not checking on our contribution to the Benevolent Fund.

"I'm her cousin Bucky from Aspen," I say, shaking his hand. Good firm grip but soft hands. This guy's never touched anything rougher than a leather-wrapped steering wheel, or his stock portfolio. I have at least handled heavy-duty video equipment in my time.

"Bucky, eh? She's never mentioned you," he says with barely-suppressed suspicion. At least his Valium hasn't knocked him out completely. I probably don't look much like a Bucky—he knows plenty of them, I'll bet.

"Black sheep of the family," I explain. "Ski all day, party all night. Keeps the administrators of my trust fund busy, you know how that is."

He smiles, that uncomfortable smile native to people who've always had so much money they find it distasteful even to mention it. God, it's amazing how much enmity I can stir up in myself over money, whenever I don't have any.

"Well, the flowers are very nice—thanks," I say, reaching for the bouquet in his arms. He looks almost ready to resist. "Unless you have someone else to give them to," I add.

He stiffens. "Well, of course not," he says and hands them over. Yes, loyal and faithful like a good St. Bernard. I wonder if he has a flask. He's got to have some virtue other than the Mercedes. Can't she get her own Mercedes, from the profits of Mondo the Man-God? What does she need *this* guy for, that I can't give her five times more, and in more interesting positions? "You just make sure she knows it's from me, will you?"

"Of course," I say. "Biff, right?"

"Derek."

"Sorry—Derek. I'll make sure she knows," I tell him and he heads back to the Mercedes, trying to decide if I'm making fun of him.

Ten minutes later, the next-door neighbor, Warren, shows up, checking on the car he saw pull into the garage. Nice guy—very soft-spoken and concerned, good manners, Bass boat shoes, khakis and Pendleton flannel shirt. Very outdoorsy, salt-and-pepper hair. None of these guys ever overeats or raises his voice. I hate them all. And they're both very concerned for Nora's welfare and that she's okay. They obviously haven't seen her in a business negotiation—she could eat them both for lunch and not in a way they'd enjoy.

In the course of the next hour-and-a-half, I hear three phone messages—men, all sounding about the right age, just 'checking in', 'seeing how you're doing', wondering 'when we can get together again.' God, the woman's the Queen Bee, and I'm staying overnight in the Hive Palace.

All of a sudden, I'm back in the Real World—there's *competition* out here and plenty of it. They all speak in rounded tones, including the Canadian 'aboot', and all of them have plans—'take in a show in Toronto' or 'going to visit the boat in Naples' (Florida? *Italy*?)—that say their mutual funds didn't suffer too much when the dotcoms went under. Unlike my bank balance. Why am I thinking about my bank balance? Forget Bin Laden—*that's* depressing.

I'm thinking about it because I feel out of my league all of a sudden, and it bothers me. The feelings her first email aroused in me shouldn't be threatened by a bank balance or a trust fund.

Says *who*? My bohemian soul? I laugh at my own adolescent dreaming. I have already seen Nora the businesswoman. Maybe I'm the only one surprised by her acumen. Maybe guys like Derek and Warren just know it instantly. Maybe that's the world they live in.

On the other hand, considering she had enough money from the family trusts to be comfortable in the first place, could Nora really be in business just to make money? There must be some pride involved, some need to show herself she can do it. It's the girl who always felt too young in school, the woman Nick underestimated, who needs to prove her ability to herself. Maybe she's capable of responding to some of the more intangible things I cherish. And embody. I hope to hell I embody *something*—at the moment, I'm not sure what it would be.

More precisely, how could she possibly be interested in me and the Wonder Bread boys here? Is that all they make up here? What about Robbie Robertson and Neil Young and Burton Cummings—the Canadian greats? They all moved to Los Angeles is the answer. Not to mention the long list of Canadian writers—name one other than Margaret Atwood. Saul Bellow doesn't count—you could live your whole life in New York or LA and be Canadian, but if you live in Chicago more than a year, you're an American. Hmmmm…I'm a real contender for the Condescension championship at the moment, but I can't help it. My mood is sinking fast.

In the course of traversing the house, I discover that Nora has three floor-to-ceiling closets filled with matching sheets, pillowcases, comforters, bath towels and furry bathmats to match the towels. Leaning against a cabinet in just the right place, I discover her videotapes—several hundred—alphabetized by title. The TV episodes are further categorized by date—in order—on this massive hideaway-rotating shelf, like something from a haunted house in an old Abbott and Costello movie. The middle shelf also holds the latest computer printout of the Nora Hill video catalogue. Alphabetized and dated, of course. Separate lists for Titles and Actors.

I'm not sure which of these items disturbs me more. Osama Bin Laden might want me dead, but so far he hasn't got me. Nora's got me but I'm not sure why she wants me, and I'm beginning to wonder whether I fit her. Without allocating percentages, I have more than enough reasons to feel unsettled. Salvation, or at least insulation, appears in the form of half a bottle of expensive 12-year-old Scotch on the kitchen counter. Hey, it was there, asking to be drunk. And I am, thanks very much.

Around 2 am, in the darkened living room watching the middle of "Sullivan's Travels," I hear a noise, a rustling around the side of the house. One of the dogs perks up his ears and starts sniffing. I head for the back windows and peer into the nightscape. It sure looks like someone is moving through the bushes along the fence—the bushes across the way are wagging back and forth as well.

Burglar? SWAT team? Do they know I'm here? Have they been waiting for my 24 hours to expire so they can pack me off to some penitentiary in the Maritimes?

I've had half a bottle of Scotch. I sway behind the drapes, mulling the possibilities: it would almost certainly have to be a minimum-security facility; I can't imagine them convincing anyone I'm a real threat to society. If it's built for guys like Derek and Warren, snagged for stock fraud or insider trading, it can't be too bad. Probably cable TV and conjugal visits. If they let me keep the laptop, I could probably get a bunch of writing done. It's not like my other offers are that inviting. Maybe I've been hasty hiding out like this.

A moment later, I hear a scraping at the sliding doors in the kitchen. SWAT teams usually burst in, yelling incomprehensible legalities—I watch TV, I know this for a fact. Which would make this, by process of elimination, a burglar. I heft the Scotch bottle—it's heavy; feels like it would hurt a *lot*—and stand near the curtains, waiting.

Twenty-Three

The wind whips open the curtains all at once and a figure steps lightly into the room, confounding my expectations. I don't expect my burglars in Capri pants and cream turtleneck sweaters in the dead of night. They have glamorous cat burglars in movies but I doubt they moonlight in Waterline Ontario.

It takes another moment for my drowsy boozy eyes to catch up to my memories of twenty-five years ago.

"Hi Kate," I say, and she pulls up gasping. I turn on a light and realize I'm still holding the bottle of Scotch, holding it over my head. I pull my arm down, turning the bottle into an offering. "Can I get you a drink?"

She looks at me for a moment and then the eyes widen—those lovely eyes of hers.

"Ted," she says, like a breath. Now it's my turn to gasp a little. How on earth did she recognize me? "Nora told me she got an email from you," she continues, as though reading my thoughts. She's regarding me with an open hunger I find absolutely delightful in a woman. "You look *good*," she says. My first thought is I'm not all that good-looking, but judging from her expression, I might be wrong.

"You look terrific," I say and it's not an empty compliment. God, if karma exists, this family has never done anything wrong in history. Or at least nothing that shows.

When I first met Kate, she was simply Nora's younger sister. Two years younger, which made her 15?—13? I've got to straighten that out. One way or another, enough years younger that I didn't pay attention. Now, those years have caught up with a vengeance.

She's stunning. Not as stunning as Nora by conventional standards, but maybe even more by mine. Auburn hair that shines red even in the dim light of the kitchen and those mischievous bright eyes, the same eyes in my photo, the Hill family at dinner on the cruise ship twenty-five years ago. Just like her sister, the body's filled out very nicely, though she's slimmer, more the dancer profile.

"I came to walk the dogs," she says.

"At 2 am?"

"*They* don't care," she replies, bantering. "I'm a creature of the night," she hisses, an evil smile on the family lips. God I love those lips.

Oh, this can't be happening. I'm getting really hot—for *Kate*. Kate, the sister of the girl I came up here to court—and the married sister, no less. I don't have lots of scruples where sex is concerned, but I had such a lousy marriage without anybody cheating (that I know of) that I've never wanted to get in the middle of someone else's (lousy — ?) marriage.

"Is Nora here?" she asks.

"I've got her locked up in the back room."

"Is she enjoying it?" she snaps, her eyes doing a beckoning dance, I swear.

She's coming on to me so openly I have a hard time believing I'm reading her right. If I knew Nora was serious about me — if only she hadn't made that remark about coming to New York in the *spring*!! — I'd have to lock Kate out of the house right now. The pheromones alone would drive me insane. She's so delicious I can't remember if I have any scruples, or if I do, what they were. And the fact that she'd be cheating on Art really eases my conscience way too much.

Then I play back what she's just said about Nora. I snap to for just a second, fighting the influence of the Scotch, the hour and the fact that I've slept very little since the SWAT team burst through my door or in the last 4 or 8 or 12 weeks or whatever.

"Would Nora *enjoy* that?" I ask. Might as well get some pointers, in case I really have to beat off the competition.

"Nora? Are you kidding?" Kate says. "Nora's idea of danger is playing tennis without a designer outfit."

She's standing very close to me now. We are both breathing in these little sharp panting motions. If the look in your eyes could be considered action, we'd be in jail right now without hope of parole. How can this happen so fast? Who cares?

"What's *your* idea of danger?" I hear myself saying, and the next second I'm ripping the turtleneck off her while she somehow pulls my pants down around my knees. They're not totally unzipped, which leaves me totally incapacitated. All she has to do is push a little and I go over like an oak onto the carpet. And then she jumps me, I swear. The woman has the most delicious mouth I've ever tasted, with any part of my body. And the rest of her tastes even better.

Actually, as I write this, having come to the next morning, a bit more is coming back to me. I remember her pausing for just a moment in the middle of a pitched battle to clear everything off the glass coffee table—"It's Nora's house," she cautioned, "we'll have to put everything back in exactly the same places"—before we commence humping there as well.

Our clothes are all over the room, there are jars of Vaseline and peanut butter scattered in the corner, the cradle and wood from the fireplace are scattered all over the floor by the sliding doors and I'm covered in soot from head to toe. How did I not notice that right away? My head feels like it's splitting open.

Kate comes out of the living room carrying a stapler, stark naked. She sits on the couch holding the twenty-five pieces of her

Capri pants and a stapler. The remains of her sweater lie on the couch next to her, tied together with packing twine.

"What are you doing?" I rasp.

"Stapling my pants together so I can get home," she says.

"Why don't you just take a pair of Nora's?" I ask.

"Because she'll know they're out of order when she gets back."

"Seriously?"

She nods. "I don't know how—I think she has those little store magnetic things in them, like tracking devices?"

"I see," I say, though the chances of my seeing anything at the moment are very slim. No, I take that back. I see Kate Hill sitting naked on the couch. She looks *good*. I'm getting excited again. Thankfully, I suspect she'll never be able to tell through the soot.

I used to scoff at Darwin—the idea that peas would choose to mate with the hardiest future husbands was just too much for me. I might be willing to accept that level of intelligence in broccoli, but not peas and certainly not celery. Anyway, I scoff at Darwin no more. If I can be gripped with this kind of insane lust despite the most skull-splitting hangover in history, there's nothing more powerful than coming.

I try to stand up—a very bad idea. Nonetheless, I eye the delicious elfin girl on the couch, and she looks back at me, as though picking up my thought, as though reading my mind. Whoa, do we really have this level of communication? What would *that* be like during sex? Maybe if I could remember more about last night, I'd know the answer...Anyway, Kate looks up and the love light is shining in her eyes. Oh man...Marvin Gaye time.

"When's Nora coming back?" she asks softly.

"This morning," I say, and realize what I'm saying. "But," I stammer, looking around desperately for a clock, "it's only 6. Whatever time she leaves Frozen Lake, it's three hours to get here."

"She's not an early riser," Kate says, getting off the couch and standing, displaying her magnificent self for me. I'm still not dealing with reality here, obviously. I'm devolving back to that first stage of sexual development, the part where you look at Playboy and develop fantasies that in real life would put you in traction. That stage went on for years in my case, but that's when it started.

One of the traditional fantasies—if you know your Hefner—is *sisters*. Now Hef, if I remember correctly, was really more into twins—but I remember even at that age thinking it would probably keep the girls a lot happier if you could tell them apart most of the time. So I am now operating in this fantasy realm, thinking about the incredible opportunity here, ignoring the appalling massacre that is certain to result at a later date. And apparently so is Kate. About five minutes after she comes off the couch and we start touching again, I realize two hours might be cutting it close.

It's only later, after we've turned the furniture in the room right-side-up again and I'm vacuuming the soot, that I realize what a crazy thing I've done. We're still both stark naked when Nikos wanders into the kitchen and puts a tea kettle on the burner. He looks over at Kate and smiles.

"Hello," he says pleasantly to her. "You have *very* nice tits."

"*Thank* you," she says. "Ted seems fixated on them, not that I mind."

"The psychologists have lots to say on the subject," Nikos says, "but I think they take the fun out of it. I'm Nikos."

"Nice to meet you—I'm Kate," Kate says, helping me push a floor-to-ceiling bookcase about ten feet back to its original location. "I'm going to freshen up a little," she says and skips off to the bathroom.

"Nice girl," Nikos says. "I haven't met her before, have I?"

"No," I say.

"She's not the one I met the other day—she was a blonde, right?"

"Right."

"That was the one we came up here for—the one you've been lusting after for twenty-five years, right?"

"Right," I nod.

"Okay," he says and mulls for just a moment. "How many innocent questions do I have to ask before you tell me?"

"Her younger sister."

He greets this information as though translating from a foreign language. "This is always trouble," he says, suggesting he's seen this at least several(!) times. "But," he brightens, "it's *definitely* a book." His eyes are twinkling.

Kate comes back into the room.

"I had panties, didn't I?" she says.

"I might have swallowed them."

"They weren't the edible kind," she says. "I didn't know you were here when I came over." She flashes me that evil smile of hers. How two sisters—with the same dazzling lips—could have smiles that different is a wonder of nature. "Did I have a bra?"

"Absolutely not," I say. "I remember that distinctly."

"You don't need one," Nikos says.

"Your friend is very nice," she tells me. "Knows how to compliment a girl."

"Sure, *now* I know everything," Nikos complains.

"Alright, no underwear—let's see if I can get these on without staple marks," she says, contemplating the pants.

That's when we hear the scraping of key in front door lock.

"Oh!" Kate yelps and jumps naked through the sliding doors, grabbing her clothes and heading for the bushes out back.

"I'm going to the bathroom," I yell to Nikos, trying not to leave soot everywhere as I rush down the hall. "Now would be a *really* good time for the charming English professor shtick."

Twenty-Four

I rush to the bathroom and start the water running in the shower. Through the door, I can hear Nora's voice.

"Hello Nikos."

"Hi—how was the trip?" he asks, pleasant as a monk tipsy on mead.

"The trip? Oh—from the lake? I don't even consider it a trip anymore," Nora says. "I've gotten so used to it. Where's Ted?"

"He's in the shower."

"Oh. How come the furniture's been moved?" Uh-oh.

"That's Ted," Nikos says. "Does it everywhere he goes. Did it with *my* furniture too." Thanks a lot, pal. You couldn't say *you've* got a fetish?—although I guess no one would believe this old man has the strength to move around much furniture.

"Didn't move it very *far*," Nora continues, apparently stalking the room, getting a better look.

"No, that's what satisfies him, just these little shifts."

"That doesn't sound like Ted," Nora says. That's it—stick up for me, girl! "But I guess we really don't know each other, do we?"

"Well, he seems to have some ideal relationship of space and geometry in his head, and when he comes into a new environment, he has to make it conform," Nikos continues, burying me deeper. "You know, being with a creative person isn't easy—they have unusual quirks," he says, and now I begin to detect a little method behind his madness. "You never know what they'll do, or the reasons—that might seem perfectly reasonable to them—behind the things they do."

Such as sleeping with your sister, he means. He's trying to build me a cover, though I'm not sure anything short of a bunker will do.

"Can you give me an example?" Nora asks. Oh man, Nikos, just back off. Leave it for when I *really* need it. Maybe I can still worm my way out of this without it being an issue.

"Well," Nikos says, hesitating, and now I feel myself holding my breath, "...after he came to my house and moved everything around in the living room, my wife was upset—"

"Of *course* she was," Nora says and I gulp at the tone of her voice.

"—Yes—well, but then we had a feng shui person in the next week and she said that one room—the one he moved around— was in perfect harmony. So maybe instinctively he's got that thing in his head. I've seen him do that, you know—he takes a book home, and when I ask him, he says he hasn't read it but the lesson *behind* the book is in his head. So maybe he just absorbed feng shui from somewhere." Trust Nikos. When any sane answer would have gotten me deeper into trouble, he comes up with something that makes so little sense as to be inarguable. That should at least divert Nora's attention, right?

"Well, he should at least have asked me before doing it," she says, and I know I'm safe for the moment. Man, Kate was right — Kate! This morning continues to come back to me, despite my every effort to bury it.

"Do you know how to make a Greek omelet?" Nikos asks. "Let me show you." He starts to jabber about omelets and I duck into the shower.

Whoever invented the shower should have gotten the Nobel Peace Prize. I managed a couple of hours sleep last night, in the midst of cavorting with Kate, and almost none the night before, dancing with the police and Nora. The fact that ten minutes under a running spigot can make me feel almost human under these circumstances, while also washing away most of the evidence, should be recognized, I think, by the Nobel Committee. Does anyone campaign for a Nobel, like they do for the Oscars? Is there some magazine you put ads in: 'For Your Consideration: Albert Schweitzer; Nobel Prize for Medicine' or something? Who votes on these things anyway? What else do the Danes have going for them?

I come out of the shower and duck right into the bedroom. I change into some non-gamey clothes and muss up the sheets so it looks like I slept in the bed, at least. Then I wander out into the living room, where Nora and Nikos are talking business.

"We're talking about Nikos' stories," Nora says. "I'm only concerned that he'll write things that will turn off our audience."

"I just can't sign a paper giving away these characters— they're the best things I've had in at least ten years, and I got all kinds of new ideas last night. So I'm just very concerned about giving away control of them."

"You're not giving up control," Nora says. "I agree no one will write any Lore of the Ancient Trappers but you in your lifetime. All I'm asking is that we have a veto over stories that could cause us problems."

Nikos is looking at me, and I know that look. He doesn't want to do this, but if I tell him I want him to—because I need the money or I'm trying to make the girl—he probably will agree. And then he'll go back home and not even resent me, not even inside, not even silently without telling me. I've never known a real human being who could do such a thing, unless maybe it's the woman negotiating with him on the couch, the couch Kate and I overturned while...that's enough of that! Keep your mind on Nikos now, and business, I remind myself.

"Okay," I say. "I think Nikos has to keep control of his characters, and I think you are mistaken for being concerned about it," I tell Nora. I can see Nikos nod his head in gratitude. He wants my support, not that he should care a whit what I think.

"Why's that?" Nora says, and I get the full-on blast of her intelligent look here, her rational withering consideration.

"Because I think one of the things that made Mondo so dispensable—so dispensable that almost your entire crew jumped ship the first time there was an alternative—was that you dumbed him down, cut off his balls, Disney-fied him way too much," I tell her. "You can't have a *nice* primal-scream God of Maleness—that's not how testosterone works. You need Trappers in the image of Greek gods—copulating with the wrong people, wandering around in the wrong direction in the dark until they discover something wonderful by mistake, full of hubris, piss and vinegar—and pissing in the wind on occasion, for no particular reason. They'll have life, and they'll be real role-models, men and women who succeeded *and* failed, who made wrong turns and learned by making mistakes, people we can relate to, instead of White Bread characters who always do the right thing and leave you snoozing because you know they have nothing to do with life. They'll *be* life in all its rude messiness—or messy rudeness. Whatever."

I realize as this pours out of me that it really sounds like a rant against the guys who've been showing up here for the last 24 hours all concerned about Nora's welfare in cars that cost as much as my apartment building. Happily, Nora doesn't seem to have any awareness of that level of my anxiety. She stares beautifully into space—I can see the gears turning. Hers turn fast and grind fine.

"Nora," I say, "these are Nikos' ideas, his characters, his baby. They work because they're unpredictable. If you play this one safe, it'll wither and fall apart. Nikos won't be able to write safe stories and the Trappers will become predictable and fail and bring down Mondo with them. You'll end up with nothing. I think you have to take a risk here." And the question is on my lips as I realize I'm asking about a lot more than just the Ancient Trappers. "Are you okay taking risks?"

All at once, it feels like I've catalyzed every doubt, every gray cloud I've developed about her since we got here yesterday. Nora purses her lips and looks around the room and at me, and there's a very interesting look of amusement on her face.

"I decided to take a risk pulling this insane prank—Mondo the Man-God—on my ex-husband," she says. "I've taken a hundred risks since then to grow my business and meet all the challenges we've faced since we started."

She smiles at me, but there's steel in her glance. "But you should know—and I don't think it'll surprise you—that I take the most carefully-considered, thoughtfully weighed, every-option-on-the-table risks in the history of mankind. And that's how I'm going to approach this one."

Twenty-Five

During a break in negotiations, Nora and I walk the dogs in the back yard.

"Several of your gentlemen callers were in contact last night," I tell her. "I don't know if you got the messages on the phone."

"I picked them up on my cell," she says.

"Warren came by to look the place over last night. And Derek came by with white roses and a silver Mercedes. They both were very concerned about your well-being."

"That's nice," she says. Still no visible reaction. Good poker player.

"I kept thinking they should see you negotiate a business deal," I add. I'll get something out of her eventually.

"Did you mention the business?" she asks, looking like someone trying not to look concerned. Why is she hiding her reaction from me?

"No," I say. "I recognized that you hadn't told them about it. But I wondered why."

"Well, Warren would just get a kick out of it, but he lives next door so I don't want to tell him too much of my business," she says. "Derek is more traditional, so I think I would only break the news to him if it was really necessary."

"You don't worry about *my* reaction," I say.

"Should I?" she laughs, tossing her hair and throwing me that million-watt smile.

"Well, I know lots of details," I say.

"Yes, but this kind of thing *interests* you," she retorts. She pulls her dog over in my direction and puts her arm around me. "Derek would be uncomfortable knowing I have other boyfriends—he's very proprietary, you know. Very bourgeois. And I'll admit, it's good for a girl to have a few safe bourgeois guys available for when you artist types get tired of us." She puts her hand on my ass and starts feeling me up.

"You don't have much faith in me," I say.

"I think I have a lot of faith in you," she says and turns me to her. We kiss a few times. Man, there's no lack of chemistry here. "I count on you to really understand what's going on in me—I wouldn't ever expect that of Derek, not really. I count on you to care about things that wouldn't mean a thing to him or Warren. I expect you to be imaginative and adventurous in ways I know I'll never get from them. That's lots of faith in you. I'm just not foolish enough to think it'll last forever—and do you really *want* me to?"

Yes! a voice shouts in my head, and I give myself up to the kiss, pouring it on, trying to make her understand I came up here on a romantic dream, a quest after lost innocent love. Just because we had sex the first time we had two hours alone—and were at it for five hours—and that I had sex with her sister a few hours ago (did I really do that?) doesn't mean there is anything less romantic underneath it all. Sure, sometimes sex is just sex, as Freud almost said, but sometimes it can be the most eloquent depiction of innocent love, passion, tenderness and longing.

But innocence doesn't apply to much in my life at the moment. There's another thought in my head and I decide to test it.

"So these guys don't know you're seeing the others?" I ask her. Give me a nice deceitful answer and I can feel a tiny bit—1% maybe—better about your goddamn hot little sister.

"Well, I don't think I've ever *lied* to them about it," she says, "but I haven't brought the subject up." She kisses me again and now her hand is on my crotch. I hope it isn't too obvious that Bruno down there—or Little Willy, in this case—is in a state of near-exhaustion, maybe even total collapse. "They're *conventional*," she says, not quite damning them to hell with those words.

Well what does *that* mean? Am I the *affair*—the Bohemian following her first conventional husband and probably preceding her next conventional husband? Suddenly I feel objectified, like the transitional girlfriend, the sugar daddy or the trophy wife. The passionate, understanding, total-lack-of-jealousy, all-you-need-is-love artist. Wild sex and real understanding, but no hope of a normal life—no hope of a country club, a Mercedes, vacations in the Canaries, following a social calendar and finding a use for all those matching bathmats. Not that I could stand any of that stuff, but who is she to deny me the chance? Is that really what's going on here?

The next question is inescapable. The other guys are conventional—?

"And what are *you*?" I ask.

And having asked, I get an answer. Over ten seconds or so, Nora's whole face opens up. All the roles—the businesswoman, the electric flirt, the seductive practical tempting teasing laughing witty cautious probing intelligent occupier of roles in society—all those fly off and leave me with a completely open face, the face of that 17 (or was she 15? I *have* to clear this up, just so I don't have to keep thinking about it at moments like this) year-old who wanted to know *everything*.

"Nobody's ever asked me that," she says. "That's a great question."

Her face is breathtaking all of a sudden—it's as though, all at once, I'm staring at a clean slate. All the experience, all the hard-won knowledge is still in there, but the history, the duties and responsibilities and pro forma requirements are, for a moment at least, wiped clean.

"That remains to be seen, I guess," she says and kisses me again, kisses me sweet and long.

Twenty-Six

When we return to the room, Nora tells Nikos, "What if I said you could write whatever stories you want about the Ancient Trappers, as long as the corporation receives the copyrights for the characters in your estate?'"

"So I can write what I want—but then you get the rights after I die."

"Right. And I'll promise not to edit or change anything from the original stories—but if we want to add new material later, we have the right to do so. We'll continue to pay royalties to your heirs for any sales involving your work," she says.

"That's much better," he says. "The only thing is—I didn't think we'd actually get this far this fast; I guess I'm not much of a negotiator," he laughs, "I actually was thinking of leaving the characters to Ted. He certainly had a lot to do with their creation; I think it would really be fitting for him to take them over after I die."

"Well, that would be a more complicated issue," Nora says, raising an eyebrow in my direction. "You created the Ancient

Trappers. There's already a mystique building around you with the members. Ted doesn't have that—at least not with them—but it might not be such a bad idea. I need to think about it. Why don't we quit now and have dinner?"

"Go out—isn't that dangerous?" Nikos says.

"It might be," she answers. "I thought we'd cook."

She and Nikos cook—broiled tuna with a sauce, pastitsio, asparagus. The two of them have a famous time, tossing stories back and forth and offering suggestions for each other's cooking. I set the table, make a salad and cut up some fruit for dessert. In the kitchen, I'm manual labor.

Several times during this process, Nora drifts over to me, putting her arms around me, and I respond naturally, entwining my own around her. It seems so easy and exciting—old friends and new lovers.

Meanwhile, I'm frying with nerves. Because it looks pretty clearly like Nora's staying over and I know—I'm as sure as I can be—Kate will be back.

I was pleased to see Kate at first, and thrilled when she turned out to be so...*thrilling*. And boy, was she ever...But I was kind of stunned that she was so thrilled with *me*. I'm not hideous but I'm certainly not a standout and especially not among the Mercedes-driving tennis-playing sailboat-sailing crowd up here. From what I can see, when they're not minting money they're in the gym. She's a beautiful woman in her late 30's or early 40's.

She's married, even if only to Art (how did *that* happen?), but in this day and age, she certainly wouldn't have a hard time finding playmates anytime she wants. So I was a bit baffled by her enthusiasm about me.

At least, it was until I looked at the photo again.

I've been carrying the photo since I left Brooklyn, the photo I took the last night of the cruise, the Hill family at dinner. In the picture, I've clearly focused on Nora—everyone else is out of focus to varying degrees. Kate is close to the camera, one of the blurriest, though her mischievous smile and those laughing eyes of hers just jump off the print anyway. But what I notice now for the first time is Marion Hill, the girls' mom. She is seated next to Nora, nicely in focus. She is leaning back in her chair with a look of motherly concern for her daughter—in my head, the first thought I have looking at her face is she's concerned her daughter should not get *too* interested in the photographer. The interesting thing, the thing I'd never noticed before, in all these years, was that she was looking at *Kate*, not Nora.

All at once, it all makes sense. Kate had a crush on me on the boat! Sure, it's 25 years ago—but I know how powerful such crushes can be, don't I? Seeing me in the living room produced the same wave of feeling in her that Nora's email did in me. All those innocent hopes and dreams, those overwhelming sensations of teenage romance and lust—lust at an age when the consequences aren't as clear as they become later—came flooding back in our first moments together.

And we responded as only two grown-ups filled with innocent (irresponsible/childish/you name it) memories could—by fucking our way through every piece of furniture in the living room. So now she's coming back. I know it. I know it if only because of the dogs. If she *doesn't* show, it proves she knew Nora was coming back today—or that she knows I'm here walking them—either way, I'll have to admit I saw her last night.

Then again, why *can't* I? What's wrong with having seen Kate? That's the answer—the way to warn her off.

"Kate was here last night," I say. "To walk the dogs. Maybe you should call her and let her know she doesn't have to do that tonight."

The room goes silent. Nikos looks like he's having one of those silent strokes. Nora immediately stops what she's doing and turns to me. It is at that moment that I realize I haven't really slept much in several days and my good judgment might be just a memory.

"Oh—when did she come by?" Nora asks with a very studied nonchalance.

"I don't remember exactly—it was pretty late." I'm sweating already. God, I'm so bad at casual.

"What did she have to say for herself?" Nora pursues. This is not idle banter.

"Nothing much—she said hello," I say. "She was here to walk the dogs. I told her I'd walked them already and she left." I'm going to stick to my game plan until it explodes.

"That's it?" she says. "She didn't ask why you were here?"

"Well, she read the papers, remember?" I say, thanking God that I remember Nora mentioning this, "but I didn't expect you to be staying over tonight, so you might as well call her so she doesn't come over again."

"Well, she knows *you're* here, so wouldn't that tell her she doesn't have to walk the dogs?"

Oops. "Oh—well that's a thought," I stammer. "But—uh—I didn't say how long I was staying."

"Because you didn't know," Nora says and it sounds simultaneously like finishing my thought and a threat. Nora has dogs—does she have a doghouse? Because I might be in it very soon.

"Why don't I just call her just in case. What's her number?"

Nora pulls a cellphone from her bag and tosses it to me. "Number 3, if it'll make you feel better," she says. But she is watching me like a hawk. I punch the key and listen to the little beeps. The lines rings and rings until I shut it down.

"No answer."

"She's probably *out*," Nora says, with a tone of disdain I can't mistake or quite understand. Sisterly friction—it's an old story.

I've known lots of sisters in my life, though never before in the biblical sense.

She and Nikos bring the food to the table and Nora says, "Let's forget about business till tomorrow. I know we'll find a way to bridge the gaps."

We clink glasses and everyone digs in but me. The food is good, but I pick at it listlessly. Disaster is stalking me around every corner.

Nora leans over and whispers in my ear, "Don't fill yourself up. I want you energetic tonight" and I start sinking through my chair. Omigod, how am I going to do this? In the past two days I've had three or four hours of sleep, 5 hours of business negotiations, 6 hours driving back and forth, 3 hours in police custody and 9 or 10 hours of fucking and I'm *old*. If I wasn't old before, I'm getting there now. Everything aches, just in anticipation.

Once dinner is cleared away, Nikos says he's tired and wanders off to bed. Thanks a lot, pal, just when I could use some cover.

Nora and I finish the dishes. I'm jumpy as a cat—any second, Kate could come through the back door, expecting fun and frolic, and I could be in the bedroom with her sister. Then again, maybe she's *not* on the way—I told her Nora was coming. No, she was actually *here* when Nora's key entered the lock. God, I'm not keeping things straight at all.

The funny thing is, somehow I don't even feel very guilty about it yet. I'm usually the King of Guilt. Maybe once I get some sleep I'll feel guilty. Rested but guilty. Maybe I'm just so petrified about the possible consequences—alienating Nora forever, losing her, losing Kate, losing *somebody*, losing *everybody*, the possibility of personal firearms at short range—that I have no synaptic capacity left for anything else. The least I can do is try to get us into Nora's bedroom, for safety's sake.

Nora puts away the last dish, carefully folds the dishtowel and hangs it from its silver ring over the sink—everything in its place. She wanders over to me at the edge of the kitchen island and begins brushing her breast against arm. She does this several times.

"Hi," she says in a breathy voice and I nearly faint. I get so hard so fast it feels like an animal has taken up residence in my trousers. I kiss her neck and shoulders and all at once the aches and pains are gone. I'm lost in wanting this woman. All the years of longing are part and parcel of the desire I feel, flat against her, our hands all over each other. Ooooh yummy.

And then she leans over, panting a bit, and just scatters everything off the top of that same glass coffee table that...oh God...

"Why don't we get a little *daring*?" she says, somehow unzipping her dress with the same motion.

"Umm—*there*?" I say. "You don't want to go to the bedroom?"

"I thought you were the *artist*!" she cries, unzipping my pants and letting the bra straps fall. Oh, is there anything sweeter in the world? But *there*? "Don't you like a little *variety*?" she demands.

Yes, I do, which is why I wanted to go to the bedroom, the only place we didn't use last night...ohhhhh she's got my pants off now and she's not shy.

"After this, we'll try the *bookcase*!" she yelps and for a moment, I have the sinking, wrenching thought that maybe she has cameras in here and knows every single solitary thing Kate and I did last night and is repeating them on purpose just to freak me out. Except, underneath all the craziness and all my concerns about the hundred million ways this could go wildly wrong, the central feeling that's taking over is that I want to make this woman *happy*. *Real* happy. I want to fulfill her in every way I can think of. All those dreams about her over all the years—and here she is now, giving herself to me as a free, joyous, groping adult. I want this to pay off for her. And for Kate—Whoops! Wrong thought. I'll straighten it all out later, but for now, I get lost in Nora and do everything I can think of and physically manage without prosthetics.

By midnight, we're spent. At least I am, and she seems content.

"I'm going to bed," I say, "if you're okay."

"I'm *fine*," she says. She kisses me again, soft and sweet. "Don't want to join me?" she asks.

"I do," I say honestly, "very very much. But I didn't sleep much last night—new place, you know—or the night before—"

"I remember—"

"—so I really need to just close my eyes and not be distracted. And you're *very* distracting." I kiss her lovely shoulder again. "Very."

"You know how to say 'no' to a girl," she says, and lopes off to her bedroom.

I crawl into my bed and am snoring before I pull the covers over me. I sleep for at least an hour before I feel a finger or two poking into my ribcage.

"Hey!" a whispered voice says.

I roll over. Kate is sitting on the edge of the bed in a very flimsy bra and panties, smiling at me with that look on her face. If Helen of Troy could launch a thousand ships with a look, Kate could sink them all with hers. Just a glance like that, and they'd all go flaming to the bottom of the ocean, smiles on the faces of every crew member. I feel myself stirring, though by this stage of the marathon, it actually *hurts*.

"I wore the *edible* underwear tonight," she says and I almost pass out.

Twenty-Seven

Please understand that I consider myself, generally speaking, neither an ingrate nor an overly arrogant person. I feel fortunate for the blessings life bestows upon me and I try not to squander them. This has become especially true in recent months, when those blessings have been so few and so forgettable in the worldwide blizzard of shit. Nonetheless, I can't just jump in here, as much as certain parts of me are aching to.

"Kate," I say, "I'm a bit confused."

"I'm sorry to hear that," she says. She looks very sympathetic, particularly around the nipples.

"I find myself really drawn to both you and Nora, but I can't help feeling this is going to lead to very nasty consequences down the road."

"Well, I understand your concern," Kate says as though impressed by my thoughtful consideration. Am I missing something here? I'm *sleeping with your sister*—isn't this a red flag the size of Montreal? On the other hand, I'm lying in bed with the sister of the girl I've been pining for most of my life, she looks like a goddamn ice cream sundae, she wants me and wore the edible underwear for me, so the whole concept of discriminatory logic is becoming real elusive at the moment.

"I don't know about you and Nora," she says finally, "I know that *we're* meant to be together. I know that you like me better than her—or at least that you're better suited to me than her."

All of a sudden, I'm getting flashbacks from *Fatal Attraction*. I hang one leg off the bed to help with a quick getaway if necessary.

"Umm—well, that's...very interesting," I say. "But when you say you know—"

"It's not a compliment, it's a fact. I can *see* it." I put *see* in italics because she pronounces it differently than the rest of the sentence. I feel as if I should cross myself when she says it, and I'm Jewish. What's *this* about?

"You could see it this fast?" I ask, careful not to sound challenging or threatening in any way. God, she is gorgeous—I could lose myself in those eyes. Don't think about them, you fool—she's a Siren, singing you to doom on the rocks. Think about French Fries or Disney movies. Forget that—look at her tits. Nikos was right about her tits. Aauuggh!

"No," she says, "I've seen it for more than a year. You don't know we've been dreaming together?"

This is where I put the patently phony smile on my face and make sure that outside foot is firmly on the ground.

"Dreaming together? No, I hadn't realized."

She laughs, quietly but naturally—the laugh is disarming in its directness. "Oh God, of course this sounds odd," she says. "I'm sorry. I'm really not nuts. I was just sure you'd given permission."

"For what?"

"For me to dream with you. I understand now that you weren't aware of it," she says quickly. "It's impossible to dream with someone who hasn't given permission. It probably didn't come to you explicitly—it probably was just someone talking to you in a dream and you spoke back."

"You mean, any time I answer a question in a dream I'm allowing some stranger into my head?" This is a disturbing thought, almost as disturbing as the fact that we're discussing it with straight faces.

"No, of course not. Most of the time when you speak in a dream, the words come from your dream sense, the part of the brain that governs dreams—which is why that conversation so rarely means anything when you wake up."

"That's for sure," I say. "You should see my dream notebooks."

Kate crawls over the bed and lies against me. Her skin is so soft and she smells wonderful, like a forest near the ocean or a flowerbed near a perfume factory or oh God I'm losing my ability to create *metaphors!* Her eyes are sparkling as she continues to fog my mind.

"But once you've made the breakthrough," she says, "once you're dreaming with your own intuitive spirit—not your dream sense, but your day-to-day intuitive mind— *then* if you talk to another spirit entering your dream, you have given them permission to dream with you. And then you can mingle your spirits very very closely together. You can become quite...intimate."

"Uh huh," I nod as though that wraps things up. There are lots of things I could do instead—say 'fire truck' or 'dogma' or some other random sound, stick out my tongue at her, choke myself to death—makes no difference; I still wouldn't know what the hell she's talking about. For good or ill, she sees my confusion.

"Let's put it this way," she says. "Most of the time when you dream, you'll see things that might relate to your daily life but they're all jumbled up. You feel like you're watching a movie and one that doesn't make any sense. You're disconnected from it."

"Yes, that's right," I say. My foot is still firmly on the floor, I should point out.

"But haven't you ever done more than that?" she asks. "Haven't you ever meditated deeply before sleeping, or started using your dreams on purpose to channel issues in your life?"

"Well, I started meditating before going to bed about a month ago," I admit, the words coming before I can think twice about them. "I haven't been sleeping well and I thought it might help—it didn't. And I remember actually making myself go back to sleep and continue a dream because I wasn't satisfied with the ending."

"And you changed it?" she asks.

"Yeah I did," I answer, only now remembering clearly. "It was just as confused but different."

"That's still changing it," she says. "So, when you start dealing with dreams like that, you're no longer just watching a movie. You're no longer disconnected. You're a *participant* in the dream, making it happen. And once you've made that change, you can agree to let someone else dream with you. And I've been your partner now for a while."

"You said over a year? How much over a year?"

"I don't know," she says. "Maybe a year and a half." About the time the novel started coming intensely—when I really started living through that novel, with the character suggested by Nora. This raises all sorts of interesting, if insane, possibilities, but it also leads irresistibly to another question.

"So we were dreaming together long before Nora emailed me?"

Kate falters. Her eyes flit away. She blushes and I get a clear sense of something I shouldn't know.

"Whose idea was it for Nora to contact me?" I ask and her cheeks go crimson.

"I never said a word to her about you," she protests but I've spent too much time lately in negotiations—I immediately find the loophole.

"Do you have permission to dream with Nora?" I ask. Kate looks like she's scanning the room for an exit sign. "You don't," I conclude, "but you planted the idea anyway. Isn't that a little sneaky?"

"I knew you wouldn't remember me," she says, "but I knew you remembered Nora. I'm the little sister—you learn sometimes to be the sneaky little sister."

And the sneaky wife, too, I can't help thinking. But then, cheating on Art probably lessens the otherwise-uncontrollable urge to kill him, so it's a *mitzvah* for both of us.

"I'm sorry to drop this on you," she continues. "I can imagine how disorienting it is to hear it explained." The disorienting thing is that she really seems to understand just how crazy she sounds. Crazy people aren't supposed to know they're crazy, are they? But it's far more comforting to think she's crazy than that she's on the level. "But is this really so new to you? Haven't you ever read Castaneda?" she asks.

"Yes, but I was stoned at the time and can't remember a word. And wasn't he kidding anyway?"

"He was dead serious. It's what killed him," she says. That makes me feel *much* better. "But really—take stock of what's happening here—do I really seem like someone you haven't met in

25 years? Or do you have feelings for me that don't make sense if we've just met again?"

Wasn't I just thinking that? Isn't that what I was thinking when I used the word 'innocent' about us a little while ago—a word I will never have any right to use ever again, and certainly never again about us. I try to remember what I felt when she came through the open curtains last night. After the first shock of seeing her—and drinking in the sight of her—I remember this overwhelming, instant lust. But the more I think about it, the more muddied the waters become. I've been excited by women continually since the age of 14 but I've never been the kind of guy who assumed women wanted me that fast. And in truth—and it's surprisingly hard to admit this—I've never surrendered myself as willingly or completely as I did to her. It just isn't like me to let my guard down like that, drunk or sober.

"I don't usually sleep with someone the first minute we meet, even if they're willing," Kate says—Jesus, can she read my mind? "And I don't think you do either, do you?"

Is this a trick question? I pause to ponder, but what I realize is that the real answer is pretty clear. I've always been ridiculously selective about whom I sleep with, protective of my feelings and cautious of getting physically involved with anyone with whom I'm not already emotionally involved. This hasn't always been easy, since men are told from puberty that they're supposed to be rutting pigs and certainly the desire for indiscriminate fucking is always present in the muscles and hormones and genes. And lately I've found myself regretting some of the opportunities I passed up. So when we leaped into each other's arms etc., I assumed it was just a sign that I'd given up that old bourgeois caution. But was it?

"No, I don't," I admit, feeling somewhat sheepish about it.

"Well, there's my point," she says. "We don't feel like strangers. We've gotten to know each other over the last year and over a lot of difficult nights in the last month. It may not be the way we'd know each other if we were dating—I don't know the details of your divorce and all your other statistics—but in some ways maybe this is deeper."

I have never mentioned my divorce to Kate or even to Nora. It might not be hard to infer but she's not speaking as though it's an inference. Maybe it's listed on the Web somewhere—everything in the world is on the Web. Did I dream about the divorce and not remember?

"I mean," Kate continues, "you trust me despite the fact that this all has to be making you pretty uncomfortable. At least, you haven't thrown me out of bed yet."

"Sweetie," I tell her, as if it needs to be said, "a man doesn't throw a beautiful woman in edible underwear out of bed over a little discomfort."

She laughs, holding her hand over her mouth to muffle the noise. "You're funny," she says. "Funnier than when we were younger." Then she puts her hand on my cheek. "I'll tell you what," she says. "Why don't we try it together and then you'll understand what I mean?"

"You mean—dreaming?" I ask, and I can hear the quiver in my voice.

"Yeah," she says. "No sex—we'll actually *sleep* together. You'll see—it's just as good."

I doubt that—but at least I can't get dragged into court for it. I roll over and put my arms around her and we both doze off.

Twenty-Eight

It's 3:30—I can see the illuminated clock on the night table. That would mean 3 hours solid dozing. That's more undisturbed sleep than I've had in a month. But 16 hours straight with Valium is what I really need. Why is she poking me?

"What is it, sweetie?" I say, rolling over. In the light seeping through the windowshades, I see *Nora* standing over me in a very fetching—but probably inedible—nightgown. I glance around the room, wondering if Kate's hiding in a corner.

"There's someone in the backyard," Nora says. "Would you mind--?"

Of course. Kate finished her mumbo-jumbo and took off. She's stumbling around the backyard and Nora heard her. Yes— far better that I check.

"I'll give it a look," I say, in that very manly tone of voice you use when there's a woman to impress and you're really really sure there's actually nothing to be frightened about.

I pull on clothes and head for the back door. "I'd suggest," I tell Nora, "that you stay in the bedroom until I get back." I'll attend to you later, young lady...

That's when we hear Kate scream, very clearly and loudly, from the backyard.

We both go hurtling through the back door. I grab the same bottle of Scotch with which I almost brained Kate last night. Now that there's the possibility of real danger, my knees are quaking like elms in the wind.

Kate is crumpled among a grove of trees behind the garage. It's only when we reach her that we see what caused her scream.

In the garage door, illuminated from behind, is the figure of Mondo The Man-God, in his cape and ceremonial headpiece. This strikes me as odd on a couple of levels. As dull as Art is, I can't help thinking he would have used the getup somewhere along the line to spice up the matrimonial bed, though adding spice to Kate is surely coals to Newcastle. But in this light, sneaking out of the house at 330 AM, he's a shock. Of even more interest, what's he doing here?

"Art," I say, "always nice to see you. On your way to play golf?"

"I wouldn't wear this to play *golf*," he says, playing to type. Then he turns back to Kate. "What are you doing here?"

"I came to walk the dogs," Kate says. Art and I both reach for her hands at exactly the same time, I swear. If he'd gotten there first, I would have pulled back—really. We both pull her up—not exactly in competing directions, but with a little tussling that doesn't escape Nora's attention, says my radar.

"Why don't we go inside?" she says. "It's cold out here."

A moment later, we're all in the living room—Nora, Kate, Art, me and Clint. Clint?

"He's the emissary of the Trappers," Art hisses.

"*What*?" Nora and I both say simultaneously.

"The guys that are left—they're calling themselves the Trappers," Art explains. Clint, a dark stocky fellow with a bowl haircut and Beelzebub beard, stands quietly in the corner trying to ignore the fact that we're talking about him. "They're very upset Nikos left and they wanted their money back on the spot. I showed them it says they can't get a refund once the program begins—that didn't do much."

"No," says Nora. "That would just antagonize them."

"I didn't press the point—I just hoped it might slow things down," Art continues. He's lost all his hubris—I almost feel sorry for him. "I told them we're merging and that calmed them down a bit, but they insist on proof. So they've taken me hostage until we give them proof."

This is not the first time in recent days, but once again I find myself blinking like someone's shining a light in my face.

"Art—you can't be a hostage," I say. "You're here."

"No, I'm their hostage," Art says, pointing rather impolitely. "That's what Clint's here for." Clint nods his head, as if to say, 'that's right, I'm the hostage-keeper'.

Kate is sitting on the edge of the couch behind Art, rolling her eyes with every word that comes out of his mouth.

"Art, he's just one person," I say. "He's not even that big. You and I could take him."

"I wouldn't try it," Art says. "He's the one who threw the rocks at the bears—both of them. He killed the second one with it." He turns to Clint. "Show 'em, Clint," he says gravely and Clint pulls two big rocks out of the pockets of his parka, hefting them both to show us their weight.

"Well, I think cause of death will always remain a mystery, as there won't be an autopsy," I say. "But I get your point."

I turn to Clint. "What is it you guys want, exactly?"

"We started our training as Ancient Trappers," he says, very quietly. "We want to finish. We went through nine of the eleven levels of self-defense—we want the other two. Mondo here says the Ancient Trappers are part of the plan. We want to finish."

"Well, the Ancient Trapper is asleep in his room," I tell him, gesturing toward Nikos' side of the house. "And I'm sure you understand just how important it is for him to have his dream time—keep him in touch with the spirits of the Mountains and all that stuff."

"You mean the Mountain Wraiths?" Clint asks.

"Right, of course, the Mountain Wraiths—he needs to commune with them at night. Right?"

"Of course," Clint says. He looks at the Scotch bottle still in my hand.

"You should really just lock that stuff up" he offers.

"Well, feel free to remind me after lunch," I tell him. "Anyway, maybe we should all just go to sleep. In the morning we can head back to camp and solve this problem," I say.

"How are we going to do that?" Nora whispers in my ear.

"We'll have to negotiate in the car on the way up—clearly we have a deadline now," I whisper back. "Does that work for you, Clint?"

Clint nods. The strong silent type. A born bear-killer, if you ask me. Nikos knows how to pick 'em.

"Okay," Art says to Kate, with far more deference than I would have expected. "I guess we should head home."

"No," says Clint. "The Trapper is here, so I'm staying here. And you're my hostage, so you're staying here too, where I can watch you."

"Well, I guess you guys can take the guestroom—Ted can move in with me," Nora says, flicking an eyebrow in my direction.

"No, that won't work," Kate says.

"Oh?" Nora says.

"I'll take the guestroom," Kate continues. "Art can use the couch out here."

"That would be better for me," says Clint. Everyone ignores him and he doesn't seem to care a whole lot.

"What's going on?" Nora asks her sister.

"We're not—together," Kate says, shrugging and throwing her eyes in Art's direction.

"I'm not accepting that as permanent," Art says.

"You'll *have* to," Kate responds.

"What happened?" Nora says, and then remembers they're not alone.

"I would think you would know, of all people," Kate replies, staring hard at Nora.

"Me?" Nora gasps. "What are you talking about?"

"I know what you're up to," Kate pursues. "I lived with it for years—six weeks a year alone in a cabin in the woods."

"With *Art*?" Nora laughs, and then realizes she's insulting her sister's husband. She stands, very confused, trying to figure out a direction she can go that won't make things worse.

"Never," she finally says to Kate. "Never. Nothing like it."

"He knows about your birthmark," Kate says with certainty. "He knows your left breast is larger than the right."

It *is*? I'm going to have to check on this later.

"How?" Nora says. Then she stares bullets at Art. "You son-of-a-bitch," she says. "That's why we always get the same cabin— you've got a *peephole*."

"Don't try that on me," Kate continues. "I know his thoughts. I know he's slept with you a hundred times."

"*Never*," Nora says, shaking her head. "*How* do you know?"

"I've dreamed with him," Kate says.

"Oh, *that* again," Nora screeches.

"He knows every inch of you—he's certain of everything about you. It's all in his head," Kate says.

"That's exactly right," Nora says. "It's all in his head."

"Maybe so," Kate shrugs. "It doesn't matter. He's with you now, not me."

"*I* don't want him," Nora says.

"Hey, *excuse* me," Art tries to interrupt but the two sisters turn on him simultaneously and he shrinks into the corner.

"He gave you permission to dream with him?" Nora asks.

"Are you taking this seriously?" Art cries. The sisters again stare him down—he slumps back into a chair.

"You may not have realized you were doing it," I tell him and realize immediately this is a bad move. Kate looks at the floor, trying to maintain her poker face, but Nora shoots me a glance that makes me want to join Art in the corner.

"He's my husband," Kate says. "It's implied."

Nora stands, a triumph of posture over psychic distress. Finally, she walks over to the linen closet and starts pulling out matched linen. She throws a heavy pile of very nice aqua patterned material in Art's face.

"You can make up the couch," she says. Then she turns to Clint. "Where are you going to sleep?" she asks.

"I'm not sleeping—I'm watching him," Clint says. A born bear-killer, I tell you.

"Well, it gets chilly here at night," Nora says, obviously forgetting where this guy's just come from. "Here's a blanket for your chair," she continues, throwing him wool in tan and black stripe.

"Kate," she says, "you can take the bed in the guestroom. There's fresh sheets here if you want to change the one's that are there." Then she looks at me. "You can fend for yourself, I suppose."

And then she stalks off to her bedroom, closing the door firmly behind her—and audibly locking it.

The rest of us are left standing rather awkwardly in the living room, staring at each other. I'm trying to figure out if there's some way for me to get back to my own—and now Kate's—bed without Art noticing I'm not around. I can't pretend I'm going to Nora's room now, can I? Art and I and Kate are all arrayed around the central couch, smiling these very fake smiles and thanking God that telepathy hasn't been perfected.

And then the door opens at the far side of the house and Nikos comes out, walking quietly and quite loosely to the kitchen. He opens a cabinet, pulls out a water glass, fills it from the tap and heads back toward his room. He is wearing a t-shirt and a pair of boxer shorts. His eyes remain tightly closed throughout this entire exercise. I wave goodnight and follow him silently into his room.

Nikos takes a sip from the glass, climbs into bed and is snoring within thirty seconds. I sit down on the floor next to the bed and try to figure out if I can fall asleep sitting up.

Twenty~Nine

I remain at the foot of Nikos' bed for about five minutes before I hear tapping at the window. It's Kate—of course it's Kate, although on a night like this it could just as easily be Barney the Dinosaur or the Ghost of Christmas Past.

"C'mon," she whispers when I pull up the bottom pane.

"Are you sure this is such a good idea?"

She pulls herself very tall in front of the window, pulls her breasts out of her bra and starts wagging them around in front of my face. My head follows like one of those dog-toys in the back window of a Pontiac.

"Hurry up," she says. "It's cold."

She knows damn well I don't need any more encouragement than that. It's not only that I don't get a vote—with those things bobbing in my face, I can't even *think* and she knows it. The whole process is undemocratic.

Of course, now that she's publicly broken with Art, she's fair game after all, according to the Machiavelli DeSade Code of Fair Play, Chapter Six, Sub-Section 12.

But that doesn't really make things any simpler. On one hand, I have the really hot sister I spent 25 years pining for and wrote a book about; on the other, the even hotter sister who insists we've bonded spiritually while unconscious late at night in separate countries. How do you make a choice like that? More to the point, how could that turn out to be a difficult choice? What does that say about me? Or her? Or maybe somebody else. If I could think, I might be able to know or guess or something.

I fiddle with the catches on the screens outside the regular dual-pane windows—they have to come up as well before I can get out. "What's the point of having screens on the windows," I complain to Kate, "when your growing season is six weeks long? How many bugs can you possibly get between winter and winter?"

She rolls her eyes like she did with Art—ouch! "Such clichés. You wouldn't believe how many kids we get up here every June with skis on top of their cars—'where's the snow?' 'Just drive north—about ten hours. When your compass stops functioning, there should be snow.'"

"Well, if you don't like clichés, you shouldn't have married Art," I tell her, trying to squeeze myself through a regulation-size window without permanently wrenching my back. "He's a failed petitioner from the Ministry of Silly Walks."

"Mmm," she muses. "Don't remind me. But if it wasn't for him, I never would have learned dreaming."

"And we wouldn't want to have missed that," I say, head and shoulders through, now trying to find something to hold onto as I pull my leg out—and not finding anything. This isn't good. If I don't have something to hold onto, I will surely fall straight onto the ground as soon as the first leg comes over the threshold—not the graceful entrance I want to make back to Kate's bed.

"You know, make jokes," she says, grabbing me under one arm. "But I was the mousy little sister of the mousy big sister until I discovered I could really understand people. And you of all people should appreciate what a liberation that is—we have the same compulsion to understand. That's what binds us together. I mean, look at what we did before."

"When?" I ask, getting the first leg on the ground. Kate lets go, I pull the other leg through and manage to pull the window closed.

"What do you mean 'when?'" Kate says. "When we dreamed together just now."

"Ohhh," I moan, "yeah. Remind me."

"You don't remember?" she says, plaintive and disappointed.

"I might have just gone to sleep—I was so wiped out," I tell her. "I'm sorry."

"No, you were *there*," she says, wrapping her arms around herself. I put my arms around her and we march into the garage, on our way around the house the long way, heading back to her window without passing Nora's room—a strategy I much approve of. Having graduated from a wife who ignored me for fifteen years to rabid date sex with two sisters in the same house at the same time, I'm willing to think conservative where possible.

"We were in Colorado," Kate tells me. "I see why you loved it there—you took me to this really beautiful place with jagged twin mountains that were just spectacular and all those golden trees and there was a dead trunk in the river we kept looking at. We would walk around in the woods for a while and then we always ended up back at the same place, staring at that tree in the river."

"The Maroon Bells, right outside Aspen," I say and realize with a shock that I not only recognize the description but that it does feel fresh to me, like I've just been there. "That was the first autumn I spent there—there was good rain that summer, so all the trees went gold at the same time. I probably have twenty photos of that dead tree in the river."

"And then I took you to Banff with me," she says, "because it so reminded me of Aspen. We went to the Banff Springs--?" She's staring at me, imploring, shivering, her eyes just cutting right through me.

And then, like a glimmer through frosted glass, the image comes back to me and I *remember*.

"The twin mountains," I say. "But gray, not white like the Bells. And farther apart."

"Right!" she says, encouraging me to go on.

"And the whole town down below, on the other side of those hills."

"Right!" she says, her eyes lighting up now, thrilled, as thrilled as I'm getting.

"And we—" I look at her now, afraid I'm going to fuck it all up, "we—were in some kind of *castle*?"

"It's a hotel," she says, jumping up and down and whacking me hard on the shoulders. "We were there!"

"You don't mean we were really *there*, like out-of-body or something?" I shrivel all at once.

"Noooo," she says, like *I'm* the crazy one, "out-of-body— that's all mumbo-jumbo. But we dreamed going there *together*— you see?"

And I *do*. I actually do. I remember this place that I've never been in or even seen in pictures, as clear as a bell—and in some way I don't quite *get*, I know she was there with me.

Her eyes shine like emeralds, but she's shivering. I pull my shirt off and give it to her and we sprint across the front lawn— thank God this isn't a high traffic neighborhood—and over to her window. She slips through in a second and I push myself in behind her—if I fall on the floor now, as long as it's quiet, I'm too cold and too carefree to worry about it.

We huddle under the covers, bodies together for warmth and because it's how we both want it.

"You see?" she whispers. "You believe me a little bit now?"

"There's something about this," I tell her—she's still shivering; I fold my arms around her without putting my hands on her back, because they're frozen—"there's something I don't know how to describe. I know we went to these places—I can feel Colorado in me fresh, so I really believe I was dreaming about it just now. But when I think of this other place—"

"Banff," she whispers back—she's now taken my hands in hers and is rubbing them all back and forth to warm them up. "It's a resort in Alberta—the Canadian Rockies."

"God, it's amazing looking," I say, immersing myself in the memory now. "But it's not quite like I've been there—I mean, I can see it but there's...something more to it, something else that comes with it that I can't place."

Kate stops rubbing our hands together—they're warmed up now anyway—puts her hands on my cheeks and focuses the most ravishing tender look I've ever seen at me.

"Okay," she says, "hold onto that feeling and try to pretend you're not you for a moment. Pretend you're a girl—maybe a little girl. See what you get."

This is not the kind of suggestion I get every day, but at the moment, I won't—can't—deny her anything. I know enough about imagination games to know I'm not going to be able to really feel like a girl—I just relax and try to find the girl-feelings in this vision of the town and the mountains and the castle—the *castle*...

"The magic, enchanted castle," I murmur to her, and I can see her eyes jump. "The kind of castle where I could be a princess," I say, and then realize what I mean, without really understanding it. "I mean, where *you* could be a princess," I say to Kate.

"That's it," she says. "You've got it."

"What have I got?" I ask.

"You didn't go there and you didn't just watch a dream I was having. You went there *through* me, through my feelings about the place. My parents took us there when I was little; it was my enchanted castle and I was the princess. I always feel like a fairytale princess in my memory of that place," she laughs. "So you've not only gone to the hotel in Banff, but inside *me*. You have actually felt what I feel about that place, which is really precious to me, something I could never explain in words."

She is luminous—I put my fingers to her hair to brush it back and am surprised it's actually there, that there is substance to this corporeal wraith hiding with me under the sheets.

"Just as I understand," she continues, "how you feel about Aspen—it's where you discovered yourself, where you became a man, where you started taking control of your own life. All kinds of empowering man thoughts involved in that place for you."

Her face gets darker now, solemn all at once. "And that's how I understood you had to come up here," she says. "You had to get away."

"What are you talking about?"

"You were really losing it," she says. "You're a creative person—your dreams aren't just a mental framework or a wish-fulfillment like they are for most people. You live in them all the time. They're what you draw on for your work. And they were failing, weren't they?"

I feel all at once like I'm choking, like some force inside me is clawing to escape and not finding a way. Kate puts her arms around me and pulls me to her. I resist for a moment, afraid I'll smother her—I'm so much bigger than she is—but she says, "It's okay. You don't scare me" and somehow, though I have no clue what the words mean, they're just the right words. And tears pour out of me like a torrent.

When it's over, we sit on the bed and I'm stunned. I feel drained and totally relaxed for the first time I can remember.

"I could see what was happening," she tells me. "When I dreamed with you this last month, you were shriveling. You couldn't sleep more than an hour at a time and your dreams were just drying up. I got so afraid for you."

"So you made Nora write me—and you convinced me to come up here."

"It's not quite that simple," she says. "But I was able to get my point across eventually."

"I was surviving," I say, defending myself.

"You'd lost your sense of humor," she says. "It's your perspective, it's your protection. It's where you've grown over the years. You were so serious and earnest on the cruise."

"'I was so much older then; I'm younger than that now.'" There's a Dylan quote for any occasion. I'm stroking her hair; she's tracing lines in my cheeks. We're so close together. I'm so intoxicated with her.

"By the way," she says, "edible underwear is only good for one night. And I'm morally opposed to wasting food, aren't you?"

Thirty

As daylight comes, I scamper back to Nikos' room, climbing nimbly through the window and dropping onto the floor heavily enough to stir but not wake him, thank goodness.

I actually get a little sleep on the floor—on Nora's nice plush carpets. Two hours later, I'm awakened by Nikos stepping over me, still functionally asleep. He says, "Excuse me" but continues with his eyes shut. I get up and follow—this could get interesting.

As he steps into the living room, Clint nearly jumps to attention. I hold a finger to my mouth to quiet him. Art is snoring loudly on the couch and Nora seems just to have arrived—she's pulling a bathrobe taut over her nightgown. Which means she sees me come from Nikos' room, for whatever good that'll do me. Nikos heads directly to the kitchen. He pulls eggs and bacon from the fridge, eyes still closed, and several pans from beneath the counter. Then he sets to work making breakfast.

In minutes, he's got a nice mound of scrambled eggs and bacon going. He's smiling pleasantly and even whistling at times, but his eyes are still fluttering half-opened. Clint and I settle onto stools at the kitchen counter, drinking orange juice and watching this in awe.

"Never seen anything like it," Clint says.

"He's a man apart," I tell him.

"How are you feeling this morning?" he asks and I see him eyeing the Scotch bottle still sitting on the counter.

"I'm fine. Not going near it," I say and he beams.

Nora is clearly under some form of torture here. This nice man she likes is making breakfast in her kitchen. Clearly she feels obligated to help—she would sincerely like to help—but is too wise to interfere with sleepwalking short-order cooks. She's not totally ignoring me but she's not really looking at me either. I'm not sure if I'm supposed to act guilty or not—I don't feel guilty, not that I can imagine why not.

Now Kate emerges from that lovely bedroom, that lovely bed, that wonderful soft shag carpet, that nice bathroom with the really sturdy upright counter that you can balance on while—but I digress...

Nora looks at her and then at me. She saw me come from Nikos' room this morning, and here comes Kate, looking amazingly demure, considering. Will this work? For a second?

Nora looks at Kate and then gestures to Nikos, who is still making eggs, whistling happily to himself while still visibly asleep.

"Are you sleeping with *him* too?" she says.

"You mean 'dreaming with him,'" I tell her *sotto voce*, stabbing in the dark.

"What did I say?" she asks.

"Never mind," I answer.

Kate wisely turns her attention to Nikos, closing her eyes and leaning heavily on the counter for a moment. We both watch her work, Nora with a good deal more seriousness than I would expect. How about that? When her back is turned, part of Nora believes in her sister, or at least wants to.

After about thirty seconds, Kate's and Nikos' eyes open at the same moment. Nikos looks around and says, "Was I asleep?"

"How'd you know?" I ask. He doesn't look all that different from a moment ago, except his eyes aren't fluttering.

"This is what I make when I'm asleep," he says, gesturing at the almost-finished bacon and eggs. "Haven't done this in years. I hope it's breakfast time."

"Bingo," Nora says and goes to the cupboards for plates and silver. Kate and I grab settings from her and the three of us start laying out the table, with Nikos following close behind, spooning the food onto the plates as soon as they've been laid down. Clint goes over and tries rousing Art, who continues to snore while being poked and spoken to.

"Nikos is amazing," Kate whispers to me. "I just figured I could wake him up—I used to have to do that with Art. I just get inside a little bit and push him back out to the land of the living. But we went on a little journey there—how long were we gone?"

"Less than a minute," I say.

"I think we went to Piraeus, Mykonos, White Plains—is that where he lives?—and someplace in Arizona where there are a lot of really big lizards."

"Anything interesting you two want to share with the rest of us?" Nora asks, not all that politely.

"You're not the school monitor anymore," Kate says.

"Just asking," Nora says, politely now. The polite is no more reassuring than the biting.

"We're talking about Nikos," I tell her.

"Behind my back?" Nikos says.

"No—you're behind us."

"Oh, well then it's okay," he says, laughing his little laugh and spooning eggs.

"Where was that place you used to go in Arizona?" I ask him. "Where Kara's brother lived?"

"Taos," he says.

"Did they have lizards there? Big lizards?" I ask. Nora starts laughing.

"*That's* what you were talking about?" she says.

"It's not all brilliant stuff," Kate shrugs.

"No kidding," Nora says. The two of them can go from flat-out animosity to being amused with each other in a heartbeat.

Nikos has been thinking about the question all this time. "Wait a minute," he says. "You mean BIG lizards—lizards the size of dogs."

"The size of *Nora's* dogs," Kate says.

"Yes, they had those," Nikos says, shaking his head. "I thought I'd imagined them."

I look at Kate. "So did he remember them in the dream or does he imagine he remembers them now because you had the dream with him?"

She holds her hands up in the air. "That's above my pay grade," she says.

"That's Kate," Nora remarks, cutting her bacon into uniform bite-sized pieces. "Never takes responsibility for cleaning up her mess."

"How am I supposed to know whether I helped him find lizards in his memory or if I planted them there?" Kate says.

"Well, maybe you shouldn't mess about with things you can't control," Nora snipes.

"That would rule out just about everything in life," Kate says.

"Not in *my* life," Nora responds.

"Okay," Kate smiles, "let's say anything worthwhile or meaningful—how's that?"

"So how about them lizards?" I say to Nikos, flailing a bit

"I hate 'em," says Clint, who is now whacking Art on the shoulder to no effect.

"Ugly things, God," Kate mutters. "But Nikos finds them interesting. You find *everything* interesting, don't you?"

"Uh-huh," I answer for him, nodding and smiling. Nikos smiles back, happy at his effect on people, happy to be having an effect. I see him on Kate's face, the same calming appreciation he brings to everyone who knows him. Except maybe the new order of Ancient Trappers.

Clint has now progressed to poking Art's arm and speaking loudly in his ear. None of it is working.

"That won't do any good," Kate announces. "He'll sleep all day like that unless you really push him."

"What do you think I'm doing?" Clint says. He pushes on Art's arm, pushes pretty hard from what I can see. Art rocks back and forth on the couch but he doesn't rouse. Kate finally gets up from the table and walks behind the couch. Clint politely steps out of her way.

She leans over, sticks both arms down as far as they'll go behind Art's back and then snaps them taut. Art rolls forward and straight down onto the floor with a deep thud. He sits up, stunned but awake, as Kate walks back to the table, wiping her hands together.

"That should do it," she says.

An hour later, we're all getting into cars for the trip North.

Thirty-One

Clint has to drive his car and insists on keeping his hostage with him. This happily leaves the rest of us to pack into the relative luxury of Nora's SUV for the drive north.

Easier said than done.

"You can sit with me," Nora says as we approach.

"He can keep me company," Kate chirps.

"You have all your multiple personalities to keep you company."

"You have to negotiate with Nikos. You want to look each other in the eye, don't you?"

"Not while I'm driving," Nora cuts her off.

If you've read this far, I don't have to tell you that I'll go with the flow far longer than is normal or even sensible. But there is a limit and we're clearly just about there.

"Okay, this is no good," I announce. "Everybody in the car knows what's going on here. Either we start talking about it or we'll explode."

"I don't know what you're referring to," Nora insists, banking on dignity. I gave up on that about the time we reached Denville.

"Sure you do," I reply. "Look at the way you're acting!"

"I'm acting perfectly normal and nice," she protests and who could reasonably argue with her? Me.

"Of course, you are. The two of you are too damn polite to kick or curse. You'll just nice each other to death." Kate is staring at me—and her sister—with wide eyes, taking it all in. She's a little too comfortable with all the fuss she's created. Though I guess I helped, didn't I?

"Nora, Kate and I...are involved." It's the best word I can come up with on a mere twenty-four hours notice. Nora makes an effort to look shocked but it doesn't last long. She ends up sad and upset, which cuts a whole lot deeper. "And so are we—you and me—we're involved too," I continue and now her expression changes completely.

"Excuse me?" she says, with a real sense of outrage in her voice. "You expect to continue *sharing* us?"

"Well, I don't know if I'm sharing you—I don't *feel* like I'm sharing you. I'm just—with you—separately...at the same time."

Nobody even makes an attempt to reply to this. It's possible none of them can figure out how, even if they want to.

"You said you came up here to see *me*," Nora says finally, puncturing the silence and if there's any way I could sink into the ground now, I'd do it. It's an amazing naked statement, so stark it's almost heroic. Heroine-ic? I'll figure out the syntax later, after I get over feeling like shit. It's not like I could possibly be surprised by this response—how I ever thought I was going to muddle through fucking her sister now seems a mystery on the order of the disappearance of Atlantis.

"I *did*.. I drove 700 miles for you. And if I'd stayed up at Tundra Lake with you instead of coming down here—which was your idea—or if Kate hadn't come over to walk the dogs at 2am while I was blind drunk and jumped me—"

"*Jumped* you?" Kate isn't happy with my choice of words.

"Well, I helped, I'll admit. It just—well, we really—it happened so fast, I don't even think we said three or four words—I mean, I didn't even have time to defend myself—" The explanation is collapsing. before I the words come out of my mouth. It's like tapdancing on the edge of a sinkhole—you can make a tremendous effort but the ground just keeps dropping out from under your feet. It's fascinating to watch, but if you're doing the dancing, you'd rather eat live cat.

"Besides which, you just about told me I was the bohemian affair between Rex and Chipper and your other lumberjack millionaire boyfriends. So why am I feeling guilty?"

Memo: Never ask women why you're feeling guilty unless you're at the gate and the plane is boarding in the next three minutes.

Nora is the one who's hurt, of course. Kate knew she was stealing me, even if she'd had me in bed—or at least in dreams-- first. If I can ever afford to hire a shrink again, this is still going to be hell to explain.

"I never said that," Nora chokes out. "I just—well, you're the free spirit, right? I didn't want you to feel tied down. Artists aren't supposed to want normal, are they?"

I would hate this if I didn't understand it. We all buy the myth, even those of us who know we can't live up to it—or down, in this case; if there's any free spirit in me right now, it's all on the downhill slide.

All, at once, I'm boiling, mad as hell, though not at anybody in the car. At least not at anybody *else* in the car.

"If I knew what normal was," I answer, "maybe I could rebel against it. You know what I've starting doing lately? I turn on the radio to check if they're announcing any new catastrophes. As soon as I know they aren't, I don't care what's on—music, commercials, people talking, doesn't matter—I turn it off. That's all I want to know. The world's not over? Okay, I'm going back to my box.

"The 'normal' world went down the tubes a month ago—or maybe when the economy collapsed last year or when I got divorced two years ago, I can't tell anymore. But I'll make you a bet I go on listening to the radio like that for a long time.

"We're driving north now to mediate between the Ancient Trappers and the followers of Mondo the Man-God, so you can continue to help stock brokers become he-men in a world where too many men are muscling each other around already. If a cop stops us on the way, I get deported—from Canada, the last country in the world to take offense to *anything*— because my Super-8 projector failed to explode the other night. And all this is interfering with my dreamtime with your sister, who I didn't mean to sleep with but I'm not sorry about it, not really. Just like I'm wasn't sorry thinking I was stealing you from Art the other night. If I die tomorrow, I'm going to be seeing both your faces— and other parts of you—with my dying breath and I'll die with a smile on my face and no regrets, despite the fact that I know this is making you miserable. In the midst of all this craziness, you think I'm worried about *normal*?"

Nora's smile is breaking through—God, her smile puts diamonds to shame. Kate's eyes are wide—I forgot to mention the Super-8 projector. She'll love the story when I tell her later. Despite the fact that she set this whole thing up, all I can think about is how much fun she'll get hearing it—and how much fun I'll have telling her.

"We didn't grow up in 1911," I run on. "You're juggling six boyfriends from what I can tell and you haven't offered to give any of *them* up for me. I've only got one other, even though she's your sister. And *you*—" I turn to Kate, "—you've been sneaking around dreaming with other men without telling your husband."

"I told him," she protests. "He thinks I'm nuts."

"Imagine that," says Nora.

"Please forgive me just enough that we get through this weekend?" I beg, "and then we can figure out the next step, okay? In a civilized way. I'll drive and Nikos can sit up front next to me."

"No," Nora says with a sigh. "I'll negotiate with Nikos up front; you two enjoy yourselves in back."

"Really?" Kate says, a broad smile on her face.

"You won't be novelty forever," Nora warns her. "My turn will come." She fixes me with her most piercing negotiating face. "Enjoy yourself now—pay later." I grimace and she adds, "Don't worry—you haven't had a problem so far making the payments."

Once we get on the road, the book deal gets settled pretty quickly. I told Nikos back at the house that I didn't want him to leave me his characters. I love him but I don't need a bequest. After he's gone, let Nora own it, as long as his family gets the royalties. So now he does what he routinely does; he ignores me and tells Nora she can own the rights after his death, as long as she hires me to write any further Trapper stories. I'll split the royalties with Kara. Solomonic hair-splitting, a venerable Greek Jewish tradition.

"You know," Nora tells me in the rearview mirror, "this means we'll have continued, um, contact. I drive a hard bargain."

"I thought that was *my* job," I answer. Kate flashes me a look (*I'm not sharing*, is how I read it) while subtly driving me insane with her knee in my lap or thereabouts. I really do like them both—isn't there any possibility of that working out? I've heard of sheiks with fifteen wives, but they have oil money to pay the 782 charge accounts.

"We're going to the back seat," Kate tells Nora and virtually drags me over into the wayback, a foldup bench facing the rear window. It doesn't offer much privacy, but we're already far enough from Waterline that the traffic is almost gone. In fact, the only car close enough to see anything would be the one containing Art and Clint.

"Isn't this a problem?" I ask Kate, pointing to the two wide-eyed men a few carlengths back. "I've never aspired to be an accessory to—what's it called?—'alienation of affection?' " Her blouse is wide-open, her breasts calling to me in several dead languages I've suddenly begun to speak fluently.

"You didn't alienate anything," she says. "I told him I was leaving a month before we met."

Another loophole! "But does he know you've been dreaming with me for a year and a half?"

"He says it's all in my head," she gasps. Then it gets hard to talk, what with removing each other's belts and pants and her blouse slapping me in the cheek and space being very limited and

I don't care what they say, the quality of carpeting in those rear wells isn't quite as dense a shag as upfront.

In the distance, I hear Nora saying, "We're trying to negotiate." Nikos replies, "You know—this is one of those sexual situations my wife and I could never manage, because we didn't have someone to drive us. When you get over seventy, you feel inhibited asking friends to take you around town while you have sex in the back window of their car. You young people are lucky to be so free."

A moment goes by and then Nikos continues, "You know— *there's* a book that would sell—an updated Kama Sutra, with positions only made possible now by technology. You know, the back seat of the car; twenty positions—the laundry room; thirty."

"We'll volunteer for the companion DVD," I yell from the floor in back.

"Don't I get in on any of this?" Nora says, a little plaintively.

"Do you want to?" I yell. Omigod—does she *mean* it?

"You said you came up here to see *me*."

"I *can* see you, every time I raise my head above the seat," I pant, throwing both pairs of pants onto the bench. "I'm still really excited about you." Kate glares at me, in between removing our underwear, but I shrug. While they both still want me, I've got leverage. We'll see how long it lasts.

"You don't think this is kind of obnoxious, screwing my sister in the back of my car while I'm driving?"

"It's all good," I reply, gasping. "Kate can drive later."

Chapter 32

When we reach camp, Clint pulls into the spot next to ours. Kate and I have retrieved our clothes and returned to the back seat, and I jump out of the SUV quickly. In case Art decides to attack me, I at least want to be in the open where I can run.

I'm standing bravely, holding my ground, my heels firmly dug in. Art walks right up to me, hands at his side, not rolled into fists—I'm checking.

"You think this is all pretty funny, don't you?" he says. "That was disgusting!" Then he turns and walks away, just like that.

"Which is why you're here and he's there," Kate mutters, taking my arm. But once again, I'm stunned. For the first time since I've known him, Art was totally genuine. He was hurt and open and entirely transparent. It was the same look I saw on Nora's face a few hours ago. I feel like a cynical exploitive self-centered sister-swapping New York stereotype. This guilt is only slightly mitigated by my remembering all the years I despaired I'd missed my chance.

"Come on," Kate says, pulling my arm, "let's go."

"Go where?" asks Nora. "You had him in the car—my turn."

My legs are getting wobbly. I wonder if the country store has ginseng? Viagra would be better—I've never needed it before but this is sexual Armageddon.

"I'm trying to think of some precedent for this in serious literature, as opposed to erotica," Nikos says, admiring the view. "Updike wrote about an affair with his wife's sister, but I think he'd divorced her first."

"The wife or the sister?"

Sensibly, he ignores me. "Henry Miller must have something like this somewhere."

"Maybe I'm blazing new trails," I tell him, marveling.

"No no," he counsels. "There's nothing new under the sun. But it still feels good when it's shining on you, doesn't it?" and he heads happily off for the cabins.

Nora takes my other arm now and she, Kate and I grapple and stumble together up the path, which is really not wide enough to handle us side-by-side. When we reach the cabin, Nora pulls us up short.

"You know," she tells Kate, pointing at Art's cabin, "*your* husband is over there."

"Nora, it took me forever to tell him I was leaving," Kate says. "He begged me to wait till after this weekend, but you can't ask me to move back in with him."

"I did it with Nick."

"I'm not you," Kate says and I see the two of them so clear in this instant. When you see them toe to toe like this, Nora's a rock and Kate's all static electricity. "You really don't want him?" Kate asks.

"Are you serious?" Nora says.

"Well, he worships the ground you walk on," Kate says. "I figured you knew. He thinks about you all night every night. He's dreamed better sex with you than he's ever come close to having with me. I didn't even think he *knew* half that stuff till I started seeing it in his dreams of you."

"Maybe there's something lacking in your marital skills," Nora says and instantly looks ashamed of herself for saying so. I want to say 'No, there's not' because there certainly isn't but this doesn't seem like the time.

"He's dreamed of you since the day I started dreaming with him," Kate says. The pain of this is clear in her voice.

"Pardon me if I don't take that as a reliable indicator of *anything*," Nora answers. "But this is a problem. I can't go in there either."

"You've been in there with him six weeks a year for the last ten years."

"I didn't know about the peephole. And I didn't know how he *felt* then."

"I thought you didn't believe in my dreaming."

"I don't say I believe," Nora says. "But he has been looking all dreamy-eyed for a while."

"Yeah, like several years," Kate says. I can see her resentment. "So just toss him out like I did," she suggests.

"He's Mondo the Man-God," Nora says. "I'd have no business if he hadn't come up with the idea—and if he hadn't played Mondo." She laughs. "It was one thing to get up in that stupid costume when we were just fooling Nick. But we've got paying customers and repeat visitors now and they expect to be impressed. I can't exactly have Mondo sleeping in the back of his car. I can just hear them gossiping—'the Man-God's pussy-whipped.'"

"You know," Nikos says, "this is actually just a geometry issue."

"What do you mean?" Nora says. She has become very attuned to Nikos—I can see her appreciation of him, the immediate attention and respect she gives his every remark. She's right but it still adds to my admiration for her.

"Well, wouldn't it make sense, considering the merger, for Mondo and the Ancient Trapper to share the central house?" Nikos says. "We can come out together, do everything jointly. Shows our mutual respect and ability to work together."

"It'll add a visual image to the words," Nora says. "That's brilliant."

"And it solves your problem," he says. "You can all just share *this* cabin." But his eyes are sparkling with laughter as he looks over at me. His eyes say, 'Boy, your problems are just starting.' And don't I know it.

He heads off to join Mondo and we march into the main room of the cabin. Once inside, no one really knows what to do. After a short uncomfortable interval, Nora begins organizing furniture, placing plates and nick-nacks on the open shelves. Kate checks out the view from the various windows. An eerie silence reigns.

Generally speaking, I've spent my whole life solving problems. At work, I was always the operations guy, ironing out the kinks and anticipating them so they wouldn't arise. In relationships, I've always sought to talk about things so they wouldn't fester. My wife wouldn't talk and I wouldn't shut up. She couldn't show her feelings and I cried easily. It never really reached the point of me baking cookies while she built cabinets in the garage, but ours was a poster child marriage for gender role-reversal.

Nonetheless, in this situation, I decide not to intervene. I'm stuck with two gorgeous women who for some inexplicable reason both want me. Two gorgeous women who happen to be sisters. Considering the capacity for disaster here, I see no reason to rush things. I go sit on one of the Super Bowl chairs and take in the halftime action.

Finally Kate says, "OK, there's only two ways I can see this working. I'm the guest, so I could stay here in the living room. Nora, I assume you brought enough extra sheets that I could make up something to sleep on the floor here?"

"Of course," Nora says. Of course she did. "But I'm not real comfortable with you sleeping on the floor."

"Well," Kate continues, "the other answer is, each of *us* takes a bedroom and *he* shuttles back and forth."

I feel my cheeks redden. The two of them burst out laughing, watching me.

"That *is* how it's going to be, isn't it?" Kate says. The two of them are having a merry old time at this all of a sudden.

"My turn next, though," Nora warns. "No quickies while I'm off tending to business."

"I could keep notches on my belt," Kate says. "You can catch up later."

This is getting frightening. "What's going to happen when I run out?" I wonder out loud. "What happens when I collapse, which could happen at any moment?"

"My suggestion," Nora says, "is that you sleep by day. I suspect you're not going to get much rest at night." She isn't laughing.

Thirty~Three

I'm sleeping. In Nora's bed. It used to be my bed when I had this cabin. But now I'm just a visitor here. I'm sleeping in Nora's bed despite the fact that she's not going to be sleeping in it for a while, simply because I need sleep.

She made the bed before letting me use it. She took a look at the mess of sheets and scraps of notepaper I left here, shook her head ruefully and said, "This won't do." She pulled all the covers and made the bed new with her own 500-thread-count sheets in less than a minute. The corners are square. The sheets lie without a wrinkle. The bed is a work of art—I mean this literally.

"This really makes you happy," I told her.

"My mom used to tell me anything worth doing is worth doing well. It took me a while, but I get it," was her answer, and she meant it without irony. This is Nora's great gift—she lives without attribution. She doesn't have that rebellious determination to make over the world in her own image that causes the rest of us such trouble and she's so much better for it. She walks right past self-doubt, not because it's unfamiliar but because it somehow doesn't scare her.

I could see, watching her tuck and fold, that she gets real satisfaction from these modest triumphs, from conquering these day-to-day challenges. A home Nora Hill resides in—even overnight—is thought-out and reflected upon, and a reflection of her grounded, balanced nature. It's no less beauty for being less flighty than most art.

And then she leaves to talk business with Art and Nikos, and I slip off to sleep.

I am in a house. I sense this only, because the first thing I actually see is the door being thrown open. I step out to view the street knowing how the street will look, the way you always know how your street will look. And I particularly know this street as it is the street I grew up on in New Jersey—at least I tell myself this in the dream. There is a big old turn-of-the-20th-Century house right across the street and another just below it, down the incline. The area is full of trees, not thick with them but filled neatly, in almost Magritte-like neat rows. They are thin trees, with no branches until well above the first floor of any houses nearby.

But the houses are shredded. . It's as though someone applied a load of very heavy-gauge buckshot to the walls—they are stripped to the bare wood in spots and worse. Some places have been cut through so you can see inside the walls and cupolas—the house across the street has turret-like round ends, with windows and a conical roof in charcoal tile. I can see houses dotting the slight hillside behind. There's no one on the street. I realize in distress that I've been here many times—I've dreamed this dream endlessly, over and over again lately.

Then it's dark and the door opens again. It's the same hill and the same houses but they've moved. They're still in the same frightening condition and there's still no one around but they're in different places. At least, the one across the street is missing altogether and the ones behind it on the hill are in different places. But now I step onto the street and walk down the hill.

The first thing I realize is that everything in sight is the same ashen gray. The ground, the trees, the houses, even the sky are all monochromatic variations in a narrow scale. The stillness is overwhelming at first. The sunlight seems filtered through some kind of thick mist. I can barely hear my own footsteps on the paved street but I can see them in the dust. And then I see the street still has a thin plywood frame with little posts placed every so many feet—this is a new development, but they've taken some of the better houses left over after Dresden and placed them on this hillside. And then the road ends and I'm walking on bare ground—no grass even planted yet—but the old houses are placed neatly where the street will lead when it's finished and the trees are grouped neatly throughout the lots to be and now people in groups are beginning to come from between the trees, talking excitedly in loud voices and appraising one house versus another.

Put a tennis court in there. Nice view over the hillside. The houses need work, yes, but much better than Delaware.

And then I'm further down the same hill, the same hill I grew up on, but the whole feeling has changed. The houses are gone and the light has changed. The colors are back with a vengeance. From the color temperature and intensity, it's an autumn afternoon, that incredible light where you feel you can see every blade of grass miles away. The same sparse high-branched trees dot the hillside in neat rows, but the whole expanse of ground is lush with a manicured blanket of grass. Not a leaf in sight. No bushes, no undergrowth—the Magritte analogy really fits. A surreal, domesticated landscape.

The place is filled with men and women in convict suits—I am among them. We wander this stately vast space, stoned or otherwise impaired. It's impossible to move at a normal speed— everything is slowed, muffled, though time seems to pass normally.

There are art books scattered at the base of the trees. The convicts—an erudite group—keep approaching the books, studying them from a standing or kneeling position, gazing down at the big pictures filling the pages. Either the pages are turning by themselves or dissolving one to the next—I can't tell which.

I hear discussion—words floating on the breeze. I can almost *see* the words at times, like smoke hovering in the air and then dissolving. I can't understand anything being said, but this doesn't seem to be of any concern to anyone.

Near a twin-trunked tree—a tree that stood on my front lawn; I remember it was my fort as a kid— is a flip-book with big chunky cardboard pages of people's faces, people injured—can't tell what from—could be war photos or accidents on the highway. A blocky red cross appears on the back of each page, across from the next photo. I move on.

At the next tree is a Cartier-Bresson book. Kate is bent over a log, face down, face buried literally *in* the book. I hear someone in the distance say about Cartier-Bresson, 'Yeah, he's against the whole Honda Civic thing.' And I say, "You mean there's a blood test?" and he says, "There's *always* a blood test."

This makes perfect sense to me—and then I come to, feeling that shaky combination of rested and off-kilter from a dream just before waking. I put some water on the boil for tea. The other door opens and Kate comes over and puts her arms around me. The world floods with affection. Such a simple act. I try to return the same simplicity and stroke her hair as she comes fully awake. Awake?

She looks into my eyes finally and says, "So did you see it this time?"

"What?" I say first. Then, "Yes, I saw it. Have I had it a while?" but again I know the answer already.

"For a month," she says. "Every night, at least the first part. The second part, the books change—I've gotten a real refresher course in art history and other things. Those accident photos were *sick*."

"I think that's driver's ed," I tell her.

"Huh?"

"I remember a movie in Driver's Ed, in high school, of people killed or disfigured in car crashes. I think the Ohio Highway Patrol did it. The idea was to scare the shit out of us. Worked for me. I remember the teacher introduced it by saying 'Look at the two people on both sides of you—in the next five years, one of you will be in a serious car accident.' And, four years later, I was in *two*—totaled the car in the last one. I remember thinking after the second accident, I just saved both the people around me, and a couple others in class. Some joke, huh?"

"It didn't feel like a joke to me," she says but she doesn't push the point. "Were the photos real?"

"The Cartier-Bresson book?" I say.

"Is that who it is?"

"That's who I told myself it was. I couldn't really see the photos—you were lying with your face actually *in* the book."

She starts laughing. "Wow—that's why I was getting the peripheral-vision view. Hah!" She looks at me and I'm overwhelmed a little at the moment. "You see?" she says. "I might be crazy, but I'm not lying."

She seems utterly transparent, like I can see right through her, like I know everything she is. Which is, in the world of adults, impossible and breathtaking. How did this family contain the two of them! Maybe it didn't—maybe they didn't try. Maybe that's the answer.

And then we hear a crash of gongs and a thunder of drums.

"C'mon!" Nora yells, throwing open the door from outside. "It's time for The Game!"

Kate's eyebrows go up nearly to her hairline. "Ohh yes," she bursts, pulling me to the door. "You don't want to miss *this*."

Thirty-Four

We step out onto the grassy knoll overlooking Frozen Lake. The sun has dropped below the mountains and lights are going on at odd intervals along the shore. Nikos and Art have emerged from their cabin together as planned but it's hard to imagine an odder-looking duo. Nikos is bundled in layers—a shirt, sweater, scarf, long pants probably covering long johns, a parka and a big floppy hat with earflaps. Art is in ceremonial headpiece, cape and a loincloth. It's 12 degrees out—?

"Does he have to contract pneumonia to prove his manhood?" I ask.

"I don't know," Nora says. "He's never dressed like that before."

"He's trying to impress you," Kate tells Nora.

"Well, he's got some muscles—and not a bad butt," Nora murmurs. *Excuse* me—I'm standing right here, you know.

"His best feature—it's not enough," Kate responds and winds her arm around mine.

Now I hear a little audio hum—Art's turned on his headpiece microphone. Then he pushes a button on a black box he's carrying and a fanfare of trumpets rings out of the speakers, followed by the pounding of kettle drums.

Slowly, from the docks by the beach, two rather odd-looking vessels emerge. They're sort of like ships—at least, they're like the front end of ships, if ships were really short and weren't actually expected to float. I guess they sort of *suggest* ships—Viking ships, like in the movie *The Vikings*. Which is to say, these ships would be really convincing to any audience that could accept Anthony Quinn, Richard Widmark and Tony Curtis as Vikings. These ships have pointy noses, planked sides curving to a truncated open rear end and a mast in the center with a little sail—well, not a *real* sail; this wisp of cloth wouldn't propel anything larger than a Tonka truck. A towel suggesting a sail, maybe.

The 'boats' are propelled by skaters—two for each team, one pair in red team uniform, the others in white—pushing from the rear. Two other guys in Viking helmets stand in the bow holding telephone poles like the ones everyone was burning the last few nights. The two ships take up positions across from each other in the center of the lake.

"This is a game?" I say. Kate starts giggling wildly—Nora elbows her, demanding she shut up. I don't mean anything by it— I'm just trying to understand. Nora nonetheless stares at me as though I've drowned her dog.

The rest of the Lost Boys—the ones not participating—are seated on the banks, yelling and chanting slogans in no language I've ever heard. In between chants, they pull out water bottles in unison, take a swig, gargle loudly and let loose a stream that drops, steaming, onto the ice.

"What's that?" I ask helplessly.

"Razzling," Nora says. I just stare at her, waiting for an answer that helps.

"It's *spitting*," Kate says.

"They were doing it anyway—we wanted to make it a salute to your fellow warriors," Nora says ruefully.

I look around now and notice two guys hovering alone at the edges of the ice, away from the others.

"Who are *those* guys?"

"Those are the goalies," Nora says. Kate starts to giggle again and Nora kicks her.

"Where's the puck?" I ask. I swear this is a perfectly innocent question, but Kate goes into convulsions and Nora blushes red as a beet.

"It's the pole," she says.

The two guys in the front of each 'boat' are holding the telephone poles at their chests, one arm steadying the shaft, the other holding the back end of the thing, ready for launch.

I find myself blinking again. This time, it's hard to stop.

"They're going to *throw* those things?"

"Of course. Hockey is a religion up here. So, just like hockey, you have to put something into the cage to score."

"A telephone pole?" I stammer.

Now two other guys with what look like big spongy baseball bats start swarming around the ice between the goals and the ships, swinging their bats menacingly in the air.

"Go ahead—I have to know," I say.

"Defenders," Nora replies.

I can't help myself—I start losing it now.

"They're going to try to stop an airborne telephone pole with a baseball bat?"

"Not really," Nora says. "As soon as someone throws the pole, everyone just gets the hell out of the way. But it gives them something to do in the meantime. And they seem to distract the throwers. It's really rare for anyone to actually hit the target."

"Which is probably really good news for the goalies. How do they score then?"

"Usually they don't," she shrugs. "Time runs out and we set the ships on fire and everyone gets drunk and happy before going home."

I take this in to the best of my ability. Finally, I can't control myself.

"What *possessed* you to come up with this game?"

"We needed something big for the last day," Nora insists without conviction.

"I didn't ask what possessed you to create a game—but *this* game?" I say. "Viking ships, throwing telephone poles, defenders with baseball bats, setting ships on fire—what were you thinking of?"

"Actually," Nora confesses, "I was thinking of Quidditch."

"We'd had a bottle of tequila at the time," Kate adds. "I came up with setting the poles on fire."

Before I have time to consider this, Art raises his arms high over his head and shakes the fringe at the bottom of his cloak.

"ARE WE READY TO BEGIN THE TRIBAL TRIAL?" he bellows.

There is no sound for a long time. Finally, a voice from the lake says, "Do we *have* to?"

This is followed by a *really* funereal silence. Finally, Art clears his throat, the sound echoing like cannon fire through his mike.

"THIS IS MONDO'S CEREMONIAL TRIAL," he says, his voice faltering only slightly. "IT IS A TRADITION OF THE MONDO BREAKTHROUGH WEEKS."

After a respectful interval, another voice comes from the ice. "What do we learn from it?"

"Yeah," adds another voice. "All we ever do is throw the goddamn sticks. We never hit anything anyway."

Nora has gotten totally silent. Her whole plan is collapsing in front of her.

It becomes clear quickly that the whole group are staring at Nikos, who stands silently next to Art looking rather embarrassed. Finally he stammers, "Well, you know games throughout history have been a test of valor and initiative. Games are not about skill really—that's what we've forgotten since we created all these professional leagues. They're about character, about grace under pressure."

"Not this game," someone says. "The only pressure we're under is we might set ourselves on fire."

"How does this teach us about the top two levels of self-defense?" calls a deep raspy voice. "We always do the same things and they never really work."

"Well, change the game if you don't like it," Nikos says. Nora slumps into my arms as though stricken.

"The game has rules," someone says. "We have to stick by them."

"NO WE DON'T," bellows Art now, coming to life and sliding on his bare feet down the slope and onto the ice. "BECAUSE IMPROVISATION IS THE TENTH LEVEL OF SELF-DEFENSE." He heads directly for the red team ship and begins barking orders, switching off his mike mid-word.

As one, every set of eyes swivels back to Nikos. He pauses momentarily, visibly replaying Art's announcement. "Improvisation is the—" Then his face lights up. "That's good," he says, then steadies himself. "I mean, that's *right*. Improvisation is where the Trapper takes the Great Leap Forward."

At this, the two groups begin swarming around, conferring with each other and setting the ends of the telephone poles on fire.

"I'm not sure that was a good idea," Nikos says, wandering back to us. "But we had to improvise," he adds, and of course his quiet wheeze of a laugh follows.

"One way or the other," Nora says, "the game begins."

Thirty-Five

The boats move out from their positions, moving toward the middle of the lake. Art has gotten a pair of skates from somewhere and is now sliding around on the ice yelling instructions to his team.

"Isn't it unfair," Kate asks, "for one team to have Mondo?"

"Two minutes ago," Nora says, "no one wanted him."

"Now," Nikos adds, "here he is, a leader of men." He looks immensely sympathetic. It's dangerous leaving Nikos in anyone's company for more than five minutes—he ends up buying all their shtick. Of course, most of the time he also infects them with his humanist philosophy and consideration. It's a bit spotty in me, of course—we'll find out soon whether Art has caught the contagion—and what he's going to do with it.

"So now, generally speaking," Nora narrates, "the two boats will fake attacks for a while, to see if they can rattle the other guys and find a weak spot in the defense."

"Why not just chuck the pole and watch 'em scatter?" I ask. "You said everyone runs when they toss the thing."

"That's not traditional," Nora says. "I'm not saying it wouldn't work, it's just not how things have always—ohh..."

The sound of that exclamation immediately throws our attention back to the ice, where Art's Red Team is deploying.

"That's not right," Nora says. "He's got the defenders attacking along with the ship."

Yes he does. Art's team rolls like a tank squadron through the middle of the White Team, with the defenders swinging their clubs at everyone in sight and the ship plowing right on almost into the goal itself. The pole never gets thrown at all—once the ship stops moving, right next to the goal, the throwers just move forward till the pole touches the goalposts.

"Score one for Griffyndor," I announce.

This new attack seems to have stunned everyone—the Whites have been standing around watching just like us. The first to recover from the shock are the spectators, who respond with a chant and a razzle onto the surface of the lake. Then the Whites notice that Art's strategy has left his goalie totally undefended. A mad scramble begins as the White ship begins moving toward the Red goal, the White defenders scramble back to take their usual positions and Art and the guys pushing his ship—the Pushers?— desert the thing altogether and head for the White ship, Art again yelling instructions on the fly.

At first it seems as though the defenders can't possibly get back in time. But Art and the Pushers reach the White ship and grab on, trying to slow it down. The White Defenders see this and skate over, swinging their clubs in the air and pushing Art's boys off the vessel.

"Jesus!" Nora yells. "Someone's going to get injured!"

"Well, when chaos takes over, anything can happen," Nikos says in his quiet voice. "Clearly they wanted something more physical than you were providing them."

"Maybe they're thinking of the cardboard tomahawks," Nora fumes.

The Reds are actually rocking the White Ship now. The Red Defenders have almost gotten into position in front of the goal. But somehow the White Throwers get off a toss—and it's good!

"How the hell did they do that?" Nora asks no one in particular. "We haven't had a throw on goal in two years."

"Under pressure, men rise to the occasion," Nikos says. This raises bemused looks from the sisters but I'm not going there.

"Tie Score," I announce in my best Announcer voice. Beats Mad Bomber or Morose Moper-Around-The-House, I suppose.

"Well," Nora consoles herself, "then we'll end with a tie score. No time left for another goal."

"How do you figure that?" I ask.

"The poles—the poles are the time clock. They're too heavy for any one of our guys to throw. You set them on fire at the beginning. When they burn down too short for the two guys to throw, the game's over. And they're almost there."

This is true. I can see the White Team vaguely reclaiming their pole, with no plan to use it again. The Red Team is staring at their pole, which is burning pretty close to the first Thrower's hand now. The ships move back into their positions facing each other in the middle of the lake.

But now Art skates over to his ship, yelling and gesturing to the Throwers in the front. They yell back and forth for a second and then the Throwers toss the pole into the air—but not at the goal. The shortened, burning log wobbles in midair for a long moment and then Art skates up underneath and catches it with both arms. He leans forward, almost thrown over by the weight of the thing, but somehow remaining on his feet.

"That's insane," Nora says. "That's got to be illegal."

"There's nothing against it in the rules," Kate says, sounding impressed. Art is now skating alone, with everyone on both teams pursuing him, heading relentlessly for the goal.

"Actually, "Nikos remarks, "they played football for years before Knute Rockne invented the forward pass. It wasn't officially adopted until they had 18 fatalities one year and decided they had to make some changes."

"Jesus!" Nora says.

"And," Nikos concludes, "we *were* talking about improvisation."

Art's totally outflanked the White defenders, who can only chase after him. The goalie wisely gets the hell out of the way and

Art rams the pole through the back of the enclosure, setting it on fire as well.

At this point, things become entirely predictable. The boys from both teams raise Art to their shoulders, chanting to Mondo the Man-God. They set fire to both Viking ships ('They do it every year,' Nora sighs. 'Tradition is expensive.') and the other goal.

"This clearly is not intended by the rules," suggests one white player, who approaches us carrying a printed rulebook.

Nikos pulls the pile of papers from his hands and rips them into tiny pieces.

"Game, set and match," he says. "Now go put out the fire."

The lawyer sets off to help the rest, who are dumping snow on the various blazes.

"That felt good," Nikos says, letting the papers go and watching them flutter in the wind. "I *like* this game."

Art dances by us, jangling his cloak fringe and waving his arms. He's either celebrating or shivering to death. He heads straight for his cabin and, surely, the fireplace. Nora watches him skip by and says, "What the hell got into *him*?" She turns to Nikos. "Was he doing drugs or something in the cabin?"

"We were talking about the game beforehand," Nikos says. "He described it and I warned him the guys might not want to play. It sounded like too many rules and not enough fun to me. He said, 'They've got to play—this is *important!*' And I said, 'Importance is the enemy of Freedom' and he stopped dead. He looked at me as though I'd said something brilliant. He even wrote it down."

"What does it mean?"

"I have no idea," he replies, laughing again. "That's all I've done since we got here—I open my mouth and see what comes out. But it seemed to fire him up."

"I'll say," Nora muses. "Do the trappers play games?"

"Sure," Nikos replies. "You kill a moose and throw the entrails at a bear. Then you see if you can beat the bear back to your cabin. If you don't, you lose."

By the time he's finished, he's laughing so hard he can barely stand.

Thirty-Six

I spend three-quarters of an hour staring at the sky tonight. It's sick that I've been here four days without ever noticing those insanely dense heavens. Sure not the same sky as New York City, boy.

I keep finding my own constellations, clusters of stars that look as though they go together but which doubtlessly do not appear on the star charts. I'll have to convince Nikos to invent a mythology for the clusters I see, in place of the traditional ones I suspect I'm missing.

I'm heading inside when I see a dark form wandering through the snow toward me. It's Art. I immediately tense—last we saw each other, I was fucking his wife in the back window of a car. In certain sections of New York, this would quickly lead to me splattered all over the second level of a parking garage with two slugs to the back of the head. With Art I know whatever happens, he'll clean up and place all litter in the trash receptacles before leaving the area.

"How are you doing?" he says, but I'm not buying any, thanks. I head for the front door and he follows me. The faster I move, the faster *he* moves. I reach for the door handle, but his hand immediately covers mine, preventing me from pulling it open.

"Pardon me," I say and he replies, "Yes." That's it—'Yes' in a dead-serious sober tone of voice. He will pardon me for trying to escape him. Again, I can't tell if he's stupefyingly dull or truly witty. I can identify the odds-on choice but that doesn't make it a slam-dunk.

He looks me straight in the eye and says, "Kate's a good girl—she deserves better than I gave her." His face is all crinkly and sentimental in the moonlight. It doesn't take me long to figure out the loophole.

"Alimony laws work pretty much the same way up here, eh?" I ask.

"I guess," he says.

"Well, no promises," I tell him and try to pull on the door. Again, he holds me back.

"Kate *is* the one you want, right?" he adds and now I see it. Boy, Kate wasn't kidding—he wants Nora so bad it's scary. North Woods, starry sky, happy drunken Vikings/Trappers/followers of Mondo all around us and all he knows is that Nora is inside and he still hasn't gotten to her. Yeah he had a peephole and that's juvenile as well as pathetic but he also had to sit there for years watching her so close. I found that painful for a day and she still had her clothes *on*. He's staring at me—of course he is, I'm standing at the door in a silent funk.

"No promises," I repeat and pull the door open.

Nora is making some kind of soup—pots are boiling and lots of cut-up vegetable remains litter the counter. It's a vegan soup in honor of Nikos. A big improvement on the soy burgers and macaroni and cheese we've survived on up to now.

Kate is standing behind Nora, nursing a glass of wine and acting as prep cook—that is, she's offering whatever help Nora will allow. Nikos is sitting at the table—having cleared a corner, he is pounding at the laptop.

"I'm trying to write the commencement address," he says.

Art slinks into the kitchen area. Kate takes one look at him, rolls her eyes and heads over to the couch. Her cell phone rings and she takes it to the other room. Art heads for Nora. If he had a hat, it would be in his hand. It's kind of pathetic, watching him moon over her like this. I did exactly the same thing, of course, but I was mourning my lost youth and the really pretty 17 (15?) year old I didn't kiss. It's different for him; he's had the real thing in front of him for years and, unless Nora's a much wittier liar than she seems to be, hasn't done anything about it.

"We have a problem," he says quietly.

"No *you* have a problem," she answers in her captain of industry voice. And all I can do is take this as a cautionary. There isn't much I've touched that I haven't fucked up one way or another. How long would it take before she started using the captain of industry voice on *me*?

"No I mean we *all* have a problem," he says. "A problem we may not be able to solve but one that at least demands some attention." Something fascinating happens now—we all stop what we're doing and *pay attention to Art*. Kate drifts back into the doorway to listen, holding her cellphone to her ear. This happens because, without raising his voice, Art has begun to sound like a grownup—it's that same tone he used to announce Improvisation as the tenth level of self-defense. He's such a buffoon sometimes that it's stunning to realize there's anything more to him.

All of a sudden, I get a glimpse of one of those life-comedies so intense you miss it when it's right in front of you. Here's how it plays out in my head:

Art grows up the gawky, headstrong, sensible, reliable nephew of Do-Right the Mountie. He wants Nora from the beginning but—does Nick get there first or is Art just not sure enough of himself to go after the girl he really wants? I know how *that* works.

Kate is the wild younger sister, flakey and fascinated by *everything* but lacking the family's unerring mastery of all they undertake. This renders her kindly and graciously pitied by one and all, until she begins to see herself that way. Art courts and marries the younger sister, promising to take care of her and keep her pointed in the right direction, all the while staying close to Nora.

Kate feels privileged to get such attention and undeserving of it and Art sees her that way too. She lives a few years as a consolation prize and then, in one of those lovely accidents of experience, ripens into one of the great wholesale life-force sources, while Art shrivels through his passionless marriage into Pompous Do-Right the Lawyer—good intentions and uprightness given their just punishment.

Art is left in the greatest imaginable crater—unhappily married and crazy for his sister-in-law, the more conventional by far of the two Hill girls, the one for whom an affair with the brother-in-law would be unthinkable. And he's so reticent about his obsession that Nora doesn't even know he's interested until she finds out about the peephole in the bathroom wall.

This guy is the George Armstrong Custer of lovemaking— assuming the Indians had let Custer live on in disgrace after Little Big Horn and he'd then built the Titanic, invented the Hindenburg, discovered Fabian and set the explosive bolts on the hatch in Grissom's Liberty Bell 7. He is the Babe Ruth of romantic futility. I feel like a master of women by comparison.

"What's the problem?" Nora asks.

"I got a call from Jeff Mortenson," Art replies. "He says Shrader's been calling people, saying he's checked the history books and the Trappers are a fraud."

"What—he accepts Mondo as genuine?" I say.

"No one *ever* accepted Mondo as genuine," Art says. "He is a stand-in for all kinds of male gods and role models and primitive spirits."

"Let's face it," Nora says. "He was a joke we had to find a way to take seriously."

"Like the Trappers," Nikos says.

"But the guys take the Trappers as real," Art says. "This whole thing is about a minute-and-a-half from collapsing."

A moment of silence follows, then Nikos speaks up. "I'm not sure how much we've fooled anyone," he says. "I've been a fiction writer for 50 years. A story is always a collaboration between the teller and an audience that *wants* to believe—and they usually know inside that they're making that choice." Art scowls but Nikos persists. "Our whole lives are based on all sorts of assumptions that we pretend to believe—whereas, if we thought about them for two minutes, we'd know they were as phony as our cardboard tomahawks."

"Such as?"

"Such as: There's someone out there for everyone. The priest talks direct to God for us. Daddy will keep us safe till we're older. The ice cream with the pretend Swedish name tastes better. This diet makes it easy to lose 20 lbs in two weeks. It's *safe* to drive your car on the highway but it's *not* safe to work in a tall building because some terrorist might fly a plane into it. We don't live our lives by these stories because they're true—we live by them because we *need* to. Who wants to confront how scary and confusing daily life is? So we have these convenient lies that are more comforting than big truths. I think that's what the Trappers are for these guys—a buffer, a way to handle things that might otherwise be overwhelming. And I'll bet underneath they know it."

"Fine," Art says, though he seems to be fuming underneath. "But there's a risk these guys don't want to admit they know you're lying to them." He pauses, as though trying to figure out if he actually said what he meant.

"*We're* lying to them," Nora corrects him. "As of yesterday, our survival depends on the Trappers and Mondo working together. So let's not start fighting amongst ourselves now."

"I'm just trying to protect your interests," Art says and again he's so solicitous of her that it's almost painful to watch, sincere to the point of being touching, in a pathetic sort of way.

"I know," Nora says. She puts her hand on his shoulder and he melts an inch or two into the floor. It's the codependency of the Upright.

"Um—" Kate breaks the silence, "—can I say something about dreams without anyone jumping down my throat?"

"Does it have to do with anything?" Nora asks, but there's no condemnation in her tone.

"I think so," Kate says. "When you wake up from a dream, you always tell yourself 'Oh it was only a dream.' I've decided that doing that—announcing to yourself the dividing line, where the dream ends and your 'real' life begins again—is really important. Maybe that's what you have to do here."

"What?" demands Art. "We should announce the Ancient Trappers are a *dream*?" Kate doesn't appear even slightly intimidated by him, but it feels like a glimpse of what went wrong at home.

"Look," Kate continues, "the images in dreams are very powerful. Some people believe that if you dream you die, you actually die. So I think the reason we announce to ourselves that we just had a dream is so we can hold onto those images. Once we separate them from reality, we can own them. Otherwise, they scare us too much. And that's the buffer the Trappers offer, like Nikos said. Tell them it's a story but not *just* a story. If you make it myth, the Trapper stories become *more* powerful, not less."

"Okay," Nora says, visibly replaying this in her head as she speaks, "so it's the Myth of the Ancient Trappers—that sounds okay in theory. But the devil's in the details, sis. How do we say the trappers are myth without making it sound like they're just a lie?"

"Well, in dreams, the devil's *not* in the details," Kate answers. "A dream conveys a mood over all else. In fact sometimes you'll see something in your dreams—something really striking—and your mind is telling you it means the opposite of what it appears to be. So you have to forget the details here and just go after the core: What was it these guys liked so much about the Trappers? I don't think they just found them more authentic. I think there's some message in those stories they liked better, or something about Nikos' presentation that beat out Mondo yelling at them through a tribal headpiece. If you focus on the core they liked, authenticity stops being an issue."

This actually makes sense but doesn't exactly point to any answers. Another long silence follows.

Then Nikos says, "I still have a few Trapper biographies to write. What if they were so ridiculous they couldn't possibly be taken literally?"

"That's a start," Kate says. "That would lay the groundwork for something more overt in the commencement."

"These are men," Nora says drily, "who bought dung hollows, mountain wraiths and throwing rocks at grizzly hallucinations. Finding something too ridiculous for them to accept could be a challenge."

Nikos raises his hands above his head and flexes his fingers like a concert pianist beginning a recital. "Well, let's see what we can do. We'll make it group participation—gather round the typewriter."

The four of us pull our chairs to Nikos' side of the table. Nora ladles out soup and puts bread within reach while Nikos begins typing.

"'Sondra the Red opened new territories by marching barefoot through dangerous woodlands. She was never seen after leaving Ottawa in 1763, and was identified only by the clumps of long red hair she left to mark her trails and the string of red-headed Native American children to be found in each tribe she encountered.'"

"Ah, those lusty Native American men," Kate says with what sounds like real nostalgia. I raise an eyebrow—she just shrugs.

"'Cletus the Short left an oral history to'—what's an old Canadian University?"

"McGill—it's in Montreal," Kate says.

"Great—I don't have a Greek to help out the French yet," Nikos smiles.

"That isn't wise," Nora says. "We English-speaking Canadians don't care if you screw up our history, but the French will put you on a hit list."

Nikos looks down at his body. "I'll take my chances," he says. He starts typing again. "Okay, 'Cletus the Short left an oral history to McGill University of his adventures in the Great North. These stories are one of the greatest troves of knowledge of the culture of the Beaver known to mankind. Cletus lived with beavers for decades, and came to be accepted by them as one of their own. He even lived for several years in the' —what's a river in Quebec?"

"The St. Maurice," says Art.

Nikos types some more. The tears are slowly beginning to pour down his cheeks. "'—for several years in a beaver lodge in the St. Maurice River, along with several beaver families.'"

"The Mertzes, the Cramdens and the Nortons," I say.

"Don't forget the Rubbles," Nora snipes.

Nikos is making those rheumatic heaving noises again, the ones he makes when he's really enjoying himself. "'Eventually, Cletus tried to marry a beaver girl, but her parents wouldn't accept him—'"

"Obviously Orthodox," I say, and he nods through his own laughter.

"'At this point, he left beaver society and went on a campaign to outlaw beaver trapping. As it was only 1863, this campaign was premature and doomed to failure. But on his deathbed, his last words were 'Tell Myrtle I will never forget her furry tail' and this is generally taken by scholars to refer to the beaver girl he was never able to marry.'"

By now we're all laughing. Nikos starts to rock back and forth, lost in convulsions.

"I don't know if these Trapper stories are that funny," he says finally, sitting up. "but they're so *silly*. Why would anyone care if they make sense? They're just *fun*."

"Maybe that's the point," Kate says. "Maybe that's the core."

"You really intend to read that to the guys?" Nora says.

"He absolutely should," Kate says. "He should read them because he'll read them like that—laughing, enjoying them for what they are. You watch him, it's impossible not to join in."

"That's true," Nora nods.

"So maybe it'll solve the problem—even if it doesn't, they won't go away mad."

"You know, she may be right," Art says and Kate and I both sit up at the sound of him saying it. "It's funny as hell. If they enjoy it enough, they might not care if it's true."

"That's fine," Nora says. "But I'm not building them lodges in the river next year."

Chapter 37

Art leaves shortly after dinner and returns a few minutes later to take Nikos and Nora to the other cabin for 'business discussions.' As Nora leaves, I find myself relieved not to have to make a decision about whom to sleep with.

A few moments later, Kate jumps up and announces she's going to her room.

"Okay by me" I say, jumping up to follow.

"No, no" Kate recoils and ohh, the rejection bites me hard, in that one second before I realize its source.

"Nora says it's her turn and you said you didn't want to decide between us," she says, every word a misery. She breaks into a queer smile. "I want to win this one clean."

For a moment, it seems like she's finished but I can feel there's more coming.

"I was always the hand-me-down. All through school, I was the sister of the tall blonde who got 4.0's in everything. When it turned out my husband really wanted Nora all along, I wasn't even surprised. So okay, I connived to get you here but you're here now. Now it's for real. You'll make your decision and…we'll see."

As should be obvious by now, impulse control is not my strong point. I have a nasty question in mind and before I can gauge the wisdom or the hurtfulness of asking, I hear it coming out of my mouth.

"When you arranged for Nora to write me, you had to know there was a chance I'd just fall for her completely." I guess it doesn't write as a question but Kate knows it is.

"Of *course*," she says. "That's what I'm *used* to. I just felt—I knew you from the dreaming. I—."

She's stymied by words—but for once, I don't need words. I know what she's feeling. When Nora tells me how she feels, I can understand and appreciate. Her logic is impeccable and even when it isn't, she knows how to explain so I can put myself in her shoes. But now, when Kate *can't* tell me how she feels, can't find the words to explain, somehow, I know anyway—our understanding lives somewhere beyond words, underneath words, however you want to put it.

As I'm mulling this, she adds, "By the way, you don't have cancer."

This hits me like the nice man who just lit my cigarette reminding me that the firing squad is waiting for me to finish my last puff.

"You've been dreaming about it for weeks," she says. "I had to get to where I understood the message. But I know you don't have it."

My head is reeling. I'd managed to forget the bloody subject, to put it out of my mind. At least, that's my first thought—a moment later, I realize what nonsense it is. That subject's been the dull moan behind the concerns of the moment ever since the doctor got that concerned look on his face. I ran away to Canada to escape it but it's not far enough. There is no far enough.

"I'm not suggesting you shouldn't see your doctor or have the tests or anything. But I've been inside you and you've been inside me—and I don't mean *that* way," she laughs, "and I *know*. I want to relieve that fear in you, so we can just enjoy being together." The look in her eyes gets very fragile now all at once." And—if we're going to be together—I need you to trust me, to be willing to trust *all* my abilities, not just the ones I got grades for in college."

And again, I know so much more than she's saying. I can feel what she feels. No one she respects has ever accepted this berserko gift of hers. Her sister and husband patronize her and everyone else just ignores it since she seems such a nice girl otherwise. But I went to Banff inside her—that really happened.

And, if it didn't, so what if she's a little crazy? A week ago, I was sitting at home counting up all the magic moments in my life that I'd failed to capitalize on. There were job moments but they sure didn't cut as deep as the women who might have cared if I'd figured out how to respond the right way at the right time. Coming up here was an attempt to balance the scales, to let myself go just a little bit cautiously crazy. And here's my match—a girl who drives me way crazier than I planned, in many different directions.

Let's face it—when you decide you want to go just a little cautiously crazy, aren't you really looking for an excuse to go *farther*?

I look at Kate's wonderful face. This woman embraces every aspect of vitality that approaches her. All she asking of me is to trust the gifts she's already given me. In a world that doesn't really offer unconditional love, isn't being taken on our own terms what we all want?

"I believe you," I tell her and feel the tension in my head— and the room—slipping away. "If you tell me it's so, it's so."

"But you're still going to the doctor when you get home."

"Of course," I say and we laugh—but it works. Kate settles into the lazy and exhausted smile of the sleepwalker, who's been fighting something invisible forever and feels like the fight is finally over.

"Competition's over," I say. "I want to collect my prize" and she pulls me into the bed for a quieter, sweeter kind of love.

An hour later, I hear the front door bang open loudly. I throw on some clothes and step into the main room to find Nikos banging away at the laptop and Art and Nora barreling through the door. Behind them through the open portal, I can make out the Squad of Lawyers, a phalanx of gray-suited robots, tramping through the crusty snow on the other side of the lake. Nora slams the door on the image.

"We have to talk," she says to Nikos.

"What's with *them*?" I ask, pointing to the approaching hit squad.

"It's Shrader," Art answers, real tension in his voice.

"We've been on the phone all morning, trying to prevent a disruption of the commencement ceremony," Nora says. "There could be a problem—"

"A little disruption isn't all that unusual at commencements," Nikos rambles. "I remember back in '74—"

"In this case," Nora interrupts, "I think it's important that we settle—"

She never gets to settle anything, as the door sets to banging. I'm right beside it. I wag my finger back and forth—should I? It's clear from Nora slumping in her chair that there isn't much choice. I pull the door open and Shrader and his three lawyer sergeants step through.

Examined up close, their gray suits are not actually identical. There is a degree of difference in the pattern of the weaving or the original material between one man and the next. Shrader seems to have the nicest wool to start with, at least to my eye. Nonetheless, it's kind of amazing that three grown men would be willing to go out in public dressed like clones. Women would never agree to such a thing.

"Good morning, Ms. Hill," Shrader commences, sitting at the table and flipping open his briefcase with that you're-not-really-worth-more-than-three-minutes-of-my-time attitude lawyers must practice alone in the office, or maybe the shower. His henchmen sit on the couch and a chair in the far corner. They're strategically placed like bodyguards, in case we should attack Shrader for violating the dress code up here—or for otherwise being an asshole. "I understand from the incorporation papers on file in Ottawa that you are the CEO of Gimmick Enterprises."

"That's correct," Nora says, squirming.

"Well, I should be direct. I'm here to take over your company. Obviously we'd prefer to negotiate something amicable. We would be willing to offer you the position of Founder Emeritus, with a salary and use of the corporate jet on available dates."

"The corporate jet?" Nora says, going nearly cross-eyed at the thought.

"Oh yes," says Shrader. "There are several large corporations interested in this project. Mondo Weekends will become a nationwide phenomenon, along with Mondo clubs, Mondo outerwear, etc. You can profit from your work, so long as you give up actively running the program. What would you say the odds are of us reaching agreement on this?"

"Slim to none," Nora says immediately, her posture even more upright than usual but uncertainty lingering in her eyes.

"Then we will lead a hostile takeover," Shrader continues without any change in his inhuman tone. Wait a minute! Maybe these guys really *are* clones! It would explain the suits. "Your organization has been embarrassed and disrupted by the Order of Ancient Trappers, who are themselves a fraud. This reflects badly on your leadership."

"The Ancient Trappers are now part of the Mondo universe," Nora says. I love business jargon—so grandiose and familial all at once. Not that anyone could ever mistake it for anything but bullshit anyway. "We've agreed to merge our assets."

This is technically not true. A verbal agreement was reached in the car yesterday, but contracts still have to be written, and signing was to wait until after we got back to Waterline.

"Well, that's a wise move," Shrader says. "All the more reason the company should be attractive under new management."

I remember Shrader now. While the other guys participated in their various activities, he remained on the periphery, chattering with his henchmen, the now-pinstriped band of brothers. The guy's a weasel. The Trappers are an excuse—he sees a weakness and decides to pounce. His kind are one of the cancers that have taken over everybody's world recently.

Nora is rubbing her foot against the floor now, rubbing hard enough to wear a groove under her chair. While it may have started as a joke, Mondo is now her baby, the linchpin of her financial success. It's the proof she is no longer the little girl too young for her classes, proof that she can swim with the big fish, who come to her to be revitalized in their Mondo Breakthrough Weeks. To have all this pulled out from under—especially as a result of someone's silly prank (mine!)—would be endless pain. I've already seduced and abandoned her—I don't want her livelihood and independence on my conscience as well.

"I won't work for you," Art tells Shrader. Good ol' stolid Art—at least he's loyal.

"I can get any guy I want in a headpiece and a cloak and no one'll know the difference," Shrader retorts. "We may dump Mondo altogether and stick with the Trappers."

"Well, then you have a real problem," Nikos says. "I have a contract that says no one can write Ancient Trapper material but me in my lifetime." Good move, Nikos—I can see Nora rousing at this boost.

"Fine," says Shrader. "We won't write anything down. We'll develop our own verbal traditions for the moment. Eventually, we'll be able to write things down. We'll just wait you out. It shouldn't take too long," he says, giving Nikos an appraising look.

Now I *hate* the son-of-a-bitch. I can feel the electricity go through the room.

"I'll contradict you," says Nikos. "Whatever you say, I'll write the opposite."

"You'll be in White Plains, getting whatever money you were promised by the corporation," Shrader says, smooth and threatening. "You will be an employee and legally bound. You'll make the coop and car payments on time, in contrast to the last couple of months."

Nikos settles back in his seat. He has a bb gun with no ammo and Shrader has an Uzi.

"I'll fight you," Nora says, sounding a good firm note, but Shrader smiles.

"Fight away," he replies. "The word's got round about this. Between the stories of the Ancient Trappers circulating among the diehards on the Web—which we can prove are bogus, if we need to—and the fact that a woman runs the company—and that she was recently questioned for attempted assassination of the PM— I've almost got the majority of your stock in my hands already. I'll have what I need well before the annual meeting next month."

"I doubt that," says Kate's voice from across the room. She's come out to join the party and is leaning against the door, watching all this with big eyes.

"I'm *certain* of it," Shrader counters. "I've assembled several large blocks of stock and have offered an attractive buyout to more than I'll need. In one night, I've already gotten pledges just short of a majority. I wouldn't have shown my cards otherwise. She—"

he points to Nora, "has let her holdings dwindle. She's taken profit. She only has 18% now."

"I understand," says Kate. "But *I've* got 35%."

Every head in the room swivels like we're compasses and she's True North. Kate throws her hands into the air and starts laughing—it all must look ridiculous from where she stands.

Shrader opens his portfolio and begins moving his finger down the list of stockholders.

"I've got two blocks," Kate says. "There's stock Art and I got when the corporation started—we're officers—that's 5%. The rest I bought myself as Dreamstreet Holdings—a little here, a little there over the years. I just told my broker when he saw shares to buy them."

Shrader has his finger, obviously, on Dreamstreet Holdings in the stock list. Now he's the one making grooves, with his other hand in the tabletop.

"I thought—" he stammers.

"I know—you called last night," Kate says. "I told you, you were very persuasive. But I also said I couldn't make any decisions right away."

"You misled me," Shrader says.

"Sue me," Kate says.

Shrader sits for a long moment. I can almost see the little dark cloud gathering over his head. He keeps looking back at the list, as though there's another answer lurking there between the lines. But we all know the score—until they change the rules of mathematics, 35 plus 18 per cent equals a majority, period. Finally, he gets up, closes his briefcase and heads for the door, joined by the phalanx in gray.

"Would you be interested in an Ancient Order of Washed-Up Lawyers?" Nikos calls as they march off to the parking lot.

For a long moment after the door slams shut, we stand stupefied, staring at each other, realizing we've just witnessed a small miracle. In a world that continually justifies the most cynical expectations, the good guys just won one.

"I got a call last night from one of my friends," Nora explains a moment later. "I gave her 1% of our stock when we first started as a joke gift. Shrader called, strong-arming her to sell or proxy to him. So Art and I have been on the phone almost the whole night. He really did have the whole lot of them in an uproar."

"It'll settle down now," Art says, continuing in his new manly tone of voice. I wonder if he had the Mondo mask on last night as they were working the phones together. "We'll make a new start with the Trappers, and if any stockholders don't like the new direction, they'll sell to people who do."

"We should add to the Board of Directors," Nora says. "If there are large corporations interested in this business, let's get them on our side."

"And you've got to explore those outerwear sales," I laugh. "Think about the Trapper parkas!"

"And dresses," Nikos adds. "There are several lady Trappers, remember, and Damian the Hairless is a cross-dresser."

"Why don't you make Cletus the Short the cross-dresser?" I suggest. "It would explain why the beavers wouldn't let him marry their daughter."

Nora turns to her sister, who's still leaning against the bedroom door, looking exquisitely as though she just got out of bed. Our bed.

"Why didn't you tell me you were the largest stockholder?" Nora asks.

"I didn't *know*," Kate replies. "I just told my broker to buy when he could. So when I got the call from Shrader last night, I had my broker check what I had. When he told me 35%, I knew we were okay."

"Barely," Nora says, embarrassed.

"I thought you had more stock than you do," Kate admits.

"But why the open order?" Nora continues. "What made you think of it in the first place?"

"I don't know," Kate shrugs. "I just figured if I had to count on someone to make me money, it would be my big sister."

"Thank you," Nora says. Kate shrugs and the two just smile at each other, the Canadian equivalent of deep emotion. The tension flies out of the room and thirty seconds later we're all in the kitchen throwing a huge breakfast together.

Thirty-Eight

About an hour later, everyone else is out preparing for the Commencement Feast at the boathouse. Nikos and I sit at the table with laptop and legal pads.

"Um, I think you should know," Nikos says, "that Nora may be thinking of straying."

"You mean with Art?"

"Oh, you noticed," he sighs. "Thank goodness. I hate getting in the middle of other people's sex lives and yours is like a spider's web lately."

"It's okay," I tell him. "I'm with Kate now, period."

"Does Nora know this?" he asks. I can't blame him, after the past week, for making sure he has all the details of my life straight.

I nod. "Kate and I told her. She graciously accepted her sister's happiness as a defeat, but I have the feeling she was doing that for Kate's sake. I think she's been expecting me to leave since I got here."

"And did Kate get any satisfaction out of defeating her sister?" he asks. Nikos spent most of his lifetime teaching women.

Men like me came to Sarah Lawrence toward the middle of his tenure. We have both spent decades studying and appreciating women's psyches—without ever, of course, really understanding them.

"I don't know," I admit.

"I don't think women ever allow themselves that sort of satisfaction," he says. "Men gloat after defeating an opponent— women can be just as ruthless and competitive, but once they've won, they feel guilty."

"What *is* that—insecurity? Or are they really on a higher moral level than we are?"

"I don't know," he muses. "It could be that they take some moral satisfaction in recognizing their own flaws. Or maybe it's just self-devaluation—the best women all seem to suffer from it. Men always assume they're handsomer and more special than they are; women are the opposite. I've spent my life fascinated by women. Just my luck, I'll end up remembered as the nurturer of overly masculine men."

"Overly masculine Canadians, no less."

He smiles again. "I was thinking this morning that if these idiotic stories came out of me so easily, there must be some more in there keeping them company. I've got a few ideas for when we get back. And it's all because of this trip." He claps me on the back at this, harder than I thought he possibly could.

He picks up the legal pad he's been working with. "I've been thinking about what I said to Art the other night: 'Importance is the enemy of Freedom.' I had no idea what it meant when I said it; now it's the whole theme of Commencement."

All of a sudden, we're back at Sarah Lawrence, discussing our writing projects. In the last year, while I was writing up a storm, Nikos had nothing—not a story, not a glimmer. Now he has his commencement address and a commission from Nora for two or three lady Trapper stories. He's productive again. Through no fault of mine, this trip actually did him some good.

He clears his throat and begins to read.

"From the beginning of time, human beings have struggled between two impulses—the impulse to control everything and the impulse to enjoy themselves. Let's call it the friction between Importance and Freedom.

"Importance has given us the Pyramids, the exploration of Earth and outer space, religion, science, public relations, social climbing, focus groups, lawyers, wars and marriage. Importance is purpose and ambition and obligations; the drive to leave something bigger than yourself and that really miserable feeling you get Monday morning when you're trying to convince yourself to go do the things you can here this week to get away from.

"On the other hand, there's Freedom—doing what feels good in the moment. Real freedom gets a bad rap in our society. It has no track record because it leaves nothing behind except sometimes a hangover or a good memory. Whatever felt good last time won't feel the same if you do it again and sometimes it won't even feel good a moment after it's over. But nonetheless, freedom is the core of a creative happy life. Freedom is improvisation and taking value in the moment, enjoying life for what it's worth while we have it.

"I was in Westchester, consumed with medicines to take and therapies to undergo—and my wife and I sat around feeling depleted because of the *important* things we couldn't do anymore. You can hear the weight in the damn word just by repeating it: *Important. Important.* Makes you feel like you're carrying barbells.

"And then I came up here and met you guys. Suddenly I was walking around in the woods, making up stories of the Ancient Trappers and having fun. As it turned out to my surprise and maybe yours too, those stories actually had a purpose, had some meaning behind them. They gave me a door into a different way of approaching life, one that finds wonder everywhere. Now, as my friend Ted reminds me, I was like that before I came here. But I'd lost track of myself, because the things I found pleasure in didn't seem Important to me. But once I started screwing around in the woods with you guys, not worrying about what I was supposed to do or all those Important things—once I was just free and in the moment, they popped right out. The result is, I feel like a new man and I think some of you do, too.

"We make the wrong things important. Our jobs, our ailments, our reputations are things we have to deal with but they're not the things that make us happy—and if they don't give you some happiness, how important can they be? The happy moments live on inside us after all the other stuff proves to be bullshit. And as Cletus the Short says, you can't make a dung hollow from bullshit.

"So today I want to leave you with a tool to help you separate the freely, truly important from the bullshit. And that is Laughter. Laughter is the Eleventh Level of Self-Defense of the Ancient Trappers. Laughter puts everything in perspective, it is the most subversive force on earth and it possesses a built-in shit detector. And when your only choice is between two different kinds of shit, it will at least tell you which one seems to be more *fun*. In this world, that might be all the meaning and satisfaction you can get."

"That's what I have so far," he says, staring at the page. "I think I got the gist of it down."

"It's a new voice for you," I say. "More conversational or something, I can't figure out what's different."

"It's more *masculine*," he says, the hiccups of laughter starting. "I'm getting in touch with my masculine side."

"It's all that time in a cabin with Mondo that did it," I answer and the quaking rises to his shoulders, tears streaming down his cheeks.

The door bangs open and Nora stands there, holding a weathered deerskin coat and Nikos' floppy hat with the built-in earmuffs.

"Voila," she says. "Trapper Outerwear. I've got twenty pair from the store—we'll see how they sell at Commencement."

After the two of them take off, brainstorming the love life of Diana the Badger Killer, Kate comes in, looking to change for the Feast.

"It should be fun," she reports. "There's moose liver pate."

"Keep Nikos away from that," I warn her. "It'll be six days before we can get on the road."

"So, you really have to go?"

"I have to take him home. And I don't know if Canada would welcome me without an income—and being a Super-8 killer to boot.

"I don't know," she chirps. "Our father *is* a media mogul, at least a local one—there's got to be a job somewhere. I'm sure the Prime Minister will forget about you eventually."

"I don't know if I want back into television," I tell her. "A middle manager in TV is a professional son-of-a-bitch; it's in the job description. I want to do something that makes me feel good."

"And get paid?" she asks and it's a good question, dammit.

"Besides, I have a son in New Jersey, living with his mom. And he still wants to spend time with me despite being a teenager. That's hard to pass up."

"I didn't know you had a child," she says. "You don't dream about him."

"I guess I *worry* about him instead. How about you? Your sister won't leave town—you any different?"

"You mean, live in New York?"

"Yeah. Live with me in New York."

"I have a practice here," she says.

"Don't tell me."

"I'm a psychologist," she says, as though I should have known. And it does seem obvious, though in a more ironic way than she intends.

"Well, hey! New York! Psychologist! Like being an oil driller in Kuwait!"

She gives me a long look, not exactly sad but not happy either.

"You want me to drive around every day with a bullseye on my back?"

"I'm willing to do most of the driving."

~~~~

Read a Preview of
'Swindler & Son,'
The new novel by Ted Krever
On Sale December 2018

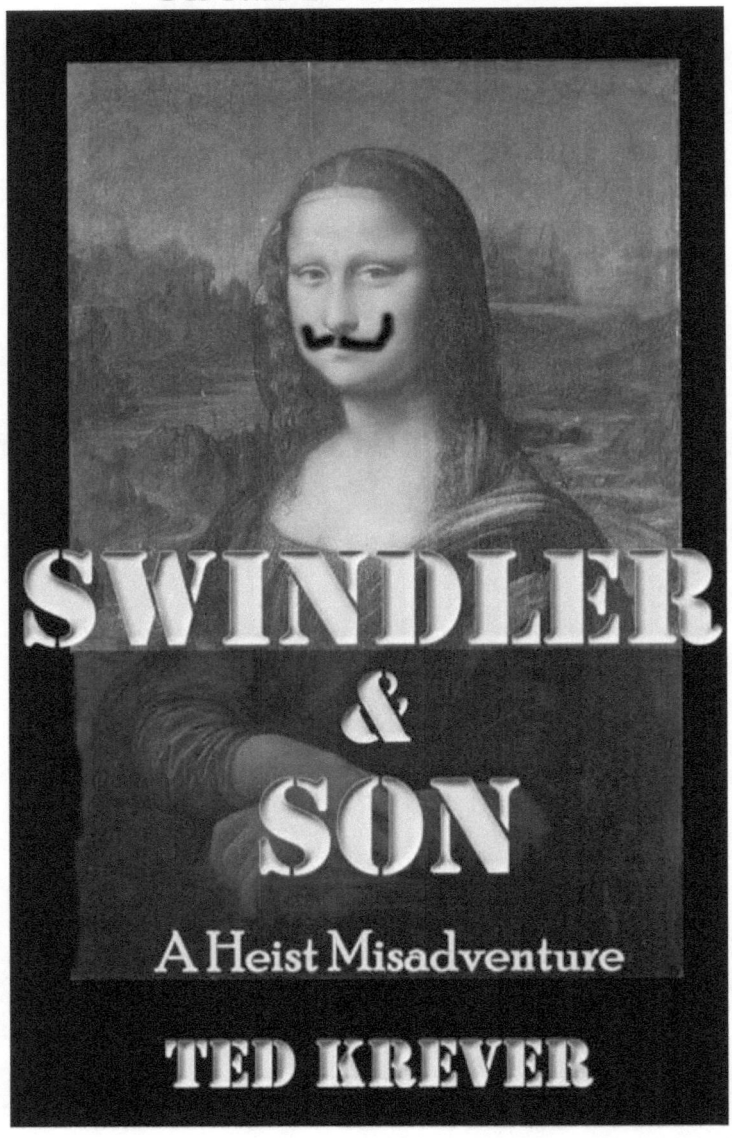

THE START

−So how does it start?

It starts with the sound of my own name spoken aloud.

Call me Nicholas, I'm fine. Nick or Nicky, even better.

But 'Nicholas Marsh' enunciated, first and last, all the way through—when I hear it *that* way, I know I've done something I'm about to pay for.

Hearing it in French, every syllable twisted and slurred and leaking from the earpiece of a Parisian counter-terrorism officer in a Kevlar vest, his back to me and his binoculars trained on my kitchen window—*that's* rock-bottom.

That's how it starts, in the snowy garden of the *Hopital Saint-Louis* in the Tenth Arrondissement, just past sundown on Christmas day, at what I fervently hoped was the end of one of the worst days of my life.

Well, actually, no...

Actually, it started about fifteen minutes earlier, on the other side of the canal, where I was mugged by some twenty-five-year-old junkie in a purple-tinted mohawk and a leather jacket. And several nice tats on his neck that distracted my attention when I should have been focusing on his oncoming fist. He took my wallet and phone and left me aching and dizzy, which is why I wandered groggy several blocks out of my way and approached home through the garden.

I love that garden but none of the official exits land anywhere near my apartment. A few years ago, I found a back door, through the *Musee des Moulages* on the hospital grounds, that let me out near a construction gate right across the street from my building.

I'm just opening that back door when I hear my name and see GIGN, French Special Forces, two officers, huddled like Martians in flak suits, gas masks and sniper rifles, peeking through the construction gate at the wide corner, the entrance to my building and, eight floors above, at the dead coleus drooping from my night table.

Frozen in place, I scan the rooftops and find a squad of dark gray uniforms—and, in case I harbor any last doubts, hear my name one more time from the headset hanging from the blonde officer's right ear. I back instinctively into the doorway, sweating and making twenty-five different plans at the same time.

The bus! They won't be checking the bus on the Boulevard de la Villette, that's an answer. Having any sort of answer helps calms the quiver in my legs, brings them back into something like working order.

This is a mistake—it's got to be. If I'd done something to deserve counter-terrorism, I'd remember it, wouldn't I? More importantly, why in hell didn't somebody tip me off? Who do I know at GIGN?

Out through the door and the museum, retracing my steps, back out the far end of the compound, past the *Chapelle* to the *Rue de la Grange aux Belles*. Up toward the roundabout at a regular clip, walking briskly like a Parisian.

Am I thinking of escape? Hell no, I'm just getting pissed. Why hasn't somebody warned me? Why haven't they given me a chance to buy my way out of this?

Oh sure, GIGN makes it look serious but that just raises the price. I know somebody in every department of government and what they cost. Serious things have been undone before.

By the time the bus makes three stops, I know who to talk to—Beltoise, the second man at the *Surete*. He was at our Christmas party just last night.

I *own* him! At least, I should. If I had a middle-class clientele, if I dealt pot or owned a brothel, I could expect a phone call 24 hours in advance of a raid. It's common courtesy!

He'll be at *D'Azur*, of course, charging his dinner to us as usual.

When I arrive, he's tucked into a dim corner. He rises before I can reach him.

"Why is GIGN all around my apartment? You don't warn me?"

His eyes bulge like marbles. "Where's your phone?"

"Phone? Stolen. I got mugged."

He looks *relieved.* "That's why they're not here yet," he mutters and pulls me into the private room in back.

"Nicky, our past history—and the fact that I like you—is why I'll give you a minute's grace before I call you in." He's serious! His face goes cold—not like he doesn't know me, like he's never *seen* me before. "Normal corruption is one thing—but this?"

Normal corruption? Normal corruption is my *specialty!* He's reducing ten thousand years of civilized give-and-take to a catchphrase. Not to mention, it's fed him quite nicely, thank you, over the years.

I look at his face, at the disappointment and condescension there, and realize what a farce it all is. You treat them like princes but the first time you actually need them to put out...they might as well be in insurance.

Faced with this ingratitude, something inside me just gives up.

"Okay," I tell him. "I surrender."

"What?"

"I'll confess, right now. It's the jet ramps, isn't it?"

He looks confused.

"We have this client, a dictator...you know the old joke about, you're not really a country unless you have your own stamps, your own airline and your own beer? Well, he's got commemorative stamps, a brewery, a Mercedes stretch limo and a portrait of himself as Julius Caesar. But he gets embarrassed when his guests have to descend a staircase off the plane.

"There's a staircase on Air Force One' I tell him and he says, 'They could have a ramp if they wanted one.' So when Kumbatta collapsed, we flew a cargo plane in and liberated a couple of jetramps. The guy was so happy, he painted two Cessna's and proclaimed them the national airline. I don't think we *hurt* anybody."

Beltoise settles into the nearest chair, not saying a word.

"That's not it?"

Silence.

"Okay, Napoleon's penis — that was a good deed, I swear."

"*Excusez moi?*"

"It's your Minister of Defence's fault! Not the present Minister, the old one. He had this…thing about Napoleon's penis, that it should be back in France where it belongs."

"It is in France! Napoleon's body is at Les Invalides!"

"The body, sure, but his penis was removed during the autopsy and it's floated around ever since from collector to collector. It's now owned by a urologist, naturally, in Philadelphia."

"Don't be funny."

"It's true. The BBC measured it a few years ago and found it a bit small. Naturally, that outraged the Minister, who insisted the English don't know how to measure. The urologist's price was just *outrageous* so we found a...more generously-sized one around the same age, for a price the Minister could afford. It made him *happy.*"

"You found him another penis?"

"Another *old* penis! You think that was easy? How many three-hundred-year-old penises you think are floating around?"

Beltoise stares at me with—I can't tell if it's respect or concern. The odd thing is, to me, this is actually beginning to feel pretty *righteous.* Confession really *is* good for the soul. "Okay, not the answer. Give me a chance. The eighteen identical one-of-a-kind Moroccan emeralds—"

"No."

"The Van Gogh with the wrong ear missing?"

Beltoise rolls his eyes. "We've never met," he warns, "except for a few state dinners with hundreds of other people I've never met either—but my advice is, you find a quick way out of France now. And don't bother replacing your phone—they'll find you as soon as you do. You understand?"

This is terrifying—Beltoise is a glorified flatfoot with a fancy office. I'm *begging* to be arrested and he's not biting. It's *unnatural.*

"Throw me a bone here," I say. "I don't understand what's happened."

He grimaces. "You know damn well it's the bomb."

"The *BOMB?*"

Of course, I know all about the bomb. I'd arrived back in Paris the day before, just in time for the funerals. Twelve dead, 37 injured, a miracle it wasn't more. A mountain of flowers in plastic sleeves heaped on the rubble, candles arrayed like soldiers in front of the dress shop left somehow intact on the corner.

And a march from the *Place De la Republique* to the *Place de la Nacion*, thousands, orderly and dogged, middle-class families and university students, *Le President* and his rivals, butchers, bakers, artists and computer technicians shuffling through neighborhood streets between broad public squares, solemn and chattering, sombre but fashionable—Paris, formal but somehow intimate. Great buildings and beautiful women dressed in black. Paris is a grand dame, maybe a bit past her prime, but she still knows how to put on a funeral.

'It's an escalation,' they say, the voices that multiply in crowds. Just a few years ago, 'they' were content to shoot up a restaurant or concert hall. Now, somehow, they bring in a bomb the size of a safe to bring down half a block of five-story apartment buildings.

The size of the explosion makes people nervous. Nobody builds a bomb that size to bring down the Rue Breguet. We all sense a grander plan that went awry and the fact that no one claimed responsibility only seems to heighten the tension. You don't even have the consolation of knowing who to be afraid of.

Beltoise, however, has made up his mind.

"It's your shipping certificate!" he yells, no longer caring who hears. "Your company's letterhead! Your *signature* on the bloody thing! You think I will cover for *that*, you're insane!"

I stand frozen for an endless moment, until words I never thought I'd hear myself say come tumbling out of my mouth.

"I didn't do *that*! I'm *innocent*!"

And then, I run.

RUNNING

-You ran?

It's an expression. I know better than to run. I walk at my usual quick pace but not fast enough to attract attention. Okay?

I lose myself in the tangle of back streets, staying off the boulevards, sticking to shorter blocks and parks where I can change direction at will. I stop short in front of angled store windows several times, switch direction several more, take a cab for a short distance and then another to double-back on myself. I'm overdoing it, in truth—if GIGN were really on my tail, they'd just throw on the sirens and take me. Once I'm sure I'm not being followed, I find a thrift shop that's just closing in a church, buy a pair of slacks and a short dark hoodie and wear them out of the store.

-This is tradecraft. Where did you acquire your technique?

Like you don't know. I had a very brief career in—what do you tell strangers at parties? About what you do for a living?

—I don't speak of such things.

We used to call it 'compliance.' I was recruited out of college. They trained me to take in a room or a street, to be invisible when that was useful. Trust no one, calculate the odds, tote up the angles and assume everyone follows their own self-interest.

But they couldn't teach me to be shrewd. I got myself involved in an 'extracurricular' scheme supporting freedom fighters—that is, it became extracurricular once it led to screaming headlines. Next thing I know, I'm getting chewed out in front of a Congressional committee for the exact same things they'd urged us to do in private.

We were thrown out like Big Mac wrappers, three fall guys, small potatoes. A generous severance package—under the table, of course—just go quietly into the night, thank you.

That training comes back to me, now that I'm on the run. Focus! *The bomb! What have I got to do with the fucking bomb?*

I need real information. Somewhere in our files, says Beltoise, is a shipping certificate for a bomb with my signature on it. I can't go home so I almost certainly can't go back to the office. But maybe Harry's apartment is clear.

If this had happened any other time—last week, even!—I could have counted on Harry's counsel, his expertise, his instincts. For fifteen years, he's been there when I needed him.

But that's a huge part of what made this feel like the worst day of my life, even before GIGN's visit. I've no idea if I can count on Harry anymore.

-Explain this please. Who is this Harry and why can't you count on him?

Harry is the majordomo, the ringmaster of our circus, the senior partner in Sandler & Son, affectionately known to staff and select members of the governing elite as Swindler & Son. Everything that isn't about Sara in this story is about Harry.

-And Harry's got problems?

Oh hell no, Harry's got no problems. Harry *is* the problem. Everybody *loves* Harry, *that's* the problem.

And why shouldn't they? Harry makes life a party, a twenty-four-hour Remy Martin and shellfish from the little inlet over *there* and put away your business cards, this isn't some vulgar networking grind, we're here to have *fun*! Remember fun? Harry does.

If you liked the Remy, you must try this cognac—it's Venetian, Dante mentioned it (disparagingly, but he mentioned it) in the *Divine Comedy* and let me introduce you to the Ambassador's wife, she has all the good gossip about the orgies at that other embassy—maybe it was the Czechs but we're not saying. Meanwhile, other groups are discussing 70's film and sex robots and if there's anything else you want to know, the person to speak to is over *there*. The band plays good acoustic jazz, the

Argentine tango couple are giving lessons one-on-one on the terrace and the star of the national football club is kicking balls around with enchanted kids and dazzled grownups on the south lawn.

In Paris, of course. That's our home base. It's one of God's jokes—Harry hated the French so, once we'd been thrown out of every other country in Europe, the only place left to go was Paris. Which, of course, he now loves because how can you not love Paris? It's *Paris*, for God's sake.

And the French love Harry. Big gnarly elegant gay Englishman, what's not to love? He ignores their culture, conducts himself like tenth-generation nobility fallen to trade or maybe a good Savile Row tailor, speaks only enough French to be fed and catered to but laughs and charms so naturally, they can't help themselves. Seduction is the French national pastime; they recognize a Master at work.

I was in Mumbai two years ago, picking up a load of Indian cotton. There was a rash of suicides among cotton farmers in Vidarbha and I was able to pick up several farms' entire crop just by paying off the bank loans. I told myself it was a good deed and a good deal. So I'm in the hotel bar at the end of the day chatting up some girl when a man behind me says, "Oh, you work with Harry Sandler? I was in a steeplechase syndicate with him in Ireland once. Took me for £65,000 quid. Most wonderful time I ever had." He bought us both a drink.

Everybody loves Harry; that's what nearly killed us all. As I watched the Iranian commandos lining up on the deck of the ship three hours ago, in their black stocking caps and their Kalashnikovs aimed at our temples, all I could think was, *Everybody loves Harry.*

Fucking goddamn Harry.

Author Biography

Ted Krever watched the Beatles on Ed Sullivan, went to Woodstock (the good one), and graduated Sarah Lawrence College with a useless degree in creative writing.

He spent several decades creating programs for ABC News, CBS, CNN, A&E, Court TV, MTV News, Discovery People and CBS/48 Hours, and as VP/Production of a short-lived dotcom.

He has driven a 16-wheeler across the Rockies, shot overnight news in NY City, managed a revival-house movie theater and married twice, in a triumph of optimism.

He was once accused of attempting to blow up Ethel Kennedy with a Super-8 projector.

Read more at www.tedkrever.com